I0583404

THE SUMMER FOR US

GOLDEN FALLS BOOK 1

IZABELA KAMILA

Copyright © 2025 by Izabela Kamila

All rights reserved.

No part of this book may be reproduced in any form or by any electronic or mechanical means, including information storage and retrieval systems, without written permission from the author, except for the use of brief quotations in a book review.

This is a work of fiction. Any names, characters, places or incidents are the products of the author's imagination and used in a fictitious manner. Any resemblance to actual people, places, businesses, or events is purely coincidental and fictional.

Cover Design: Alison Warren

Editing: Nicole McCurdy, Emerald Edits

Andrea Halland, Editing by Andrea

Formatting: By Destiny Blake LLC

E-Book ISBN: 979-8-9988803-0-8

Print ISBN: 979-8-9988803-1-5

For my husband Michael.
Our love story will always be my favorite.

CONTENTS

AUTHOR'S NOTE

Thank you for picking up *The Summer for Us*! This is a small town, dislike to love, opposites attract romance with a grumpy hero, sassy heroine, forced proximity, found family, banter, and tension.

This story is my love letter to summers in the Midwest and the first book in the Golden Falls series, a set of interconnected standalones each taking place in northern Wisconsin during a different season.

This book is intended for adult readers ages eighteen and up. *The Summer for Us* contains explicit, on-page sexual content and strong language. Additional content notes include:

- Both characters are dealing with failed relationships (but there is no other man/other woman drama)
- Alcohol consumption
- Career struggles
- Side characters briefly mention loss of a loved one

I hope you enjoy your time in Golden Falls with Wes and Jules. Happy reading!

- Izabela

PLAYLIST

Listen on Spotify!

no tears left to cry - Ariana Grande
Heat Waves - Glass Animals
She Lit a Fire - Lord Huron
Power Over Me - Dermot Kennedy
Something in the Way You Move - Ellie Goulding
GIRLS - The Kid LAROI
She Wants to Go Dancing - Mt. Joy
Love You Anyway - Luke Combs
Bathroom Light - Mt. Joy
Into You - Ariana Grande
Dress - Taylor Swift
Perfume - Del Water Gap
Diet Pepsi - Addison Rae
34+35 - Ariana Grande
Labyrinth - Taylor Swift
Wind Up Missin' You - Tucker Wetmore
Days Like This - Joytrip
Heaven - Niall Horan

Daylight - Taylor Swift
Worst Way - Riley Green
Golden Hour - Kacey Musgraves
I'm In Love With You - The 1975
Love You For A Long Time - Maggie Rogers

REALITY WEEKLY

Leaked audio reveals the truth behind *Paradise Love* couple's shocking split

Tech entrepreneur Tony Pierce had no intention of continuing his relationship with interior designer Juliette Campbell after they won the hit reality dating show, according to exclusive audio.

Fan-favorite *Paradise Love* couple Tony Pierce and Juliette Campbell quickly stole viewers' hearts during the reality dating show's most recent season—but exclusive audio reveals paradise isn't always what it seems.

Viewers were on the edge of their seats as sixteen compatible singles gathered in Fiji to find love and compete for one million dollars. Pierce and Campbell, who won the season, paired up on night one and didn't leave each other's sides during the two months of filming.

Both have been quiet on social media since the season finale two weeks ago, and now we know why.

Pierce, a tech entrepreneur from Silicon Valley, had no intention of continuing his relationship with Campbell, an interior designer from Chicago, after they won, according to exclusive audio obtained by *Reality Weekly*. The secret recording captured a heartbreaking conversation between the couple just days after their win as they prepared to leave Fiji. Neither Campbell nor Pierce could be reached for comment.

Listen to a clip of the recording here.

Transcription:

Juliette: I'm so excited to go on a date with you outside of the show. We can finally be a couple in the real world! I mean, I know we'll have to do long distance, but we'll make it work.

Tony: Oh, babe, that's adorable, but you can cut the act now. Show's over. The cameras are off.

Juliette: W-what?

Tony: Pretending was getting so tiring. Did you really think I fell in love with you? In two months? Babe, this was never about love for me. I wanted to boost my company. I never expected to win the whole thing, but I wasn't about to stop this when I realized how well we were doing. The cameras loved us, and I'm half a million dollars richer now. It doesn't get better than that.

Juliette: But I—

Tony: No hard feelings, right? We'd never work in the real world, anyway. You're kind of a handful.

An anonymous source close to the show claims the two ended their relationship immediately after the conversation, and Campbell was devastated. But what did she expect from going on a reality dating show to find love?

Even we could've told her there's heartbreak in paradise.

Follow *Reality Weekly* online and on social media for updates.

1

JULIETTE

You're kind of a handful.

Those five words played in my brain over and over, and not even the soft hum of my car's engine or the music playing through the speakers could drown them out. I hadn't listened to the audio. I didn't need to.

Living through the moment once was enough. Being told you're a handful by a man you're falling for was something I wouldn't wish upon anyone.

My feelings for Tony on the show were real and so was my excitement to continue exploring our relationship. But my enthusiasm disappeared as soon as he said those words to me. Words that made me feel small, embarrassed, and like I wasn't enough. No way in hell was I going to pine after a man who made me feel that way or allow him a space in my heart.

The way he acted during that conversation was a complete switch from the Tony I'd gotten to know. It gave me flashbacks to my various exes, making me question my judgment of men. How did I not see the red flags from the beginning? I'd gotten it completely wrong. *Again.*

Until the article published, I didn't even know a recording of our conversation existed. We had already taken off our microphone packs, but they were still in the room. My guess was one of them hadn't been properly turned off and captured our conversation.

I thought I'd be able to give a simple reason for our breakup —*it just didn't work out*—and move on from *Paradise Love*, from Tony. But that wasn't the case.

I'd be fine if I never heard or saw anything related to the show again for as long as I lived.

My grip on the steering wheel tightened as a love song crooned through the car's speakers. I let out a groan, immediately reaching over to turn off the volume. I'd settle on listening to the low, rhythmic rumble of the tires on the highway instead.

I glanced over at my car's center console screen to see how much time I had left driving. Two hours.

Another two hours of monotonous scenery through the car window, and I'd be able to have a glass of wine. Or maybe I should skip the wine this time. A glass of wine (several, technically) was part of the reason I was in this mess.

At the end of last year, I'd come home from a girls' night frustrated with my string of failed relationships. I saw a call for applicants for a dating show while scrolling social media. I was on my couch waiting for my Taco Bell delivery and thought, *screw it*. So, I applied.

When I got selected for the various rounds of interviews, the producers convinced me this show was different from other dating shows and they were looking for contestants who were serious about settling down. They even had us complete multiple personality and compatibility tests to ensure they were selecting people who would connect romantically. They claimed the typical struggles of being on a dating show wouldn't apply here, because *Paradise Love* was different.

It didn't take much convincing for me to accept my spot on the show when they offered it. I mean, hello, a trip to Fiji to find love with someone kind, funny, and also looking to settle down? Someone I could potentially create a future with? Yes, please.

I trusted the people behind the show. It was optimistic of me —I knew that *now*—but they said all the right things. Just like Tony had. I tended to wear my heart on my sleeve, but maybe I shouldn't. So far, it hadn't gotten me anything except a few forgettable exes and public embarrassment.

Even though the producers claimed *Paradise Love* was different, it wasn't. I wasn't immune from the low after filming, having my life impacted, or hearing everyone's opinion on social media. The show used me for ratings and had no problem doing so.

I reached for a sour gummy worm from the bag in my cupholder, going for the head first and ripping the piece of candy as I took a bite.

A ring filled the car, and I let out a groan when I saw it was my older brother Grant calling. *Again.* I loved my family, but they hadn't left me alone since the article was published. I get they were worried and wanted to help, but they didn't understand how embarrassing it was to have your biggest insecurities splashed online for thousands of people to comment on.

I was tired of talking and thinking about the show, about Tony, about all of it. But I also knew I couldn't avoid my brother forever. Reluctantly, I hit the button on my steering wheel to answer. Might as well get this over with.

"Hey, Grant. What's up?"

"Hey, Jules. I have an update about your apartment."

I let out a sigh. My apartment in Chicago flooded while I was filming the show, and my landlord made it clear he would get things fixed...at his own pace. I couldn't move back in until he was done with the work.

Luckily, I'd moved most of my belongings to storage before

heading to Fiji, and Grant lived in Chicago, too, so I was able to crash on his couch once I got back. Due to his busy schedule as a lawyer in the city, I actually hadn't seen him much, which allowed me to wallow in peace. But I needed to have a space of my own—and a bed. I was only twenty-seven, but I swear my back ached more after graduating college.

"Oh, yeah? What'd you find out?" I asked curiously. When I'd told Grant about being kicked out, he'd insisted on looking at my lease to figure out a solution. It was the lawyer in him.

I heard Grant's key unlocking his condo as we spoke. "Well, I was right. Your landlord can't kick you out without giving you accommodations, especially since the damage wasn't your fault. But there are no empty units in your building, so he's going to ask the property company to find you an apartment in a different building. I also made it clear you won't be paying rent while you're not living there. Might take them a bit to find you a new place, but at least—" He stopped. "Where the hell is your shit?"

For the last couple of weeks, my makeup, clothes, and shoes had been scattered around his neat apartment. And now they weren't. They were packed up in boxes in the trunk of my car.

"About that…" I laughed awkwardly. "I appreciate you looking into the apartment thing." I waved my hand as I spoke, even though he couldn't see me. "But I actually have it figured out. Well, sort of. I found a cabin in northern Wisconsin that I rented out for a few months. I'm making the drive up now. I'm about two hours away from the property."

Silence filled the other end of the line, and I was pretty sure if I was there in person I'd see Grant's eye twitching. While I was impulsive, he was orderly. He loved routine, and I loved trying new things.

"Juliette," he said slowly, his voice gentler than I expected. "You can't keep running away from your problems like this."

"That's not... I'm not..." I stammered, reaching for words to defend my recent decisions, but I couldn't find them. The leather of the steering wheel creaked under the pressure of my hands, my pulse kicking up a notch.

"I'm worried about you, Jules."

"I'm fine, Grant. Everything is fine. The drive up here has been great. The cabin will be great. I'll be—"

Grant cut me off with a dry chuckle. "Let me guess, great?"

I held back an eye roll. I didn't appreciate being called out, even if he was right. But I needed to believe everything would turn out fine.

"Keep me posted, alright?" Grant continued. "And let me know if you need anything."

"I will," I assured him.

With that, Grant hung up, leaving me to my thoughts about his earlier words.

I wasn't running away. That's *not* what I was doing. Right?

I stared at the picturesque log-sided cabin with large windows, a wraparound porch, and green shutters. The neighboring lake shimmered in the warm sun. Lush trees surrounded the property and the water. It was private, secluded, and peaceful. Exactly what I needed.

The tension in my shoulders lessened a fraction. Getting out of the car also eased the ache in my legs from the five-hour drive.

I tried not to think too much about if my summer plans were exactly what I needed or if I was making another big mistake. Only time would tell. Yes, coming up here was impulsive, but at least things couldn't get worse. Or at least I hoped they wouldn't. I didn't think I could handle something else going wrong.

The cabin I booked was in Golden Falls, a town about three hours north of Madison, Wisconsin. Multiple small lakes, lots of cedar and maple trees, and hiking trails surrounded the town, which had a historic downtown with various local businesses. From a quick search, I learned people all across the Midwest traveled to Golden Falls, especially during the summer.

Golden Falls was going to be my private getaway—exactly what I needed to clear my head and figure out my next steps. The rental listing called it a "lakeview haven."

Even though the last few months hadn't gone my way, I had to believe I could turn things around. People would forget about me and the show soon enough. While Tony was getting the brunt of the backlash, I was getting all the pity, and honestly, I wasn't sure which was worse. I didn't need people flooding my social media comments feeling sorry for me or telling me how naive I was to think things were going to turn out differently. I just needed time.

I shook my head to get out of my thoughts, instead focusing on the view in front of me. My temporary fresh start.

First order of business was bringing my belongings from the car into the cabin and unpacking.

"What in the hell do you think you're doing? This is private property." The low, booming voice startled me. I'd been so distracted that I didn't hear the crunch of gravel behind me.

A scoff of disbelief escaped me as I turned toward the voice. A man trying to lecture me. Just what I needed.

I wish my body hadn't reacted when I turned, but my gaze was immediately drawn to him. He stood tall—well over six feet —and muscular, his presence striking. His dark-brown hair was hidden under a forward-facing baseball cap that said *Lake Ridge*. His facial hair was neatly trimmed.

And those dark-brown eyes bore into me.

Somehow, he looked rugged and put together at the same time. An addicting combination—one I had no interest in.

I wet my lips. "I'm staying here for the summer. I'm renting the cabin from Lily Richards." I peeked behind his broad frame and noticed there was no car, so I assumed he must've walked over from one of the other properties down the road. Since this was my fresh start, I didn't want my mood to taint our first impression. I opted to be friendly to the stranger. "I'm Juliette Campbell, but everyone calls me Jules. Do you live nearby?"

"Like hell you're staying here," he grumbled, completely ignoring my question and introduction. *Okay, then.* "This place hasn't been rented for years." Had I blinked in that moment, I would've missed the slight crease in his forehead and the way his jaw tensed.

His arms were now crossed, the simple black tee pulled taut against his chest and straining against his biceps. His dark-wash jeans hung perfectly on his hips.

The flicker of emotion was gone, and the irritation was evident. And any motivation I had to be polite was gone, too. This man radiated selfish, and that was exactly the type I'd vowed to stay away from. See, I could recognize red flags.

"I *am* staying here," I clarified. "And I have no problem calling Lily to confirm my stay. I'm only here for the summer."

"Of course, it's just for the summer. That's how it always is with you city girls," he scoffed, and the look on his face said it all. Whatever the reason, he didn't want me here.

My lips parted in surprise, and I let out a dry, humorless laugh. Seriously? *What an asshole.*

"What the hell does that mean?" I quickly shook my head. "You know what, never mind. I need to start unpacking, unless you planned on helping me?" I stood up straight, my eyes not leaving his intense gaze.

A muscle in his jaw twitched. "Smart ass," he muttered.

"Better than just being an ass." I faked a smile.

With an irritated sigh and shake of his head, he turned around without another word and stormed off down the gravel driveway. "Real nice," he grumbled under his breath.

"You started it!" I yelled over my shoulder as I lugged my bright-pink suitcase up the wooden steps.

I had a bad feeling I'd just met—and pissed off—one of my neighbors. Not quite the fresh start I was hoping for.

But I had no intention of leaving. I was finally looking out for myself, and he sure as hell wasn't going to drive me out.

This summer was for me.

2

JULIETTE

My phone buzzed, and I'd bet money on it being my family checking in on me. I sat down at the kitchen table, reaching for my phone to pull up the various notifications.

MOM

Sweetie, we heard from Grant that you're in Wisconsin now? Here if you want to talk. We love you. Hope you had a safe drive.

DAD

We're only a phone call away. Love you.

GRANT

Can you at least let Mom and Dad know that you're alive and made it to the cabin? They're worried.

MOM

We're not worried! Just wanting to check in.

I laughed softly to myself at the last message from my mom. She could deny it all she wanted, but I knew she was worried—even if she didn't have to be.

Like I'd told Grant over the phone earlier, I was fine.

Totally and completely fine.

It was frustrating, though, how life seems so simple when you're growing up. Or, at least, it seems like the adults in your life have it all figured out. Then you get older, and the curtain is pulled back.

No one knows anything. We're all trying to figure this out.

And, sure, things can be simple if you go through the motions: go to college, graduate, begin your career, work in said career for the next forty years, and retire. But what about when plans veer off track? What about when thinking about working the same job for the next four decades makes you break out in hives?

Not so simple anymore.

And don't even get me started on how while we're all trying to figure out life, we're also expected to get married, maintain friendships, travel, and have hobbies. How are we supposed to have it all figured out?

Maybe it was stupid, but I thought going on *Paradise Love* would help with some of those challenges. I thought it would give me time to focus on dating and finding love, so that when I got back home, I just had to worry about the other stuff.

Not quite.

I typed out a quick response to let my parents know I'd arrived at the cabin and planned to spend the rest of the day unpacking. I'd already brought in my luggage and the couple of boxes I had from the car.

I would soon need to find food for dinner. The gummy worms would only satisfy me for so long. Right on cue, my stomach growled.

Great.

I'd go into town tomorrow to get groceries and see what restaurants were around, but for tonight, delivery would have to do. I swiped out of the text thread and opened DoorDash on my phone. Unsurprisingly, my options were limited. As I scanned the list of four restaurants—and I'm using *restaurants* loosely, since one of the options was a gas station—I settled on pizza. I couldn't go wrong with pepperoni pizza with ranch on the side.

After placing the order, I turned my phone on silent and set it on the coffee table. I had about an hour until the food got delivered. I leaned back in the chair, closing my eyes for a moment and inhaling deeply.

"It'll all work out," I said to myself on an exhale. Things were already looking up. I mean, I had the summer in a cabin with a beautiful view.

I opened my eyes and got up from the chair, allowing myself to fully take in the space. The first floor was open concept, with the kitchen blending seamlessly into the living area. The wooden floors and the beams slanted across the ceiling made the space feel rustic and cozy.

There were floor-to-ceiling windows on the back wall, as well as a screen door leading to the deck. As I looked out the window, I already knew this was going to be my favorite part of the cabin. The windows framed a picture-perfect view of the lake, trees, and a path down to the dock. There were two Adirondack chairs on the deck—an ideal spot to sit and enjoy the sunset.

The kitchen was small, but everything I needed was nestled in the wooden cabinets. I had a full range of appliances, too. A color-coded binder on the kitchen counter contained information about the cabin, local businesses, and various activities to do in Golden Falls.

I made my way through the rest of the two-bedroom cabin, quickly falling in love with the place—and how quiet it was. No traffic, no honking, no people walking by.

The only place I didn't explore was the basement. Nope. Not

going down there. I was sure it was totally fine, but I wasn't taking any chances. I had seen enough scary movies.

After hanging up my clothes in the main bedroom closet and organizing my toiletries in the bathroom, I made my way back to the living room. I crossed my arms over my chest, my eyes bouncing around the space. I kept thinking about how the furniture was set up in the living room. It made the room feel too big. Usually, that was a good thing, but since it was just me in the cabin this summer, I wanted the area to feel more intimate.

Maybe if I...

Unable to help myself, I gripped the arm of the couch and tugged it closer to the center of the room, ensuring it wasn't too close to the kitchen. I then moved the coffee table and lamp closer to the couch.

With this small change, I'd be able to sit on the couch and watch TV while also enjoying the morning sun streaming in through the front windows.

Before going on the show, I was working for a boutique interior design firm in Chicago. Luxe Living was my first job out of college, and I had worked there up until leaving for *Paradise Love.*

My initial plan had been to return to work after wrapping up the show. But after the breakup disaster, going back to work was the last thing I wanted to do. My *Paradise Love* winnings allowed me to take the summer off and pay for the cabin rental, while still having money left over. It also helped that my boss Cheryl was supportive of my decision to step away for the summer. For now, I was temporarily unemployed.

I really enjoyed designing, working with clients, and turning someone's vision into a reality, but I'd been feeling uninspired. I needed to get back to why I loved interior design, which was helping people figure out what they wanted and bringing it to life. It was truly special seeing their faces light up when their dreams became a reality. I also enjoyed how interior design was like a puzzle and how rewarding it was to find the solution. Something as simple as rearranging a few pieces of furniture could really change a room.

Most of Luxe Living's clients were wealthy, and it seemed like no matter what we presented them with, they weren't happy. It was never enough, and they constantly wanted more.

I didn't expect my job to be easy, but I did want it to be more fulfilling. I was a small fish in a big pond, and I couldn't see the impact I was making.

And not only at work.

I felt small in the city, too. As much as I loved Chicago, it was overwhelming.

The opportunities were infinite—there was always something to do and new people to meet—but that wasn't always a good thing. It was hard to focus on the present moment. I was always looking toward the future and focusing on ensuring my career was successful, because it seemed like that was what everyone else was doing.

I was starting to lose who I was, what I liked, and whether or not I was happy. I'd devoted so much time to my career that the rest of it didn't exist.

I was looking to get away from the busy city life. Take a break to figure out what I wanted to do, and more importantly, who I wanted to *be*. I'd return to Chicago after the summer in Golden Falls, but right now, I wasn't looking ahead. I was *finally* focusing on the now.

And my current focus was signing into a streaming service on the TV and picking out a movie to watch while I waited for my pizza. I grabbed the remote and sat on the soft fabric couch, settling into the cushions. As much as I enjoyed the peaceful quiet, I needed some sort of background noise. I landed on *Sweet Home Alabama*, a perfect second-chance romance comfort movie with Reese Witherspoon. I'd lost count of how many times I have watched it. I was over real-life love, but I could still appreciate fictional love, especially if it included a kiss in the rain.

"I wonder if there's popcorn," I muttered, pulling myself up from the couch—it was dangerously comfortable and easy to sink into—and walking over to the kitchen. I searched through the wooden cabinets until I came across the snack drawer stocked with chips, granola bars, hot chocolate, and...microwave popcorn!

I unwrapped the plastic and placed the popcorn bag in the microwave. I set the timer for two and a half minutes and started my search for a bowl.

Not too bad for my first evening in Golden Falls. All of it was almost enough to keep my mind off the mysterious, handsome neighbor I annoyed earlier.

Almost.

3

JULIETTE

I had only been in Golden Falls two days, but I was already itching for human interaction. Sitting on the back porch and gazing up at the starlit sky had calmed something in me. It made me realize I was up for the challenge of figuring out what was next. Not everything was fixed—it *had* only been two days, and I *was* still upset—but I also felt more energized and excited than I had in a long time.

I was eager to meet people in town and learn about the best spots to eat, shop, and spend time at. As much as I enjoyed my alone time, I preferred to be around others. Specifically, people who knew nothing about *Paradise Love*.

I'd always enjoyed meeting new people and striking up a conversation. I loved connecting with people and seeing excitement on their faces when they talked about their passions. What I struggled with was long-term connections and meeting people who wanted to prioritize friendship even when life got busy. I had friends in Chicago who were willing to grab lunch or coffee when it worked for them. But when I reached out last month once I returned from filming? No one had time to meet up.

I wasn't sure about the type of friendships I'd make in

Golden Falls. The chances were high they would be short-term, too, but I was hopeful, especially when Lily reached out about stopping by this afternoon.

I'd been looking forward to it all day, although my day so far was tough to beat. I had a lazy morning consisting of a long, hot shower, an iced coffee, and breakfast outside on the deck. I went into town to get groceries, and then I spent most of the morning reading.

Now, I was happy to be back in the air conditioned cabin.

A knock at the door signaled Lily's arrival. My bare feet padded against the hardwood floor as I quickly crossed the living room to the front door.

When I opened the door, I was met by a petite blonde woman, who looked to be around the same age as me, maybe a couple of years younger. She was smiling from ear to ear as she rocked back and forth on her heels. Her blue eyes were bright, and her blonde hair was pulled into a low, messy bun with a few wavy strands framing her face. It was like being greeted by a burst of sunshine. *And* she was holding a pink bakery box. We were going to get along great.

"You must be Lily!" I exclaimed and motioned for her to come inside. "It's so nice to meet you and put a face to the name."

When I booked my stay at the cabin, Lily texted me immediately to see if I needed anything ahead of my arrival. We'd been texting on and off since then. Seeing her now felt familiar, even if it was our first time meeting in person.

"I feel the same way. I'm so happy to have you here, Jules!" She smiled, gently bouncing on the balls of her white sneakers. I could feel the excitement vibrating off of her. "Oh! And I brought you these." She handed me the bakery box, and I lifted the lid to peek inside. My mouth watered immediately. "There's two lemon raspberry muffins and two slices of cherry coffee cake. Figured this would be a good way to lure you to visit my café next time you're downtown. Your first coffee or tea is on the house."

Even though Lily's words were simple, they comforted me immediately—like a warm hug. As much as I wanted this change of scenery, it was still overwhelming being in a new place and not knowing anyone. The way Lily's friendliness from text translated to in person made me feel even better about my decision to come here.

"I'll definitely stop by this week. It'll be the first place I go to when I drive into town next."

As we moved from the front entrance to the kitchen, Lily took in the space.

"Also," I said slowly, "I hope you don't mind, but I moved some stuff around. Just to open up the space a little."

"No, I don't mind at all. I love how you've rearranged the furniture. You didn't change much, but it already feels so different in here."

"Sometimes that's all it takes. It can also be easier for someone new to come in and see different potential for the space. Part of the reason why I love being an interior designer." Or the reason why I *loved* being a designer. I was so lost in the motion of grabbing two small plates for the treats Lily brought that I didn't realize my slip up until the words left my mouth. Trying to steer the conversation I said, "And you must've read my mind, because I've been craving something sweet."

Lily's smile brightened even more. "I hope you like them. The muffins and coffee cake are both favorites around here. The muffins are a family recipe that started with my mom's grandma and has been passed down generations. I had to set all this aside in the morning, because otherwise I knew it would sell out by the time I closed up." Lily sat at the kitchen table and thanked me as I set down plates and forks. "I guess when we were texting

I never asked what you did. Do you like interior design? What brings you to Golden Falls, then? Vacation?"

I sat next to Lily at the table, reaching for a fork and immediately grabbing one of the muffins. I could tell Lily's questions were out of genuine curiosity, and when I took a beat to respond, she added, "That was also a lot of questions. You don't have to tell me if you don't want to."

Those words allowed me to let my guard down. The opportunity to choose what I wanted to share rather than people already knowing information about my life from a tabloid article was refreshing. I'd been holding a lot in, and I knew it'd feel good to let it out, share it with someone I didn't know. But I also didn't want to ruin a potential friendship before it started.

"It's kind of a long story," I warned her.

She lifted a shoulder and reached for the slice of coffee cake. She looked up at me, her expression softening and putting me even more at ease. "I have time."

So, I gave Lily the rundown of what happened. Why I signed up for *Paradise Love* and how my experience was not what I expected. I told her about the whole ordeal with Tony: our time on the show, how I fell hard and fast, what he said after we won, and feeling like it was all for nothing. I shared how overwhelming the social media and tabloid attention was—plus my career struggles—and how I needed a break from it all, bringing me to Golden Falls.

By the time I finished, we'd eaten our lemon raspberry muffins and coffee cake, moved over to the couch, and each had a glass of wine. The whole time, Lily listened intently and validated my feelings. She reiterated how I wasn't overreacting and reminded me I wasn't alone.

It felt good to trust someone. It wasn't a secret that I let people in easily, but my gut was telling me I had nothing to worry about with Lily. While my gut had been wrong before, I had to trust myself, too.

"That's why you looked so familiar," Lily admitted. "I had the first few episodes on in the background while I'd get ready to open the café in the mornings, but I never finished the season. Certainly don't plan to now." Lily shook her head. "I'm definitely skipping future seasons, too. The producers had to have known Tony wasn't there for love, right? And they let him on anyway? Ugh, the whole thing sucks. I'm so sorry, Jules." She reached over to give my hand a squeeze.

"Yeah, it really does suck, but I know it'll pass. Just need to give it some time." I let out a breath. I'd keep repeating those words until they were true. "I saw this all going differently. I thought I'd fall in love and be less stressed about the future knowing I had someone by my side through it all."

Lily tilted her head to the side as she thought. "I get that. I do think having the right person by your side makes life less scary. But having the wrong person? That makes everything *more* stressful. It sucks that everyone had to watch your vulnerable moments play out, but you only gave him a few months, not a few years. And now you know even more of what you don't want in a partner."

I hadn't thought about it that way, but it put things into perspective. It had just been a few months. Maybe I could use that same amount of time in Golden Falls to turn things around.

"You're right. I hate that the audio clip is out there and people heard what he said, but at least I know the truth *now* and didn't fall deeper for him. He's right about one thing—we never would've worked in the real world. I can't be with someone who is so self-absorbed, entitled, and willing to do anything for money."

Lily nodded in agreement. "Oh, totally. From the first

episode I could tell you were too good for him. Your person is out there for you. I know it."

I shook my head with a scoff. "I have no interest in finding my person, at least not right now. I'm focusing on myself and figuring out next steps for my career. I love interior design and working with people, but I've lost my passion for it. The clients have also been extra difficult lately, which doesn't help. I don't know. I feel...stuck."

"You're clearly good at it and have a vision. We gotta get you back to why you started." Lily tucked her legs under her, turning so she was facing me more. "What if we worked together? I've been wanting to give my café a refresh but have been struggling to find the time and motivation. I have some ideas, but it feels daunting to try to tackle it on my own while also running the business."

I thought about Lily's suggestion. Luxe Living catered to wealthier clients and businesses, and I'd always wondered if we were missing out by not offering more affordable packages. I hadn't had time to think through the idea—but now, time was all I had. I didn't want to get ahead of myself, but I immediately recognized the potential of partnering with small businesses.

"I...yes. Yes! I'd love to." I paused before getting too excited. "Are you sure?"

"Very," Lily assured me. "Let's start this week, if that works for you? Send me your rates, and we'll go from there."

"Of course, that'll work for me. My schedule is wide open." I grinned. "I can't wait to stop by your café."

I couldn't remember the last time I was this excited about a project. Since I wasn't working for Luxe Living over the summer, I'd approach Lily's request on a freelance basis and adjust my rates accordingly. Maybe there were even other businesses in Golden Falls I could work with to see how well this type of model would work. If this proved to be a success and I wanted to return to Luxe Living once I was back in Chicago, I could potentially pitch a business expansion to Cheryl.

A wave of excitement suddenly coursed through me. I couldn't wait to hear Lily's ideas and brainstorm with her. And I hoped this temporary fresh start would work out in the long run.

"I'm so glad you stopped by today. I didn't really know what I was doing when I booked the cabin, and I know it's still early, but I have a really good feeling about the summer. I appreciate everything you've done to make me feel welcome," I admitted to Lily.

"I have a really good feeling about the summer, too." Lily nodded in agreement. "You're going to bring energy and excitement into town that people will love. I know it's just for the summer, but it's been a while since we've had someone new in town, besides the summer tourists who usually stay for a week or so. I'm excited to get to know you more—and make a new friend."

My smile widened at Lily's words. "Me, too. I think we're going to make a great team."

4

JULIETTE

A COUPLE DAYS LATER, I WAS MAKING GOOD ON MY PROMISE TO visit Lily's café. Plus, I needed to go into town to restock my fridge again...and maybe grab another bottle of wine.

The short drive was peaceful, and thanks to my GPS, I didn't get lost on the back roads. Since it was still early June, I was able to roll down my windows and enjoy the breeze before temperatures got too hot.

Golden Falls was a town of a couple thousand people, which meant there was minimal to no traffic. Such a welcome change from driving in Chicago.

Lily told me it would get busier during the summer as couples and families from across the state and Midwest came to visit. Apparently, the population more than tripled. Most spent their time enjoying the warm weather out on the water or on the trails, but the historic downtown also drew people in.

As I got into the heart of town, I immediately understood why.

The historic Victorian-era buildings blended effortlessly with the newer constructions, giving the town a rustic, cozy feel while staying modern. Antique light posts lined the brick sidewalks, along with flower planters and benches. Many of the local restaurants offered outdoor seating, and the picturesque Lake Golden provided a perfect view. I loved that the calming water was in view regardless of if I was in town or at the cabin.

I pulled into a parking spot right in front of Lily's café: Purrfect Blend Cat Café. As I got out of the car, I glanced around and also spotted a clothing boutique, yoga studio, and pizzeria on the same block. The grocery store was only a short walk away.

I couldn't wait to explore downtown, and that started with my meeting with Lily at Purrfect Blend.

"What if you moved these tables from the far wall so they were closer to the windows? It'll give customers a nice view, while also providing enough space for those walking in. We can plant some flowers in front of the café to enhance the view, similar to the other businesses on the street," I suggested as Lily and I walked around the space.

Lily tapped a pen against her chin in thought, slowly nodding. Her wavy golden-blonde hair was down today and kept out of her eyes with a light-blue headband. "Yeah, I love that idea. The space will feel more open, and it might even give me the opportunity to fit an extra table or two down the line."

Her café was now closed for the day, and we were in the middle of brainstorming upgrades to give the space a fresh, new feel. I could tell right away Lily loved her business and was proud of it. For good reason, too.

As soon as customers walked in, they were welcomed by the fresh smell of coffee, cinnamon, and caramel. Muffins, coffee cake, and various cookies were neatly organized inside three glass cases sitting on top of the light oak counter. Since it was only her baking, Lily often had a limited supply of pastries that sold out before the morning was over. It was her goal over the next year or so to hire some help, but on extra busy summer days, her mom stopped in to help take orders.

Behind the counter, Lily had various appliances, syrups, and mugs to make coffee and tea for her customers. Chalkboards hung on the wall behind the register with her feminine cursive writing detailing what drinks were available. For any lattes, Lily dusted a coconut sugar and cinnamon blend in the shape of paw prints.

There were circle tables and wooden chairs set up in the main room, as well as stools off to the side near the counter so customers could chat with Lily as she made their drinks. Lily displayed art from local artists on the walls, including paintings and drawings of cats, local views, and abstract art.

Customers could also take their drinks into the adjoining room where four to five cats roamed on any given day. Because of her partnership with the Golden Falls Animal Shelter, all of the cats were available for adoption. They had toys, cat trees, window perches, and more to keep them busy.

As welcoming as Lily's café was, it was also a little cluttered when you walked in, which is why we started with rearranging the tables. There were also opportunities to add more color and Lily's personality into the space. I wanted to start with small changes that were low cost and would make an immediate difference.

The back-and-forth brainstorming with a client was always one of my favorite parts, especially if they were excited about the project. While Lily had mentioned feeling overwhelmed, I could tell she had a lot of ideas and so much passion for her business.

After earning an associate's degree from the local community college, Lily opened her cat café last year. It had always been her dream to combine her love for animals, coffee, and baking.

Not only did I learn more about her business, I also found out Lily had lived in Golden Falls her whole life. Her parents and older brother lived in town, too, and she had an older sister who was a travel nurse in Hawaii.

"Having extra seating will be great, but no rush on adding it, especially if we add extra seating to the cat room," I assured Lily. I paused to write on my to-do list to stop by the thrift store to see if they had any comfortable chairs or loveseats. "I think new curtains would also be an easy addition, and we'd talked about how you wanted to add some color to the walls. Should I pick up paint swatches?"

Lily chewed on her bottom lip, reluctantly responding, "I can't ask you to help me with that, too. You're already doing so much."

"Lily, you *hired* me," I said, amused. "This is what I'm here to do, plus it means I get to see more of the town. I assume there's a hardware store nearby?"

She nodded. "Yeah, Hal's Hardware. Hal's the best. You'll like him, and he's a good person to know around town. Which reminds me, I need to show you around downtown and introduce you to some of the other business owners and residents. I want you to meet my best friend, Eliza, too, but she's out of town for the next few weeks at a yoga conference and retreat in Madison. She owns the yoga studio a few doors down." She waved her hand in the general direction. "You probably saw it on your way to the café."

"I did! It caught my eye right away. I'm excited to meet her and whoever else you introduce me to." I was excited to form friendships and connections in Golden Falls, even if I was only staying for a few months. I could easily see this being the type of place I'd come back to visit. "The store's called Hal's Hardware?"

"That's right. Just a couple blocks away past the restaurants and shops, toward the grocery store."

Wanting to be sure, I pulled out my phone, tapping on the maps app and searching for the hardware store. "Got it!" I said once I found it. "I think a neutral color or a pastel yellow would look really nice for this main wall and help the chalkboards pop. We can keep the other walls off white to help this one stand out but add other pops of color with various decor. I'll keep an eye out when I'm shopping and text you pictures of anything I find."

Lily nodded, a grateful smile gracing her lips as she slipped her notebook and pencil into the front pocket of her apron. "That sounds perfect. Whatever you think will look good will work for me. This is going to be great!"

She rounded the counter to begin cleaning up for the day, and I followed suit by packing up my laptop and notebook.

"Oh, by the way, are you free for dinner sometime this week or next?" Lily asked. "My parents have been wanting to introduce themselves. My dad loves to grill over the summer, and we'll have a bonfire, too."

"I'd love to. Text me the address and time, and I'll be there." Sliding my bag on my shoulder, I added, "I'm going to walk around downtown and pick up groceries before heading back to the cabin. I'll let you know about the paint, and we'll go from there."

"Yeah, actually, I'm about to wrap up here. If you want, we can walk together, and I'll show you around?"

"I'd love that," I eagerly replied.

Lily untied her apron and hung it up on the wall. The hook was shaped like a cat, of course. She grabbed her purse and met me at the door, fishing out her keys to lock up.

"Next time you come by, I'll have a new creation for you to test," she said. "I've been trying a recipe for vegan strawberry muffins, and I think it's *just* there. I'll want a couple people to try them before I sell them at the café."

"Wow, that sounds absolutely amazing. You don't have to ask me twice. I'm more than happy to try. Anything strawberry for the summer is perfect."

"We're on the same page today. I knew there was a reason I liked you," Lily teased.

I had no clue how Lily had time to be coming up with new creations while also revamping and running her café. This business meant a lot to her, and it made me even more eager to be in her corner.

5

WESLEY

Damn tourist season. It was already starting.

I hated the influx of visitors who came into town over the summer. Yes, I was grateful for the extra foot traffic—both for the bar I owned and the other businesses in town—but I still hated how there were so many new people around.

I'd lived here my whole life and still hadn't fully accepted that Golden Falls needed and thrived on tourism, especially during the summer. You either hated it, or you loved it. It was clear where I stood.

It especially irritated me when visitors treated Golden Falls as just another vacation spot, ignoring the people who lived here full-time. They came for a few weeks and then turned their backs.

I had connections to this town, to the people, that went beyond a simple visit. This was and always would be my home, and I was protective of those around me. I could count the people in my inner circle on one hand: my parents, two sisters, and Cooper, my best friend who was more like a brother.

"Damn, man. What's with the scowl on your face? Is that

why this place is so empty?" Cooper had on a shit-eating grin as he entered Lake Ridge from the back door.

"Ha, very funny," I deadpanned, but the corner of my lip twitched upward. "How many times are you going to keep making that joke?" We didn't open for another couple hours, and Cooper damn well knew that.

His grin stayed firmly in place as he approached the bar, leaning his forearms against the counter with his signature messy, dark-blond hair falling into light eyes full of amusement —at my expense. "Haven't decided yet, but it got that scowl off your face, didn't it?"

I grunted in response, continuing to stack the rack of dry beer glasses before we opened.

As much shit as we gave each other, I always knew Cooper had my back. There weren't many people who always put others first, but Cooper did. We'd known each other since we were kids, and he'd been with me through everything. It was exactly why, even though he wasn't a brother by blood, I considered him family. I'd do anything for him. No questions about it.

It also wasn't uncommon for him to be at the bar, whether it was to hang out or to help. He loved this place as much as I did.

Lake Ridge had been in my family for years. My dad, who grew up in town, started it in his early twenties, wanting to leave his mark on Golden Falls. He'd purchased an industrial building and renovated it. Once he was ready to build his staff, one of the first people he'd hired happened to be his future wife— my mom.

My dad always planned to sell Lake Ridge once he was done with it, not wanting to put pressure on me or my sisters to stay and take over. But I couldn't let him do that. I loved Golden Falls and never saw myself leaving—I also wanted to put my own mark on this town. Lake Ridge was a town staple, and I couldn't imagine Golden Falls without it. I had so many memories here, and I knew others did, too.

So, a few years ago, I bought the bar from my dad. I wanted to keep the simple feel I loved while also offering a fun, unique atmosphere for people who wanted to grab drinks, dance, sit outside, or all of the above.

Since taking over Lake Ridge, I'd done a handful of renovations with the help of Coop and my dad, including a custom-built wooden bar. I added a blue neon *Lake Ridge* sign over the door. There were pool tables, dart boards, and a dance floor.

The exposed-brick walls were decorated with photos from my favorite spots in Golden Falls, as well as pictures of my parents when they were running the place and newspaper clippings of when Lake Ridge opened.

I also added to the outdoor space. Now, when the garage doors opened, it transitioned seamlessly into an outdoor patio with bistro lights and yard games. Earlier this year, I added fire pits and outdoor tables, knowing they'd be a hit.

Between the revamped set up, expanding our beer and liquor selection, and testing out a small food menu, word about the bar traveled quickly. Lake Ridge landed on a few of those "must visit" lists for people traveling to Golden Falls and the surrounding towns. It was another draw to an already popular town.

It was my third summer running Lake Ridge, and I was proud of the work we'd done. I wanted to continue to grow the bar, turning it into a destination both day and night. There was a real momentum heading into this summer, and I wanted to take advantage of every second of it.

"You apologized to your new neighbor yet?" Cooper asked, pulling me out of my thoughts. He raised his brows as he pulled out one of the bar stools and sat.

I held back a groan. No, I hadn't. My first mistake had been walking over when her car pulled in. My second mistake had been telling Cooper what happened. He rightfully gave me shit about it.

"Haven't seen her around since then." It wasn't a lie. I really hadn't, but I also made no effort to stop by the cabin.

I'd been an asshole to my new, *temporary* neighbor, and I knew it. I was caught off guard, because I had no fucking clue someone was moving in there for the summer. The memories flooded my mind. Emotions I'd avoided tried to rise to the surface.

Nope. Not doing that.

I wanted nothing to do with that cabin or with Juliette Campbell, no matter how beautiful or intriguing she was. I'd spent enough summers in Golden Falls to spot a tourist from the city. She drove her goddamn Audi up and down the road at least three times before finding the cabin, and her bright-pink suitcase nearly blinded me.

She most definitely ordered DoorDash the other night, too.

Juliette would spend her summer here and then leave. Just like they always did.

"Hmm," Cooper hummed, eyeing me skeptically. "Well, maybe I'll stop by at some point and apologize for you. Be the one to give her a warm Golden Falls welcome."

I rolled my eyes but didn't say anything. I normally entertained Cooper's various remarks, but suddenly my patience was thin.

"What?" he asked innocently, raising his hands. "I want to make sure she's all settled in and give her a tour around town. Maybe show her some of the hiking trails around here. Who's better equipped than me?"

Cooper was a park ranger and helped manage Wisconsin's state parks that surrounded Golden Falls and the neighboring towns. He was also the town golden boy and the one women flocked to. He typically went for the tourists and kept it at a handful of dates before moving on.

"Fine by me. I don't care," I muttered.

"Wasn't asking for your permission, but thanks." That classic grin of his came back into play. "Everybody's talking about her."

"About the new girl?" Louise, one of the Lake Ridge bartenders, piped up as she walked past us and started to set up her station with various drink garnishes. Louise was in her fifties and had lived in Golden Falls for nearly her whole life. "Heard she's real nice and friendly. She was out walking around downtown with Lily yesterday."

"Are you talking about Juliette?" Ruby, one of my other employees, bounced up from the host stand to join in on the conversation. Ruby was a seasonal employee and worked summers and winters when she returned to Golden Falls from college. "She was my favorite on *Paradise Love* and now"—Ruby looked around before leaning in and whispering—"she's in our town." She let out a happy squeal. "We have a celebrity in Golden Falls!"

The three of us looked at Ruby like she'd started speaking a different language.

Ruby rolled her eyes. "*Paradise Love*. The reality dating show *everyone* online has been talking about." She paused, waiting for our reactions. "Really, nothing?"

Even Louise, who had her eyes and ears everywhere for gossip in our small town, was at a loss. Usually news of tourists didn't phase the locals, except for when there was someone new and they were staying for longer than a couple of weeks. And, apparently, if they were also on some dating show.

"I think you got the wrong crowd here, Ruby," Cooper said with a laugh. He turned to me. "You think Lily would know something?"

My jaw clenched, and I let out a deep sigh. Yeah, I had a

feeling Lily knew. My sister had rented our cabin to a reality TV star, for fuck's sake. I knew nothing about the show, but Juliette had to love attention and be a damn good liar if she was willing to fake being in love for the cameras. People didn't go on those shows for love—they went on for fame.

"The last thing this town needs is someone chasing their fifteen minutes of fame," I clipped.

The three of them stared at me in silence before Ruby spoke up. "Well, I'm glad she's here. This town could use a little bit of fun and a little bit less whatever attitude you have going on right now." She waved her finger in a circle in my direction.

Cooper nearly burst into laughter and moved his hand over his mouth to cover his smile. "She's got a point," he said under his breath, and Louise nodded in agreement.

"Now, if you'll excuse me, I have work to do." With a flick of her hair, Ruby strutted off.

I ran a hand over my face. "Here, grab a towel and help me dry off the bar counter while I finish stacking these glasses," I grumbled, tossing a towel to Cooper. He caught it with ease and stood from the stool.

The start of the summer always reminded me I could use extra help. Louise and Ruby were part of my small, dedicated staff, but on busy summer nights, we could use more help to serve drinks and food. Especially if I was serious about expanding the food menu.

Ruby was the only one of my seasonal staff who had returned to Golden Falls this summer. So, I had to figure something out, and soon. Because summer was here and Golden Falls was already bustling with activity.

I needed to focus solely on Lake Ridge. I couldn't afford any distractions if I wanted the business to grow. If I wanted things to work out.

Not again.

6

WESLEY

THE UNIVERSE WAS TESTING ME—OR PUNISHING ME—BECAUSE I couldn't remember the last time the bar had been as swamped as tonight. It was a Friday night, so I expected it to be busy, but we were already drawing a bigger crowd than we had at last year's peak—and summer had only just started.

Most customers tonight were understanding of the longer wait to get a table or be served drinks, but I'd told my staff to offer a free drink or basket of fries if people got impatient.

I had to figure something out and fast.

Tonight, I didn't mind having to help with running food and making drinks, but I knew it wasn't sustainable if we wanted to continue to grow. Normally, I helped set up before we opened and then spent the evenings in the back office catching up on paperwork and payroll.

Since that hadn't been the case today, I knew I was in for an even longer day tomorrow.

"See you tomorrow, Louise." I gave her a nod as I left through the back door.

"Nice work today, boss," she called back from the bar as she finished closing up for the night. I still wasn't used to being called "boss," especially not from Louise.

My dad hired her as a bartender back when he still owned the place, and she'd been working here for the last fifteen years. The best bartender in town. Hell, the best bartender in the state.

I was grateful for my staff, especially Louise, who I'd learned a lot from over the years. I was nervous to add someone new to the mix, because I didn't want to ruin the current group's dynamic.

I got into the driver's side of my new black Ford pickup truck, continuing to think through who in town might be looking for a bartending gig. I was thrilled to upgrade my truck to an all-electric model earlier this year, and that new car excitement still hadn't worn off. As I started to pull out of the parking lot, my phone rang through the truck's Bluetooth system. Mom was calling.

"Hey, Ma. You're up late." I shouldn't have been surprised she was still up. Ever since my sisters and I moved out, Mom became a night owl, often staying up late watching crime documentaries or reading romance books. Something about how she had "so much energy" because we weren't stressing her out anymore. I knew that wasn't quite true—she still worried about us.

She laughed. "I couldn't put my book down. Had to finish it before going to bed. Plus, I was hoping to catch you before bed but knew you'd be busy at the bar. How'd everything go tonight?"

"Busier than I anticipated but...overall fine. I know if this keeps up, I'm in trouble, though. I want to hire a couple more people this summer. Just thinking through the logistics. Know anyone who might be looking for some extra work?"

"Well," Mom said, "Lily mentioned Eliza was looking for some extra work here and there when she gets back from her trip to Madison. She's a fast learner and was a bartender in college. I bet she'd be a good addition. She knows the staff and regulars already, too."

Now that I thought about it, Cooper, who was Eliza's older brother, mentioned she was looking for a second job to help fund plans for her yoga studio. Eliza taught classes during the day and into the early evening.

"I'll ask and see what she thinks. Lily didn't say anything to me. As usual," I grumbled. It was a low jab at my sister, and I knew it. I was frustrated at her for renting out the cabin, especially now knowing it was to someone who spent their free time on reality TV. But I also couldn't blame her. After all, Lily didn't know the full story of what happened. No one did.

"Oh, come on, Wes. Don't give her a hard time. We've been renting out the cabin for years." Mom paused, clearly wanting to say more. Just as I thought she'd drop it, as she had over the last two years, she asked, "Why did seeing it rented out throw you off so much?"

Wasn't that a damn good question I wish I knew the answer to.

I didn't even have time to think of a way to deflect before she added, "What happened between you and Gretchen?"

I let out a low sigh. Now that I *did* know the answer to, but I didn't have much interest in revisiting the past. Cooper knew majority of the story, but I hadn't even told him the full truth of how my heart had been broken by someone passing through.

"Things didn't work out. Not much more to tell. I've moved on and am focusing on Lake Ridge now. That's my priority." That much was true. Gretchen might have broken my heart, but I didn't have feelings for her anymore. My focus was making the bar as successful as possible, which left no time for dating, relationships, or falling in love. Besides, I was better off alone, because it meant not getting my heart broken. "You said you wanted to ask me something?"

Even over the phone, I could tell Mom wasn't happy with my answer and changing the subject, but she dropped it. For now at least.

"I did. I was hoping you'd be able to stop by Hal's this week. I was talking to him today, and he mentioned his card reader at the store wasn't working. He should really update his whole computer system, but...one step at a time. Think you'd be able to help him out?"

"Yeah, no problem at all. I'll stop by later this week," I said with no hesitation. "I'll even see if I can convince him to upgrade everything down the line. It'll be easier on him."

Hal Nelson was like a grandfather to me and my younger sisters. I was lucky both sets of my grandparents were around when I was growing up, but they didn't live nearby. Hal did.

He was at every sports game, every graduation, every milestone for me and my sisters. Even now, with us all grown up, he still found ways to support what we were doing. Helping him fix the card reader was the least I could do.

"Thanks, Wes. See if he wants to come over for dinner soon, too."

"Will do."

Hal was an honorary part of our family, but I often wondered about his own family. He lost his wife Vera a couple of years ago. He had a son and grandson, who was a few years older than Lily. Hal had pictures on the walls of his hardware store of his grandson over the years.

Hal's son and my dad grew up together, but Ron Nelson left Golden Falls and never came back. Ron made a name for himself with Nelson Group, a real estate firm based in Milwaukee that now had offices all across the country. Nelson Group focused on development, construction, and property management.

Their whole model was bringing in more "modern" businesses while keeping a small town feel. The latter was a bunch of bullshit.

They bought buildings and made local businesses think it was in their best interest. But really, most tenants were priced out when the rent increased. I knew there were likely some benefits for the businesses that were able to afford to stay, but it still didn't sit right with me for the businesses that had to close or find a new space. Especially when the companies that filled the now vacant space were chains and multi-billion-dollar businesses.

A local coffee shop closed, and suddenly the space turned into a chain coffee shop. A building filled with small businesses was suddenly getting turned into a luxury apartment complex.

It didn't feel like a coincidence. To me, it seemed like they were working against the businesses these small towns were built on, ones that spanned generations. The very type of business Hal owned.

And I could only imagine they were eyeing the building Hal owned and managed, which housed Lily's café and Eliza's yoga studio. But Hal said we had nothing to worry about, and all we could do was believe him.

I finished up the call with my mom as I was pulling into my driveway, the gravel crunching underneath the tires. I was more than ready to end the night with a beer on the back porch overlooking the water and then go to bed.

As I stepped out of my truck, I couldn't help but let my gaze wander to the property to the left, obscured by various maple and cedar trees. My evening had been too busy to think about Juliette Campbell, but now, all of a sudden, I had all the time in the world.

I thought back to our first interaction and how she didn't back down. How the golden sun lit her up like she was a goddamn angel. The fire in her green eyes ignited something inside me, something I had no business feeling.

I didn't like it. I didn't like how she'd only been in my town for less than a week and already had people talking about her, already found a way to get under my skin. A woman who looked like that—sun-kissed skin, wavy brown hair, long legs, and a sassy mouth—didn't fly under the radar. No way in hell.

7

JULIETTE

I walked carefully across the tile floors in the kitchen, not wanting to mess up my freshly painted toes. As I set my mug in the kitchen sink, I couldn't help but look out the window. I didn't think I'd ever get tired of the lake sparkling in the morning sun. I'd have to go out on the water later this week—Lily had told me there were paddle boards and kayaks I was free to use in the small shed next to the cabin.

My gaze shifted to the house down the road, or where I figured the house was. Trees obscured the property, but the dock and pontoon boat were in full view, as was the man walking down the steps with a natural, quiet confidence.

I didn't have to stare long to realize it was the same man who'd given me my not-so-warm welcome. Guess I'd been right about him living close by.

Once he was by the boat, he crouched down and started to work with his hands. Likely retying and retightening the ropes, but I wasn't sure.

What I *was* sure about, even from far away, was that he handled the thick ropes with skill, his fingers working expertly and quickly. The sun shone down on him like a spotlight and highlighted the tee stretched across his back and how his strong arms flexed with ease.

His jeans hung on his hips and hugged his muscular legs as he stood back up. He unlatched the boat's side gate and stepped onto the deck. Each movement was natural, without any hesitation; he knew what he was doing. He likely had the same routine every summer.

I wanted to walk away from the window, but I couldn't. My feet were glued to the floor. Something was pulling me to the mystery man. His confidence and how at ease he looked on the boat was how I wanted to feel in life.

We hadn't run into each other since I moved in. Maybe that was a good thing. I wasn't looking for any distractions over the summer. I couldn't help but wonder, though, where his reaction came from and why he was all prickly and grumpy.

I was pulled away from the window when my phone rang. I slowly made the walk over to where I'd been sitting at the kitchen table. I accepted the call and put the phone on speaker, starting to paint my fingernails with the light pastel-pink polish named "summer love"—the very thing I would not be having.

"Hey, Grant," I greeted.

"Hey, Jules. You settling in okay?" my brother asked, not missing a beat.

"Yeah, settling in just fine. The drive wasn't too bad, and I'm pretty much all unpacked. The cabin was furnished, so I didn't have to worry about moving my stuff from storage. I'll figure out what to do with it all once I decide what I'm doing long-term. I'm focusing on the summer for now."

Grant hummed as he listened. "And how about everything else?"

Wasn't that a loaded question.

"Good enough, I guess." I sighed. "There haven't been any new articles, so I'm hoping people are already forgetting. I haven't checked social media. Figured it'd be best to stay off of it for now." I looked out the kitchen window that faced the back deck and the lake, hoping Grant hadn't heard my sigh. I thought back to my conversation with him earlier in the week. "And I'm not running away from my problems. I'm taking a much needed break."

"I shouldn't have said that. I was just...worried about you. You were staying here one day and then all packed up and on the move the next. You deserve the break. But be careful, okay?"

I could've used that reminder a few months ago before going on *Paradise Love.*

"Yeah, I'll be careful," I assured him. "I've already made a friend in Golden Falls. Her name's Lily, and it's her parents' cabin I'm staying at, but she's the one who manages it." I filled Grant in on what I knew from Lily about Golden Falls and how we were working together on her café.

"Not surprised you've already made a friend. You always had a talent for meeting people and connecting with them, Jules. Don't let what happened deter you from that." I appreciated Grant's words, because lately, it hadn't felt like much of a talent. It felt like I'd been opening my heart and trusting the wrong people. But I knew with Lily I was finally trusting the *right* person. Talking, working, and spending time with her was natural—as if we'd been friends for years. That didn't come easily, especially not as an adult.

But then my mind wandered to my mysterious neighbor, who I hadn't seen since my first day in Golden Falls. For the first friend I made, it seemed like I'd made an enemy, too. Well, enemy might be too strong of a word, at least on my end. I had no clue what he thought of me.

"It's been a while since I've been this inspired," I admitted. "In a way, going on the show gave me perspective on what I want to do differently in my day-to-day life. Which, actually, since I'll be in Golden Falls for the summer, do you think you could get me out of my lease? I want to find an apartment with a different property company when I get back to Chicago."

"Sure, I'd be happy to," he said. "If anything else comes to mind you want me to look at, let me know. I'm more than willing to help. I'd say that to anyone, but especially you, Jules. You're my sister, and I hate to see you hurting."

Grant was a lawyer—one of the top in Chicago for labor and employment law. He quickly made a reputation for himself by advocating and helping clients with wrongful termination, discrimination, harassment, and other issues related to the workplace. In addition to working at a law firm, he focused his time on pro bono cases. His dedication and efforts, especially on those cases, landed him on the *Forbes* 30 under 30 list a few years ago.

Grant and I were four years apart and hadn't always been this close. We fought *a lot* growing up, usually over small things, and it wasn't until he went off to college and law school that we got closer. Likely because we weren't living in the same house.

When we both ended up in Chicago, we started to spend more time together. We, of course, still bickered a lot, but it was different. It definitely made our parents happy that we were getting along. Our parents recently moved from the Chicago suburbs, where we grew up, down to Florida, looking to escape the Midwest winters for warm weather and sandy beaches. Not a bad deal.

I'd considered going down to Florida for the summer, but it didn't feel right. I wanted to figure out my next steps on my own.

"Thank you for caring so much, really. I know you have a lot on your plate, and I appreciate you making time for this. I know I've been a little distant with everything, but it's only because I don't want it to be a big deal. I just want to move on and enjoy the summer. I don't want people to pity me for trusting the wrong person and getting my heart broken."

"I don't think it's that people pity you," Grant clarified. "I think some of them relate to what happened. At least from what I've seen on social media. Plus people are saying you deserve better, which I completely agree with."

I hadn't thought of it that way, that people might be thinking of their own breakups and relating to what happened between Tony and me. I'd been focused on how embarrassing it was, but everyone got their heart broken at some point. I'd eventually, a long time from now, find the person I was meant to be with.

"Wait, since when are you checking social media? You always complain about it."

Grant let out a heavy sigh. "Since I've been trying to get in touch with Scarlett."

Now *that* caught my attention. Grant hadn't uttered her name in years. I finished painting my nails and carefully closed the bottle of polish, laying my hands on the table to dry.

"Scarlett? Why are you trying to get ahold of her?" I asked.

My brother's college sweetheart was Scarlett Sinclair. Like *the* Scarlett Sinclair. The incredibly talented and successful Academy Award-winning actress.

Their romance was a whirlwind. They met during their freshman year, quickly fell for each other and were inseparable, got married toward the end of their senior year, and then divorced a few years later. My parents and I had been shocked by the divorce. We saw the two of them together—what they had was real. It was the type of love people wrote romance books about.

"Wow, you've really been off social media. I thought you

would've heard by now." Grant's words had me on edge. What wasn't he telling me?

"Well, yeah, I couldn't check my phone when we were filming, and then I haven't been online since getting back. What happened?"

"When you were filming, there was an announcement in the tabloids that Scarlett was engaged. It was all speculation, but there were photos and everything," Grant explained.

My eyes widened, and somehow, I'd managed to hold in my gasp.

He continued, "Then a few days ago, a story came out claiming Scarlett's engagement was fake because she was still married. To me."

I shrieked, unable to hold in my reaction this time. I parted my lips, about to tell Grant this sounded very similar to the movie I just watched, but I figured that wouldn't help, so I kept it to myself.

"I haven't been able to get in touch with her. I texted and called. I thought maybe I could get through to her by social media. But nothing. It's been complete silence. Whatever, it's not my problem," he scoffed.

I had no idea what happened between the two of them, but I couldn't imagine any of this was easy. He might claim it wasn't his problem, but I knew from the tone of this voice it was very much on his mind (and it really did seem like his problem!). My brother liked to help others and fix what was wrong—he wasn't going to be able to forget about this.

"I'm sorry, Grant. Hopefully, you hear from her soon," I offered.

He sighed again. "Nothing I can do but wait. And, hey, don't worry about this. Focus on yourself, okay? This summer is supposed to be for you. I gotta run, though. My next appointment showed up a few minutes early. Let me know if you need anything, and talk to you soon."

"I will. Talk to you soon," I responded before hanging up.

I wondered if the Campbell siblings were doomed when it came to relationships.

It sure seemed like it.

8

WESLEY

WHEN LIFE GOT TOO BUSY OR CHAOTIC, I KNEW I COULD AT LEAST hide out at home. Similar to the bar, this house had been in my family for years. It was where my parents first lived after they got married but before they had me and my sisters. Once they knew they wanted to start a family, they decided to buy a family home and rent this place out.

It had been a rental property for most of my life growing up —same with the cabin down the road. When I decided I was putting down roots in Golden Falls after college, I bought the house from them.

It was in good shape, but I wanted to make it my own. I fixed up the floors, changed out the faucets, and painted the walls. While I hadn't asked Lily for help, I appreciated the decor she brought in. The place had a comfortable and simple feel on the main floor. In the basement, I'd put in a small bar that matched the one at Lake Ridge, as well as a pool table, dart board, and workout area.

While I lived among rental properties—most of the road had tourists coming in and out over the summer—the house was tucked into the trees, which made it quiet and private. Plus, nothing beat looking out the window and being surrounded by water and a line of trees.

I didn't have nearly as much time these days to be out on the water. I finally had the chance yesterday to spend time on the dock and get the pontoon ready. Normally, I would've already taken the boat out at least once or twice.

Today would've been a great day to be out on the water since it was a perfect summer day—not too humid, clouds in the sky, and the sun shining bright. I had my kitchen window open, letting in the breeze as I cooked breakfast. A comfortable and quiet morning was exactly what I needed before heading into Lake Ridge in the afternoon.

I lifted the skillet from the stove, letting the two over-easy eggs slide off and onto the two pieces of toast on my plate. I was ready to have my breakfast at the kitchen table when the silence was broken by a high-pitched scream followed by a loud splash.

Great. So much for quiet.

It wasn't uncommon for people visiting Golden Falls to be reckless out on the water, and it was one of the things I hated most from the tourists. Driving the jet skis like idiots. Not wearing life jackets. I lived here long enough to see and hear about the tragedies that happened when you weren't careful— when you thought you were invincible.

The last thing I wanted was someone getting hurt. I quickly set my plate down and pulled the back door open, standing on my deck first to see if I could spot anyone.

My bare feet thumped quickly on the wooden steps until I reached the dock, nearly ready to jump in. But then she surfaced the water, pushing her wet, brown locks out of her eyes.

Juliette Campbell. Of course.

She blinked the water out of her eyes and reached for the stand-up paddle board. The ankle strap cord was submerged under water, meaning she was using it. I let out a sigh of relief. She likely lost her balance and fell in but was overall fine.

I was panting from running down the stairs, and she was catching her breath, too.

I should've walked back inside...but I couldn't.

When she pushed up onto the board, her tiny yellow bikini left nothing to the imagination, displaying her round breasts, curves, and full ass, especially when she reached over to grab the floating paddle. Juliette was undeniably stunning. So stunning it was impossible for me to keep my eyes off her.

But I also knew she was temporary. Maybe if I'd met her a few years ago, things would've been different. She would've gotten the version of me from *before*.

Juliette let out a gasp when she finally spotted me, placing her hand on her chest. "How long have you been there?!" Instead of standing, Juliette remained on her knees, turning so she was facing me on the board.

"Ever since your scream ruined my breakfast," I gritted, realizing my food was probably cold. Who wanted cold eggs? "Had to make sure you weren't drowning. I'd prefer not to have that on my conscience."

"Lucky for you, neighbor, I don't need saving. And even if I did, I'd much rather save myself than accept your help."

"Smart ass," I muttered.

I watched as she reached behind her, the thin yellow straps of her swimsuit falling to the sides. With her hand over her breasts to hold up her bikini top, she carefully lay down on her stomach. Her bare back and round ass were on full display. My fists clenched at my sides.

She'd untied her bikini top.

I pinched the bridge of my nose, closing my eyes and trying to gather my composure. I didn't lose control like this. I inhaled deeply, steadying my heavy breathing, and opened my eyes at the same time Juliette used her hand to block the sun, squinting as she looked over at me.

My eyes could've been playing tricks on me, but I swore a tiny, satisfied smile crossed her lips. This woman was going to be the death of me.

"What," I gritted, "do you think you're doing?"

"What does it look like I'm doing? I'm enjoying the water and tanning. You're not going to tell me the lake is private property, too, are you?"

"Your bikini is off," I growled.

"Barely, and it's just my top." She rolled her eyes. "I don't want tan lines on my back."

My jaw clenched as I continued to stare at her.

"What?" She raised her brows. "Were you hoping for a show?" A smirk tilted those full, pouty lips.

"That's the last thing I want, sweetheart. Are you already thinking about the next reality dating show you'll be on? Sorry to disappoint, but there are no camera crews in Golden Falls."

Her shoulders tensed from my words, and regret hit me immediately, leaving a bitter and sour taste in my mouth.

"Sweetheart?" she asked with a scoff, rolling her eyes and ignoring my insult. She lifted her head slightly, her eyes scanning down my body to my jeans, landing just below my belt, before she rested her head back down and closed her eyes. "And your body says otherwise."

I didn't have a good response, because my dick had, in fact, betrayed me. My jeans were quickly growing too tight. All of a sudden, all I could think about was ripping off those tiny bikini bottoms and having her splayed out on the board for my eyes only. My cock twitched.

I didn't know if I was more irritated at her or with myself. I turned around, stomping back up the wooden steps. "I don't know what you're talking about!" I called over my shoulder, swearing under my breath.

"Enjoy your cold shower, *sweetheart!*"

Fuck. She was right. I needed a cold shower, and I needed it now.

A couple days and cold showers later, I felt just as irritated and on edge. Images of Juliette in a yellow bikini plagued my mind, and I needed to try even harder to avoid her. It was the only option.

I pushed open the door to Purrfect Blend, immediately spotting Lily behind the counter with her back turned to the door. It was late in the afternoon, which meant she was closing up for the day.

"Well, if it isn't my dearest brother," she greeted without turning around.

"Uh...how'd you—"

"The reflection on the espresso machine," Lily answered before I even finished. "I like seeing you a little freaked out, though. Should've kept that going longer." She turned around with a grin. "I have a few cookies left over from the day. Want me to pack them up for you?"

I approached the counter, tilting my head to look at the cookies in the glass cases. Wait, that wasn't what I was here for. I was here to talk with her about the cabin rental—not get lured with sweet treats. That was the problem with Lily. Well, problem was too strong of a word. But I could never stay mad or be frustrated with her for long. Between her kindness and big heart, it was impossible.

"Sure, yeah, I'll take whatever you have left." I tapped my fingers on the counter as Lily grabbed a pair of tongs to place the treats in a pink bakery box.

She glanced down at my fingers and then back up at me. "What's on your mind?"

I wasn't exactly sure how to ease into what I wanted to ask, so I blurted, "You rented the cabin to a reality TV star?"

Lily froze for a moment, and her shoulders stiffened ever so slightly before she continued going through the motions of packing up the pastries, avoiding my gaze. "Where'd you hear that she was on a reality show?" Lily's voice was casual as she skirted around my question, but I knew when my sister was avoiding telling the truth.

"From Ruby. Something about Paradise..." I waved my hand, unable to remember the exact name of the show.

Lily swore under her breath as she folded the top of the box to a close. "I figured people around here would find out eventually, but not this quickly. Did Ruby tell anyone else?"

"Cooper was there, but I doubt he cares." Cooper also didn't participate in small town gossip—that much. "But Louise was there, too. That seemed to be the first she'd heard of it."

Lily's eyebrows raised. "Ruby was aware of town gossip before Louise? That's unheard of." She let out a small laugh. "But with Louise knowing, it's only a matter of days before it gets out to the whole town. Shoot, I need to tell Jules. I don't want her to think I shared any of this."

"So you *did* know?" I crossed my arms over my chest. I'm sure there were plenty of people Lily could've rented the cabin to, even multiple people throughout the summer instead of a short-term rental.

"Don't get all"—Lily pointed the tongs in my direction—"grumpy. It's not a crime to go on a reality TV show." She glared at me before continuing. "I didn't know about what happened when I rented the place to Jules, but even if I did, why should it matter? She needed a place for the summer, and the cabin was available. I hadn't accepted any of the short-term rentals yet, so it all worked out."

"Because she's bringing unnecessary attention and drama to our town. That's why it matters, Lily. The summer is busy enough. I don't need my staff or patrons gossiping about Paradise whatever."

Lily rolled her eyes. "Oh my god, Wes. People are always going to be gossiping about some small town drama. It's Golden Falls." Lily set the two pastry boxes on the counter. "You're being unfair. You haven't even met Jules yet. Why don't you go next door and introduce yourself like a normal neighbor? You'll see she's super nice."

I held my tongue, not correcting my sister that I technically had met Juliette (twice) and was next door already. Except it wasn't to introduce myself. Lily's other words—*about what happened* and *she needed a place for the summer*—confirmed my suspicions that this was another city girl looking to get away from her problems. That was not someone I had interest in getting to know. That was someone who was either looking for trouble or running away from it.

"Thanks for the cookies," I said to my sister as I grabbed the box.

"You're overreacting! I'm not giving you any more cookies or pastries until you say hi to Jules," Lily called out as I walked out the door. "And be nice to her!"

9

JULIETTE

YOU KNOW THE FEELING WHEN YOU'RE ON VACATION AND everything is better than it is at home? The food. The people. The weather. But then you're not sure if it's because you have the vacation high or if things are *actually* better?

That's how Golden Falls has felt so far.

I was letting myself slow down and really enjoy my

surroundings. I was going into town almost every day, spending time with Lily, cooking dinner for myself, and spending evenings reading on the back porch. If I wanted to tan topless, I did. And if I wanted to irritate a man who had no business telling me what to do, I did that, too.

I wasn't checking social media and was overall spending way less time on my phone.

I liked Golden Falls.

I'd wanted to find a place I was excited to settle down in and plant roots, but I couldn't get out of the habit of moving around. It's what I did when the opportunity for *Paradise Love* came up, and even now, it was what I was doing for the summer.

Maybe I did default to running, but that was only because I didn't feel like I had my own safe space to retreat to when things got hard.

It was similar with friendships and relationships. I kept people at a distance, because I knew eventually one of us would move away or get too busy. And then what? I'd tried long-distance friendships. They worked for a while but eventually fizzled out.

Even though I'd been in Chicago for the last four years, I still hadn't put down roots. As much as I enjoyed the city, it wasn't the place for me long term. But I couldn't figure out why. Why could I see myself more in Golden Falls than Chicago? What was I missing?

I had time to figure it all out. But the looming feeling that I should have it all solved by now? It didn't go away. Society had a timeline, for women especially. Finish school, get married, and start having kids—all before turning thirty. I *did* want that, eventually, but first I wanted to be happy on my own. I didn't want to fall for the wrong person, again.

It wasn't lost on me how lucky I was to afford a summer up

here in the first place and take the time to be passionate about my career again. I wasn't about to let this chance go to waste.

The last few months especially, I'd felt an increased sense of anxiety. That my career wasn't on the right path, that I wasn't making enough money, that I'd lost touch with people in my life. Maybe it was silly to think a reality TV show would fix all that, but I thought it would encourage me to not think about work and focus on the relationships in front of me.

Turns out, what I needed all along was getting away to a Wisconsin small town. Much more realistic than Fiji.

The cabin truly was equipped to be a summer rental, and it surprised me that it had been empty for what sounded like a couple of years. Surely it had to have been by choice, since a property like this would get booked immediately.

I leaned my head back against the Adirondack chair on the back porch, taking a few minutes for myself and admiring the view before heading downtown for most of the day. The gentle breeze brushed my face, and the warm sun kissed the exposed skin of my legs and arms. I'd opted for a pair of distressed denim shorts, a tank top, and sandals today. Much more casual and relaxed than what I wore to work back in Chicago.

As much as I wanted to sit out here all day, I had to get my day started. My first stop was Hal's Hardware.

The drive downtown was getting more familiar. I didn't need my GPS this time. Progress! The overview Lily gave me last week really helped. Everything was pretty close to each other and easy to find once I got to Main Street. I typically parked my car in front of Lily's café and then walked to where I needed to go. Today that was Hal's.

Lily told me he was a man in his early seventies who'd lived here forever. He ran his hardware store and also owned the building where Lily's café and Eliza's yoga studio were.

According to Lily, Hal was nearing retirement and was looking to decrease his responsibilities with managing the building. Lily was hoping for the opportunity to own the building and had been setting aside savings each month so she'd be ready if Hal approached her about a potential deal. She had a feeling he'd say something by the end of the year based on various hints from him.

I pushed open the red wooden door to Hal's, and the bell over it jingled. An older man with thick white hair, a round belly, and glasses sliding off his nose, wearing jeans and a checkered blue shirt, turned around from the front counter, a welcoming smile on his face. I assumed this was the famous Hal of Hal's Hardware.

"Howdy, miss. What can I do for ya?"

"Hi, I'm here to look at some paint swatches. I'm picking out a color for Lily's café. You must be Hal." I took a few steps toward the counter and stretched my hand out. "I'm Jules. I'm staying at the Richards's rental cabin."

Hal easily shook my hand, nodding as he listened. "Welcome to Golden Falls. Anyone who is friends with the Richards family, especially Miss Lily, is good in my book. I can't believe she's in her twenties already. I could've sworn she just graduated high school." There was a warm fondness in his voice.

"Lily had nothing but good things to say about you, too. I take it you're close with her and her family?"

Hal nodded. "Yes, ma'am. Those kids are like grandchildren to me, especially with my own grandson not living in town. It's been a while since I've seen him, but he's doing well for himself.

He's a couple years older than Lily." He paused for a moment before adding, "My son left Golden Falls and hasn't looked back since. Turns out this town isn't right for everyone, but I have a feeling it'll be right for you."

When Hal spoke about his son, his tone wasn't angry or upset. More so like he'd accepted this was how it all worked out. And while it sounded like there was more of a story there, I didn't want to push.

"Oh, thank you." I smiled. "I'm only here for the summer, but I'm trying to make the most of my time here."

Hal hummed, and I could've sworn there was a twinkle in his eye. After a beat, he added, "Good they're renting out that cabin again. It's a beautiful property."

That was the second time someone mentioned there had been a period of time when the cabin wasn't being rented out.

"It really is beautiful. I'm so glad I'm able to stay there and get to know this town. I haven't been here long but can already tell there's something special about Golden Falls."

The corner of his lips twisted upward. He stepped from behind the counter and waved his hand for me to follow him to the back corner of the store.

"I'll likely need to order whatever paint you pick out since my in-store supply is limited, but go on ahead and take a look. Feel free to come and get me if you have any questions." Hal extended his arm to showcase the wall filled with paint swatches to choose from. My gaze zeroed in on the section of pastel yellow.

"Perfect! I'll be sure to ask if anything comes up. Thanks so much, Hal."

"It's not a problem at all, Miss Jules. Welcome to town."

10

JULIETTE

IT WAS EASY TO LOSE TRACK OF TIME AT HAL'S AS I THOUGHT about all the ideas Lily and I had discussed. I picked out the yellow paint color I wanted to order, as well as warm beige for the adjoining room if Lily wanted to switch up the color there, too.

Our earlier conversation of flowers also came to mind, both for Lily's café and the cabin's front porch. I knew I wasn't going to be in the rental for long, but adding some flower pots would be an easy addition and add some color to the exterior.

I was looking through the aisle of colorful ceramic flower pots when the bell above the door signaled someone else had entered the shop.

"Hey, Hal. How's the day treating you?" The voice was warm, low, and familiar.

"I'd be better if this dang machine was working. I swear this thing causes more trouble than it's worth. What's wrong with taking cash? How come I gotta accommodate those plastic cards?"

A rough, husky chuckle escaped the newcomer. "It'll all be smooth sailing once we get it set up properly. It's the same system I have at the bar. I'll have it back up and running in no time."

When I discreetly peered around from the end of the aisle, I immediately realized why the voice was so familiar.

It was my grumpy asshole neighbor, and he was *smiling*. The corners of his eyes crinkled from his smile. A smile that made my knees weak. A smile warm like summer.

He tipped his head back and let out a low laugh over something else Hal said.

So he *did* know how to be nice.

He just hadn't wanted to be nice to me.

It was clear mystery man was a local. The way he spoke to Hal. His confident stance and relaxed shoulders. He was at ease here. He had the same demeanor out on the dock earlier in the week.

And he mentioned he'd owned a bar. Had Lily mentioned a bar when she'd been showing me around? I didn't remember.

I couldn't look away from him, my eyes scanning his tall, broad frame. The way his muscles flexed as he leaned his hip against the front counter. His facial hair was shorter today—stubble instead of a neatly trimmed beard. His brown hair was tousled, like he constantly ran his fingers through it.

He looked a lot better smiling than he did scowling.

My cheeks started heating up, and my palms got sweaty. When did it become a million degrees in here?

I couldn't remember the last time a man had captured my attention like this. Or the last time my body reacted this way. I'd been on my fair share of dates over the last few years—unsuccessful ones, clearly—and then *Paradise Love*. Mystery man looked nothing like Tony. Tony was always clean shaven, had his hair neatly styled, and always had on a dress shirt or polo. And my body never reacted like this to Tony—or any of my exes.

I really, *really* hoped my type wasn't arrogant asshole.

After taking a final look at my neighbor, I let out a sigh and turned my attention back to the ceramic pots. I'd already picked out two, and there was a final one that stood out when I first walked into a store. A bright-blue flower pot with an intricate, colorful design that would look perfect next to the cabin's front steps.

I leaned forward, propping my right foot on the bottom most shelf to give me some extra height. I reached my arm up to move the pot closer to the edge. Just as I got it close enough to grab it, my right foot slipped. I stumbled back but managed to stay upright.

The rest happened in slow motion.

The pot teetered, teetered, teetered on the edge of the shelf.

Then it tumbled down, shattering on the floor.

11

JULIETTE

"Fuck," I muttered as I ran my fingers through my hair. I looked around for a broom and dust pan. Anything to clean this up with.

"Everything okay back there?" a voice called out. It wasn't Hal's, which meant...

"Everything's fine!" I responded quickly, kneeling on the tile floor next to the mess and trying to gather the broken pieces.

"Huh, causing trouble already, city girl? What a surprise."

I tipped my head back, my eyes meeting the intense gaze above me. His expression was harsh, his jaw sharp and clenched so tight I thought he was going to crack a molar.

Gone was the smile I'd seen a moment ago. Gone was the laugh I'd heard.

This was the same version of the man I'd met on my first day and the version who had come barreling down the steps of his dock. The attraction flew out the window, or at least I wanted it to. Because *this* man in front of me wasn't someone I wanted to give another thought.

A warm flush spread over my face—not because of him, but because I'd created more work for Hal with the mess.

"It was an accident," I said through gritted teeth, looking up at him. I hadn't backed down before, and I wasn't going to now. "And I'm trying to clean up the mess so Hal doesn't have to."

"You should've asked one of us for help getting this down."

"Because you're so willing to help me?" I asked with a scoff. "Gosh, I wonder why I didn't ask. I'm fine. I can clean this up myself and take care of it on my own. I don't need your help, so if you could—"

As we were talking—*arguing*—I continued grabbing pieces of broken ceramic without looking. Which was a mistake.

"Shit," I hissed, finally looking down and seeing the blood dripping down my hand. I'd cut the palm of my hand on one of the sharp jagged pieces.

His eyes flicked down to see where I was looking. "Goddamn it," he grumbled when he spotted the blood. "C'mon, I think Hal has a first-aid kit in the back." He extended his large hand to help me up, and I stared at it for a beat, so ready to argue with him that I could take care of this on my own. I decided against it because, for once, I *could* use his help. My hand was stinging, and I needed a way to stop the blood.

I set my other hand in his, slowly standing.

"Hal, I'm going to take Juliette to the back. She hurt her hand," he called over the aisles to the older man.

"Do you have to scream it to the whole store?" I hissed under my breath to him.

"I think the whole store heard what happened when the ceramic pot hit the floor, plus it's just the three of us here, anyway," he muttered back as we waited for Hal's response.

"Everything you should need is in a box in my desk drawer, Wesley," Hal responded. "You doing alright, Miss Jules?"

At least now I knew his name. *Wesley.*

"I'm okay, Hal. Thanks for asking."

We first went to the store's single-person restroom where

Wesley instructed me to rinse my hand with cold water and use paper towels to apply gentle pressure so the bleeding would stop. He watched, and when I met his eyes in the mirror, I swore his brows furrowed in concern for a split second.

We then stepped into Hal's office—or what Hal claimed to be his office. The tiny room had one window, a desk, and two chairs. Hal had pictures on the walls, similarly to how he did up front, and various tools spread out on his desk.

"Go ahead and take a seat." Wesley nodded toward the office chair. I didn't know why, but every time this man spoke, I wanted to do the opposite of what he said. I listened, though. He was helping me, after all.

I got comfortable in the chair and looked around the office while Wesley opened the desk drawer, pulling out a red first-aid kit. He grabbed antibiotic ointment and a bandage.

He moved around the desk and kneeled in front of me. "Lay your hand so your palm is facing up."

I rested the back of my hand on the top of my thigh, palm facing up, and removed the paper towels to expose the cut.

Wesley had washed his hands before we left the bathroom, and he reached for my hand, his large fingers tenderly examining my injury. He let out a quiet sigh. He seemed relieved. "Doesn't look as bad as I thought. Not saying it doesn't hurt, but it looked worse with the blood. Cleaning it helped." He twisted off the cap of the ointment, and seconds before he was about to spread the cream on my wound, I pulled my hand away slightly.

"It's going to hurt, isn't it?" I asked, my body already anticipating the sharp stinging and pain that would follow, even though I knew the ointment was necessary. My other hand wrapped tightly around the chair's armrest.

"It'll sting," Wesley started slowly, "but it'll help if you focus your mind on something else. You can also look away if you have to."

I didn't expect his voice to sound so tender, so caring, so patient. It was such a sharp contrast to what I was used to with him. Slowly, I nodded and extended my hand back toward him. He met my eyes, looking at me as if he was asking permission. I nodded again, and he dipped his head down to tend to my injury.

I focused on his calloused touch, the way his brow furrowed in concentration, and how carefully he spread the ointment over the cut. I focused on how delicately his large hands touched mine, and I realized I'd never had a man be this gentle with me, this caring. And how depressing was that? That I couldn't picture any of my ex-boyfriends tending to me this way. Instead, my grumpy neighbor, who wanted nothing to do with me, was the one to make sure I was okay.

"All set," Wesley said, and when I looked down, the bandage was wrapped around my hand, covering my palm. Turns out his advice worked. I just had to focus on...him.

"Thanks, Wesley," I said breathlessly.

His shoulders tensed at the sound of his name. He ran his tongue along his bottom lip, and my eyes followed the motion. He slowly tore his gaze away from my hand and looked up at me. Our eyes met, and it was the first time I realized how close we were. The scent of mint and mahogany overwhelmed my senses. Being so close to him was too much.

"Just Wes is fine."

The corner of my lip quirked up into a half-smile. If he intended on calling me by my full name, I'd do the same. "I'll stick with Wesley for now." His name rolled off my tongue with ease, and I wanted to say it again.

Silence filled the small room as we stared at each other. I kept my eyes on him, but I so badly wanted to look away, let my gaze drop to his lips, his throat, his hands. He was so manly and rugged, but I was starting to see he was also gentle and caring—when he wanted to be.

As we stared at each other, I couldn't tell if that was heat or distain in his eyes. Did it even matter?

I swallowed and looked down at my hand, still in his grasp with his calloused thumb rubbing small circles along my wrist. All it took was that brief flicker to break whatever was happening between us. As I started to pull my wrist away, he beat me to it and quickly dropped his hold. He stood and backed away so suddenly he nearly stumbled.

My skin burned where his touch had been.

"I'm going to find a broom to clean up the mess you made," he grunted, creating distance between us and reminding me he didn't want me in his town.

"How many times do I have to tell you I don't need your help?" I asked stubbornly, getting up from the chair and standing toe to toe with him, needing to tilt my head back to look up at him. I didn't know what he thought of me, or why, but I sure as hell wanted to prove him wrong.

"Really, you're telling me a city girl like you would've been able to clean and bandage your wound?" He raised a skeptical brow, crossing his arms over his chest, which created distance between us. This man was as stubborn as I was—if not more.

"What I'm telling you—" I gritted between my teeth but stopped at the sound of Hal's voice. I wasn't sure when he'd gotten here, but I welcomed the interruption.

"Now, now, Wes. Don't you go scaring my customers away, even if I know this one can hold her own." Hal's voice was stern as he came up behind Wesley and elbowed him in the side before turning to me. "Don't worry about that, Miss Jules. I'll clean it up."

"Hal, I really—" I started to say before Hal cut me off again, this time with a sharp shake of his head.

He gestured for me to follow him to the register at the front of the store. "Let's get you checked out up front and get your order in for some paint."

Reluctantly, I followed Hal. I must've left my purse in the aisle with the ceramic pots, because he had it at the register already. "Will you at least let me pay for the flower pot I broke?" I offered as I dug through my purse for my credit card.

"Nope," he responded, popping the P. "But I will order you a new one and get it delivered to where you're staying."

Hal rung up the cost for the paint I picked out for Lily's, along with two flower pots I was going to go back and grab.

"Thanks, Hal. Sorry again about the mess." I tapped the card against the reader, able to pay without a problem since *Wesley* had fixed it.

"Don't sweat it. Accidents happen. I already forgot about it." He gave me a friendly wink before rapping his knuckles against the counter. "Have a good rest of your day, Miss Jules, and take it easy." He nodded toward my hand. "Hope to see you around soon."

"You, too, Hal. See you around."

Even though Hal had said not to worry about it, I intended to see what I could do to help with the mess on my way out. But in the short time it'd taken for me to check out, everything was cleaned up, and Wesley was gone, leaving me even more confused about what happened between us.

12

JULIETTE

Once I stopped replaying what happened at Hal's, the rest of the week went by quickly.

Word had gotten around that I was working with Lily...and also that I'd been on *Paradise Love*. Luckily, the latter didn't seem to be as much of a problem as I thought it'd be.

People had questions about the show and what happened, but they were more interested in getting to know *me*. A few of the other locals even asked if I'd be able to work with them on some design tips. Mainly focusing on how they can optimize their space and attract customers, especially those passing through in the summer. They were looking for a balance of old and new—keeping the historic downtown feel while also catering to the modern upgrades tourists were looking for. I loved the challenge.

I knew the attention was thanks to Lily vouching for me, and it meant a lot to me she trusted me so quickly. It was hard to believe I'd only known her for a few weeks.

Things felt different in Golden Falls. Like they were slowly turning around.

Even driving to the Richards's family home felt right. I didn't feel those knots of anxiety in my stomach that I often got when arriving at a new place and not knowing what to expect. I was filled with those knots on *Paradise Love*.

I drove slowly on the long, paved driveway. Lily's parents were a short mile drive south of downtown. Even though they were close to everything and had neighbors, their property was quiet and private thanks to the trees on both sides and Lake Golden along the back of the house.

"Holy shit," I swore quietly when I saw the home's front exterior. It was absolutely breathtaking. I'd been blown away by the cabin—which lived up to its name of a lakeview haven—but this was something else entirely.

It was a multi-story gray house with white trim and black shutters and a two car garage. Similar to the buildings downtown, it had a historic, timeless feel while still being modern. Honestly, calling it a "house" didn't do it justice—it was a mansion.

Once I turned off the ignition, I got out of the car and walked up the brick path to the front door.

The door swung open before I was even able to knock.

"You made it!" Lily exclaimed as she easily wrapped her arms around me in an embrace. "Mom, Jules is here!" she called over her shoulder.

I greeted Lily with a smile, wrapping my free arm around her while the other held the bouquet of flowers I'd brought for her mom.

"Come on in. Dinner's about ready." Lily waved for me to step inside the house. The interior was just as luxurious as the home's exterior.

Lily's mom met us, and I quickly noticed the resemblance. They had the same blonde hair and warm smile. "It's a pleasure to meet you, Jules. I'm Laura, and you'll meet my husband Mark once we make it out back. He's out there grilling up the hamburgers, hot dogs, and vegetables."

"It's so nice to meet you," I responded, extending the flowers out to her. "These are for you. It's been amazing staying in your rental. I'm so excited for the rest of the summer."

Laura's face softened as she took in the flowers. "That's so nice of you, Jules. Thank you. We're happy to have you, both in the cabin and for dinner tonight. My son should be here soon." Laura turned to Lily. "Do you know if Cooper's coming?"

Lily shook her head. "No clue. I wouldn't be surprised if he did, though." She then turned to me. "Cooper is Eliza's older brother and pretty much my second older brother. Fun, right? Having *two* overbearing, protective brothers who think they know everything." She rolled her eyes.

"I have one brother who thinks he knows everything, and that's plenty," I said with a laugh.

Laura looked between us with an amused smile. "Well, we'll set up enough plates, and there won't be a shortage of food." She waved her hand for us to follow her through the home and out the sliding back door into the backyard. Trees lined the property, but the yard had plenty of open space.

A patio area immediately greeted you after you exited the home. A large dining set with plenty of room for guests took up most of the space, and bistro lights sparkled over the glass-top table.

Lily's dad, Mark, stood next to their expansive grill and outdoor kitchen setup. The delicious smell of grilled food only added to the welcoming environment.

Wooden steps took you down to a fire pit surrounded by chairs, and then another set of wooden stairs took you down to the dock.

I couldn't wait to see how the stars would light up the yard once the night sky turned dark. The stars in Golden Falls shone brighter than anywhere I'd seen.

It was absolutely perfect, and I had a feeling it would be a great night.

"Your house is stunning. This view especially. I could spend all night out here," I said to Laura as we stepped onto the patio.

"I often do. Reading out by the fire pit is one of my favorite ways to wind down in the evening." Laura glanced around with a fond smile. "Lots of memories were made out here, too, which makes me even more excited for the years to come. Go ahead and make yourself comfortable. I'll go see if Mark needs any help."

Lily sat at the table, patting the chair next to her for me to join.

Once I sat, I asked, "So, who's going to be here tonight? You said your brother and Cooper, right?"

Lily nodded. "We're only waiting on them tonight. Hal sometimes comes by, but he has poker tonight instead. Eliza is still out of town. And then Marnie, Cooper and Eliza's grandma, was busy tonight, too. It's been a little quieter at dinner the last few years since my older sister Jade left." Lily's tone sounded chipper, but I could tell from the slight frown there was more there.

"But the guys should be getting here any minute, which means"—Lily grinned as she twisted off the top of the bottle of white wine to pour us both a glass—"we might as well start with some wine."

I clinked my glass against hers before taking a sip.

"I really am glad you were able to make it tonight, and you're always welcome here," she assured. "I can text you when the next family dinner is, and we'll have to have a girls' night once Eliza is back."

Her eyes lit up with excitement. "I should make a group chat with the three of us! I can't believe I didn't think of that sooner."

She picked up her phone. "That way you two can get to know each other a little before she's back." She looked up at me before starting to type out the text.

"I would love that." My heart swelled at how Lily ensured I was included. While I was still getting to know her, it was obvious she was a thoughtful friend who cared deeply about those around her. "I'll definitely take you up on the offer for a girls night with Eliza. You mentioned Jade is in Hawaii as a travel nurse? How did she end up there?"

Lily nodded slowly, finishing up typing out the text. "Sent!" She grinned, placing the phone down on the table. "Well, Jade went to college in Iowa for nursing, and then was trying to figure out if she wanted to come back to Golden Falls or move. She ended up moving to California and started her career there before deciding to become a travel nurse a few years ago. I'm so proud of her," Lily gushed proudly. "But I definitely miss her. We haven't talked nearly as often over the last few years with her busier schedule, but she always sends a postcard when she gets to a new location.

"We were really close growing up. She's a few years older than me, but we were always doing something together. My mom would always joke we were attached at the hip. I get why she left Golden Falls. I wish her schedule allowed her to come back once in a while to visit."

I reached over to give Lily's hand a squeeze. "I hope she's able to visit soon. Maybe you can even plan a trip out to where she is. And I know it's not the same, but there's always FaceTime, too."

Lily twisted her lips to the side as she thought. "Yeah, I'm glad you said that. We sometimes FaceTime her in for these dinners, but it's been a while. I'll actually text her right now to see if she's free. It should be the afternoon over in Hawaii, which might mean she's finishing up her shift." Lily picked her phone up again, quickly typing out the text. She looked up at the sound of a car pulling up. "Must be the guys! Means we can finally get dinner. I'm starving!"

Any sort of sadness was wiped from Lily's face as her mood shifted, but I could see in her eyes it wasn't gone for good.

I hoped my new friend wasn't keeping in more than she could handle. I knew what that felt like.

13

WESLEY

"Dinners at your parents' house will always be the best. I don't care how old we get." Cooper grinned as we got out of his Jeep Wrangler.

"I couldn't agree more." I'd gotten my love of food and cooking from both my parents, but their food would always surpass anything I was making that evening. Coming over for dinner was a no brainer.

Cooper and I went straight toward the side of the house and to the back yard.

"Hey, Ma. Hey, Dad," I called out.

My mom made her way over to give both me and Cooper a hug. My dad, meanwhile, was grabbing beers and setting them out on the table. If the beers were out, that meant the food was grilled up and ready to eat.

I almost didn't see her in the initial commotion. *Almost.*

But a woman who looked like that was hard to miss.

Big, green eyes. A smile so bright it lit up the whole yard. Long, brown hair cascading down her back in waves.

The bright-yellow sundress—the same color as her bikini— hugged her body and curves perfectly, flaring at her hips and hitting above her knees, showing off those long, tan legs. The dress was held up by thin straps tied into bows.

Thin straps I knew would easily snap if tugged.

When our eyes locked, a jolt of electricity coursed through my body the same way it did at Hal's. The image from that day of Juliette Campbell on her knees in those tiny denim shorts was seared into my mind, as was the soft feel of her skin as I tended to her injury. I briefly glanced down at her hand and didn't see a bandage, so I assumed her cut had healed quickly, which was good. I didn't want her hurt. I just...didn't want her in town.

"What are you doing here?" we asked at the same time, although whereas her question sounded genuine, mine came out harsher than intended. What was with this woman and catching me off guard?

I normally wasn't an asshole—at least, I *really* hoped people didn't see me that way—but she reminded me so much of what I was trying to forget. The emotions I didn't want to be feeling.

I didn't interact much with those passing through or visiting Golden Falls. I cared about those close to me and about the other residents, but I refused to let anyone else in.

Not again.

I did my best to keep memories of those two summers locked away in my mind. I had no interest in revisiting them.

Maybe it was unfair to Juliette—in fact, I knew it was—but I didn't trust myself. Juliette was here only for the summer just like *her*.

"I'm here to have dinner with my family. What are *you* doing here?" I gritted. So much for my plan to avoid Juliette. That was damn near impossible when she was everywhere.

Lily's jaw dropped, and my mom's eyes widened at my remark. My dad let out a sigh, and I didn't even look over at Cooper.

"Wesley! That's no way to talk to our guest," my mom scolded, about to turn to Juliette, likely to apologize.

"Lily invited me. Were you going to say this is private property and try to kick me out again?" She tilted her head to the side.

Another commotion broke out, and the fire in her eyes let me know she knew exactly what she was doing.

"You said what?!"

"Wes, I told you to be nice!"

"Son, you know better than that."

I deserved that.

I didn't know how to act around her. All I knew was I needed to get Juliette Campbell out of my mind. I didn't need to be thinking about her long, tanned legs. Or the way her lips tipped up into an innocent smile and eyes blazed at the sight of me.

Juliette turned to my sister. "He's your brother?"

"Unfortunately," Lily sighed, which earned a scowl from me. "I didn't realize you two had met already. I told Wes to introduce himself since he lives next to the cabin, but...I guess that didn't quite work out." My sister then turned to me. "Well, Wes, you can introduce yourself properly to Jules and maybe even apologize for whatever first impression you made."

"And for the second and third impressions, too," Juliette muttered, causing Lily to widen her eyes and look between us.

"You're going to scare my new friend away, and she just got here!" Lily exclaimed, raising her arms up and letting them drop against her sides.

Juliette locked eyes with me, straightening her stance. She was a good foot shorter than me, but her confidence sure as hell made up for it.

"Don't worry, Lil. Wesley doesn't scare me. I'm not going anywhere."

I don't think my name had ever sounded that good leaving

someone's lips. Hearing her say it for the first time at Hal's had caused my whole body to tense up—because it sounded that damn nice.

I was forced to look away from her when Cooper joined the conversation after making his burger. It was no surprise his first priority was food.

Balancing his plate in one hand, he extended his other to shake Juliette's. "Hey, I'm Cooper. Nice to meet you, Juliette. Would love to show you around town one of these days, if you'd like, or around the trails. I'm a park ranger, so I know the best spots around here." He grinned, giving the type of introduction and first impression I wished I could've given her. Cooper made it look so easy. "Don't worry about Wes. We're happy to have you in town."

Juliette's face lit up, and I wouldn't be surprised if at this point she reserved her smile for everyone but me. "Nice to meet you! And call me Jules. I really enjoyed hiking growing up but haven't been out in a while. I'll definitely take you up on the offer to show me around. What's your favorite spot around here?"

I had no interest in watching Juliette fawn over Cooper, so I stepped around them to make myself a burger, telling myself the sudden wave of irritation had nothing to do with jealousy and everything to do with Juliette Campbell being in my space.

After making a burger and ensuring my plate was filled with food, I made my way over to the glass-top table and took the seat I always did during family dinner.

I let out a grunt at the sudden sharp pain in my shin. Since it was just Lily and me at the table, it was easy to tell who the culprit was. Even with her sitting diagonally from me, she was still able to get a good kick in under the table.

"Be nice," she hissed, keeping her voice low. Juliette and

Cooper were still talking, and our parents were making their plates of food.

"I'm trying," I grunted back.

"Well, *try harder*." If looks could kill, my sister would be the only Richards sibling at this table. Everyone claimed Lily was all sunshine, but having grown up with her, I knew there was much more to her. Yes, she was kind and always had a smile on her face, but she also fiercely protected those she cared about and never hesitated to speak up. It made me proud to be her brother, except for when her wrath was directed right at me. "We want Jules to feel welcome, both at family dinner and in Golden Falls. She's been through a lot these last few months."

My brows furrowed in confusion over my sister's words. What did she mean? Had something happened on that goddamn show? The look on Lily's face gave it away that she'd said too much. Right as I was going to ask her what she meant, my parents, Juliette, and Cooper made it to the table and took their seats.

My parents were sitting at the head of the table, with Lily and Juliette on one side and Cooper and me on the other. Juliette and I were sitting across from each other. Because of course we were.

Once everyone started eating, the wine, laughter, and stories flowed with ease. The rocky start to dinner was put in the past, or at least I hoped it was. Thirty-two years old and getting a look of disapproval from my mom still hit me just as hard as it did when I was a teenager.

"So, Jules," my mom said with a smile, wiping her lips with a napkin, "Lily was telling me about how the two of you are working on the café. How has that been going?"

Juliette set down her burger, her face lighting up immediately. "Oh, it's been great. I've loved working with Lily, as well as learning about the town and meeting the other business owners around here. I appreciate the connections Lily has helped me make so much, especially since I've only been here a few weeks. I hadn't planned on working when I got to Golden Falls, but it fell into place. I've been really inspired by the idea of working with small businesses."

"What do you do again, Jules? You're a designer?" Cooper asked, and I had to admit I was grateful for the question, because I'd been curious, too.

Juliette nodded. "Interior designer, yeah. Most recently, I worked for a firm in Chicago. Things...took a bit of a turn, so I'm grateful to spend the summer here and figure out what my next step will be."

"Very cool. I can't wait to see it all come together. If you need anything from me, let me know. Happy to help or make any connections." Cooper knew anyone and everyone in town.

I could see the passion in Juliette's eyes when she spoke about her job, but there was something else I couldn't identify. Her shoulders dropped ever so slightly at the mention of it. Curious, I kept my eyes on her.

She didn't look away when our gazes locked. Instead, her right brow lifted slightly. She kept her eyes on me even as she brought her wine glass up to her lips. I liked her confidence, and I liked how she didn't look away.

The rest of the dinner conversation flowed smoothly. Juliette shared more about her time in Golden Falls. She'd only been here for a couple of weeks and was already on a first name basis with a handful of the residents, including Hal. Honestly, if you had Hal's approval, you had nothing to worry about.

Lily talked about her café and the rest of her plans for the summer. Cooper brought up how he was looking forward to spending time with the summer camp kids through the educational programming the park rangers helped out with.

I stayed quiet, mostly, more excited to hear what everyone

else was up to than to share what'd been going on with me. But when my mom asked about the bar, I mentioned the busy summer season at Lake Ridge and how I'd been wanting to talk with Eliza about picking up some bartending shifts if she was still looking for an evening gig when she got back from her trip.

Lily turned to Juliette. "Oh, we should really stop by Wes's bar one of these nights before Eliza starts working there, especially on a night when he lets me take over the music."

"You don't give me much of a choice." I rolled my eyes but couldn't help the smile that tugged on my lips. As much as I pretended to be annoyed, the nights Lily controlled the music were the nights we had the highest drink sales and people stayed right up until bar close.

She had a natural knack for reading the room and identifying what people wanted to listen to. Every time she visited, she'd curate a playlist with pop, country, and rock hits and throwbacks. I planned to use her playlists even on nights when she didn't stop by.

Juliette hummed, an amused smile on her lips as she looked between me and Lily. "Sounds like a plan. I've been needing a good night out, especially if there's dancing."

"I'll see what works for Eliza once she's back. We have so many plans for the summer!" Lily said with a laugh.

I knew my sister, and I knew how easily she got attached. And how easily she tended to get hurt.

Lily could handle her own—I knew that—but I hoped she wasn't forming a close friendship with someone who was simply going to forget about her after the summer was over. Juliette said so herself she was thinking about what her next stop would be. But after hearing about how she was getting to know everyone, how she was taking time out of her night to have dinner with my family, I had a feeling she'd leave her mark on Golden Falls.

Either way, she was leaving at the end of the summer. That much was clear.

"Oh! I got a text back from Jade," Lily exclaimed as her phone screen lit up with a message from our sister. "She finished up her shift and got back to the apartment and can talk for a few minutes to say hi."

I was close with both of my sisters, but growing up, I'd spent more time with Jade, likely because we were closer in age. I was the oldest, Jade was two years younger than me, and Lily was eight years younger than me.

When Lily and Jade weren't together, Jade was hanging out with Cooper and me.

We had countless memories of getting up to the wildest shit, sneaking around, and staying up too late. We were always up to something.

Things obviously changed as we got older, and especially when Cooper and I were going off to college. Even when we'd visit for the weekends or stay longer in the summer, things were different. Good, but different. It wasn't until Jade graduated from college and decided to go out to California that things changed. Cooper and Jade would get under each other's skin more often than not when they spoke.

"Hey, Lil. Hey, everyone," Jade greeted after picking up the FaceTime. "How's dinner?"

"It's great." Lily's whole face lit up at the sight of our sister. "We're just missing you! Thought we could say a quick hi. You must be tired from your shift."

"I am, but I'm excited to see you guys. It's been a while since I've called."

I admired my sister a hell of a lot for the work she did and how much she cared for others. It wasn't an easy task, and from the sound of her voice, I could tell it had been a long day.

Lily turned the phone so it was on her and Juliette. "I also wanted to introduce you to Jules. She's staying at the cabin this summer."

"Nice to meet you, Jules. Glad you're able to enjoy the cabin. I didn't realize Mom and Dad were renting it out. How's Wes?" Apart from Cooper, Jade was the only other person who knew more about what happened with Gretchen.

Lily didn't put the two together, thinking Jade was asking how I was doing overall. "Oh, Wes is fine." She waved her hand to dismiss Jade's concerns. "Grumpier than usual. Here, see him for yourself." Lily reached over the table, handing me the phone.

"Hey, sis. Yeah, I'm fine," I assured her with a nod. It'd been too long since I'd checked in on her. "It's good to see you. Figured you were off busy saving the world. You taking care of yourself?" I held the phone out, making sure Cooper was in the frame, too. For a second, I thought our connection had frozen or Jade hadn't heard me, because her face went blank.

"Oh, uh, y-yeah. Trying to, at least," she stammered and offered a tentative smile. "Cooper, hey. It's, um, good to see you."

Cooper, who normally was smooth and always had something to say, looked just as paralyzed. These two were acting like awkward fucking teenagers. I elbowed his side, which caused him to clear his throat and offer one of the most strained smiles I'd ever seen from him.

"Hey, Jade," was all that came from Cooper.

What the hell?

We continued to pass the phone around, my mom taking the most time as we talked with Jade over the next twenty minutes. She told us about Hawaii, her patients, and the hospital, likely sharing just the highlights and leaving out the painful or difficult parts of her day. After working twelve-hour shifts over the last three days, Jade had a few days off. She planned to do some hiking with her coworkers who also had time off, as well as spend time on the beach.

"Love you guys. Let's talk soon, okay? Enjoy the rest of your dinner. I'll be sure to send some pictures from the hike tomorrow," Jade said to wrap up the call.

"We love you, too, sweetie. Be safe and talk soon." My mom smiled at Jade before hanging up the call and handing Lily back the phone. "I remember when you two and Jade would always be out on some sort of adventure. Hiking, camping, you name it," Mom added as she looked at me and Cooper with a thoughtful smile.

"She was always looking for the next best thing, the next adventure," Cooper muttered, grabbing his beer and taking a large gulp to finish the bottle.

I reached over and handed him a new beer, having a gut feeling he needed another drink. Although I couldn't figure out why.

14

JULIETTE

By the time we were wrapping up dinner, I was already looking forward to the next one. Even though I was the new guest, I was included and at ease the whole night. Well, at least once we sat down.

It was still hard to believe Wesley was Lily's brother. Typical small town.

Wes and I didn't exchange another word the rest of the night, but every so often, I'd feel the weight of his stare. I couldn't figure out why we didn't click, or why it wasn't as easy to be around him as it was the rest of the Richards family.

By the end of the night, I'd even become fast friends with Cooper, who offered to buy me a drink when I stopped by Lake Ridge.

Lake Ridge. The words on the baseball cap Wesley had on that first day clicked into place.

I was slowly starting to see the inner workings of Golden Falls and the various connections between residents. Even though a lot of people passed through during the summer, it was the year-round residents who kept the town going.

Like Wes.

It was easy to see the impact the Richards family had in town. Cooper and Eliza, too.

I wanted to be on good terms with Wesley, but that meant figuring out why we weren't on good terms to begin with. I wasn't sure I'd ever get answers to that. Me just being here struck a nerve.

Tonight, I'd come to realize there were a few different sides to Wes. The grumpy side, which I was *very* familiar with. The natural, confident side I'd seen out on the dock. The caring side when he tended to my injury at Hal's. And the quiet, reserved side from tonight.

He didn't say much during dinner, but he was listening intently the whole time. His eyes softened when he was speaking with Jade over the phone. He refilled his mom's water glass and got up when his dad needed something. He had that same fondness when talking to Hal.

He loved and cared about his family.

He loved and cared about this town.

Maybe we could have a restart.

I glanced around the yard and caught sight of Wesley walking through the sliding door into the house and carrying a stack of plates from dinner.

Mark was cleaning the grill while Lily and Laura chatted at the table with me. Admittedly, I'd zoned out as I watched Wes enter the house.

When Cooper said he was going to help Mark clean the grill, Lily batted her eyelashes, an angelic smile on her face. "Actually, Mom got ingredients for s'mores if you wanted to get the fire started, Coop."

Cooper, Laura, and I burst out in laughter.

"Go ahead and start the fire, Cooper. I'll go help Mark while Lily delegates." Laura chuckled with a shake of her head.

"Your future husband is in for a treat, let me tell you,"

Cooper said with an amused huff as he stood from his seat. I assumed he had a lot of years under his belt of being bossed around by both Lily and his own sister. He made his way down the wooden steps over to the stone firepit Laura and Mark had in their yard below the patio.

"If he even exists! At this rate, I'll be single forever," Lily called out, letting out a sigh. She turned her attention back to me. "I love it here, but the dating pool is slim to none. Most of the guys I've either known forever, went on a date and it didn't work out, or they don't like cats. And, yes, that is a dealbreaker!" Lily made a face as she shook her head. "I'll have to visit you in Chicago after the summer. Maybe I'll find a nice, hot city guy with a cat."

I grinned. "Love that idea. I'll see who I can find for you."

"I'm holding you to it," Lily said with a smile of her own. "I'm going to grab the graham crackers, chocolate, and marsh-mallows."

I quickly shook my head. "You stay here. I'll go grab them. Need anything else from inside?"

"Nope, just that. Everything should be in the kitchen, which will be on your right after you go in through the sliding door. Thanks, Jules!"

When I stepped into the house and followed Lily's directions, I saw Wes standing at the kitchen sink. He was rinsing the plates and then putting them in the dishwasher. I watched how he bent toward the dishwater, muscles flexing in his arms as his long fingers wrapped around the plate. His jeans hung on his hips, wrapping around his muscular thighs and ass.

I paused. Maybe I couldn't figure him out, but I *could* admire him from afar. Just for a moment.

I was grateful *Paradise Love* hadn't come up during dinner, because knowing that about me would likely make Wes hate me even more. It would make me seem even more out of place in his town. Or maybe he knew already?

I wasn't keeping it a secret—after all, I told Lily minutes into meeting her, and it was getting out around town—but I was keeping it close to my chest for now. I was still trying to figure out how I felt about the whole experience. On one hand, I had no regrets, because I'd tried something new and out of my comfort zone. On the other, it was safe to say my life had been flipped upside down and my vulnerabilities aired for everyone to see.

I bet Wes had it all figured out. Maybe that's why I bothered him so much. Because I had no idea what I was doing, and he had his life put together.

Trying not to dwell more than I already was, I walked into the kitchen.

"Need some help?" I asked as I stood behind him, peering around him to see how many dishes he had left in the sink. "You can rinse and I can put the dishes in the dishwasher?"

He paused what he was doing and turned the water off but didn't say anything.

I continued, "I know we got off on the wrong foot, but I don't want to spend the whole summer tiptoeing around you. We're bound to keep running into each other." I paused. "We can at least try to be friends."

"Friends?" he asked hesitantly before shaking his head. "Don't need any more friends, city girl."

I held back an eye roll. *Of course* he would say that.

"Pretty sure it's scientifically proven that having more than one friend is good for your health. And having *only* one friend is detrimental to your well-being."

"I don't just have one friend," he grunted, turning around so we were now facing each other and crossing his arms. "I have more than that."

I tilted my head, crossing my own arms over my chest and taking a few steps forward to close the distance between us. We were standing toe to toe now, and I had to tip my head back to look up at him. "Who other than Cooper? And siblings don't count."

His jaw clenched, and I realized I liked getting under Wes's skin. I liked getting a reaction out of him. If he was going to give me trouble, I was going to dish it right back.

"I'm not looking for temporary friends. You're only here for a few months, and then you're leaving." He shook his head. "Besides, I don't think I'd be able to be friends with you."

Ouch. I took a step back. "What's that supposed to mean?" All of a sudden, all I heard was Tony's voice in my head. *You're kind of a handful.* Did Wes think that, too?

Wes uncrossed his arms and braced his palms on the edge of the counter. "I can't, Juliette."

I nodded slowly, almost in a daze. Was I too much? Was that why? I wanted to know what he was so hesitant of, why he wouldn't give me a chance. The rest of his family liked me.

I mustered a polite smile, finding that the last place I wanted to be right now was the kitchen. "Noted." I swallowed. "Well, I don't need any more friends, anyway. I'll be friends with Lily, Cooper, and Eliza, once I meet her."

I turned and grabbed the s'mores supplies I had come in here for. As I walked out, I could have sworn he whispered, "Believe me. It's better this way."

We ended the night making s'mores and sitting around the fire Cooper started. The heat from the bright flames warmed us on the breezy June night. The sun had long set, and the stars sparkled in the dark-blue sky.

I had two square pieces of graham cracker resting on my thigh—one plain and one with a square of chocolate. My marshmallow looked perfect—gooey and slightly burnt. I carefully adjusted my roasting stick to place the marshmallow on the graham cracker with chocolate and used the other graham cracker to help slide the marshmallow off.

I lifted up the s'more to take a bite, humming in delight from the sweetness and various textures. The perfect summer treat.

As I looked up, I met a pair of dark eyes that were already focused on me. It wasn't the first time tonight I'd looked over at Wesley and he was already looking at me. But...why? Did he want me to leave that badly?

Maybe Wesley didn't want me here, but I wasn't going to let him stop me from building a friendship with Lily. From coming back to the Richards's house for dinner if I was invited. From stopping by Lake Ridge. It seemed like everyone else was happy I was here, which was enough for me, because they'd actually taken the time to at least start getting to know me. Cooper already started to put together a list of beginner trails I should check out during my time here.

"We're so grateful you were able to join us tonight, Jules," Laura said, pulling me out of my thoughts.

I looked over at her, a warm smile on my lips. "I had a great time. Thank you for having me."

"You're always welcome to stop by. No pressure, but the invitation is always there if you're looking for some company and food."

"I'm already looking forward to the next one, so that's wonderful to hear. I'd love to join again."

Like I'd told Wesley, I wasn't going anywhere. For now, at least.

15

WESLEY

IT'D BEEN A FEW DAYS SINCE DINNER AT MY PARENTS' HOUSE, AND I couldn't get Juliette's defeated expression out of my mind. She hadn't let it show as we wrapped up dinner and sat around the fire pit. Maybe my words hadn't impacted her much, but the way her expression fell when we were standing in the kitchen? It gutted me.

She was trying. And I wasn't.

I knew keeping my distance from her was the right thing. Especially with the way my body reacted to her standing so close to me. Those big, green eyes looking up at me through dark lashes. The way her plump, pink lips moved as she spoke. When I got home that night and hopped in the shower, I was hard as a fucking rock thinking about her in that goddamn yellow sundress.

I couldn't be friends with her, because we barely knew each other and she already had such an effect on me. All Juliette Campbell had to do was look at me and I was fucking tongue-tied.

I wasn't the right man for a woman with so much fire, passion, and light, even as only a friend.

I let out a frustrated groan as I turned from my side onto my back, staring up at my bedroom ceiling, the room illuminated only by the moonlight. It was two in the morning, and I couldn't fucking sleep. I brought my hands up to my face, rubbing my eyes. Fuck. What a mess.

This wasn't the first night I'd replayed the interaction as I tried to fall asleep, which was why I had to do something about it soon. It wasn't unusual for me to overthink, especially at night, but I normally didn't let it impact me so much the next day. I was normally better at letting those thoughts go and moving on.

I untangled my legs from the sheets, setting my feet on the floor and getting up. I adjusted my boxers as I walked over to the kitchen, grabbing a glass from the cabinet and filling it with water. I set the glass down, leaning my arms against the counter. As I looked out the window, my eyes drifted toward where the cabin was. Trees obscured my view of it, but...my mind stayed on Juliette. Was she able to sleep? Or was she tossing and turning, too?

I gulped down the glass of water, setting it in the sink and turning my back toward the window. Our various interactions replayed in my brain as I searched for a solution.

Maybe I was going about it all the wrong way because, like she said, she'd be around. She was forming fast friendships with the people in my life, and it was obvious I wasn't good at avoiding her.

One thing was clear, though. It was impossible to forget or stop thinking about Juliette Campbell, no matter how hard I tried.

16

JULIETTE

The week after the Richards family dinner was busier than I expected. Most days, I would leave the cabin in the morning, spend part of the day working at Lily's café, and use the other half of the day to meet with people in town. A few other business owners were looking over ideas I'd put together for them after an initial consultation.

I knew people were hesitant to do business with me since I wasn't a local, but they were warming up pretty quickly once they heard my ideas and saw the work I'd done at Lily's. We painted the main wall a beautiful pastel yellow and used a warm beige for the cat room. We also added a bird feeder outside the window so the cats could watch birds and other critters.

Now that the walls were painted, my next task was rearranging the tables in the café and bringing in the new furniture I thrifted for the cat room. The loveseat I found would be comfortable for guests and was made of a fabric that wouldn't get easily damaged by the cats. I needed to find a way to get it over to Lily's since my car wasn't big enough. Plus, I still needed to find curtains for the café's main room and some other little decorations to add some color and tie the space together while staying on budget.

My to-do list for tomorrow was piling up, but it felt good to have tasks I was excited to work on. Lily was a great person to partner with, because she gave me creative freedom and trusted my instincts.

After spending most of the day downtown, I was driving back to the cabin to unwind and possibly enjoy another swim. As I pulled up the gravel driveway, I did a double take when I spotted two bright-blue ceramic planters with blooming flowers. They were right next to the wooden steps that led up to the front door. When had those gotten there?

I hopped out of my car, glancing around before making my way toward the front porch. The ceramic planters were the same design I'd been eyeing at Hal's. The same as the planter that shattered.

Not only did these two planters have flowers, but so did the other two I'd purchased myself. I hadn't had time to plant the flowers, so for the last couple of weeks, the planters had been sitting empty in the corner of the porch.

Now, I had marigolds, asters, petunias, and dahlias—one type of flower in each planter.

I took another look around the porch, this time noticing the note taped to the front door. I carefully removed it, tucking the tape back and reading the messy scrawl.

Juliette,

I thought long about what you said, and you're right. You'll be here for a while, and I want you to feel welcome. Both in town and at dinner, if you decide to stop by again. I'm sorry for our rough start.

I'm not the best with my words, clearly, but that's no excuse. I hope this can be a new start for us, if you're willing. You've likely figured this out already, but yes, I live nearby. Down the road, actually. If you need anything during your time in Golden Falls, I can try to help. I'll leave my cell number down by my name.

I hope you enjoy the flowers. Figured I would leave them out front and you'd find a good place for them.

- Wes

Once I got through the note, I read it again, in disbelief this was from Wes and that he'd been the one to plant the flowers. That was...thoughtful. It didn't excuse his actions, but I appreciated his apology and that he'd done something about it. Actions spoke louder than words to me.

This is what I'd been hoping for when I asked him to be friends, and while he made no mention of being friends in his note, he gave me his number and offered to help if I needed anything. Maybe we didn't need to be friends. Acquaintances and neighbors was enough.

We could be cordial.

I fished my keys out of my purse and pushed the door open. I made my way into the kitchen and set my purse and the note on the counter.

I wanted to move on with my day, but I couldn't stop staring at the piece of paper, mainly the phone number scrawled on the bottom. I should text him, right? Just as a thank you. And to let him know I noticed the flowers.

I pulled my phone out of my bag and unlocked it. The various unchecked notifications on my homepage caused a sigh to escape me. While I hadn't checked social media since getting back from *Paradise Love*, I still had all the apps on my home screen, which meant I saw the number of unread notifications. And it was in the thousands. *Great.* Definitely not dealing with that right now.

The number of unread texts was much better. One from my parents with some photos of their summer in Florida. Another from my brother checking in. And the final one was from Lily about some new treats she was baking.

I'd respond to those soon. For now, I typed in the new number and sent a text to my neighbor.

ME

> Thank you for the flowers. You put the blue planters exactly where I imagined them. I'm going to move the other two to the back porch.

Almost immediately after I sent the message, three gray dots appeared.

WESLEY

> You're welcome. I'm glad you liked them.

ME

> And a new start sounds good to me.

WESLEY

> I appreciate the second chance. Or is it a third or fourth chance at this point?

ME

Hmm maybe even a fifth chance. I also didn't realize you had such a green thumb, neighbor.

WESLEY

There's a lot you don't know about me.

ME

Well, maybe I'll learn another thing or two about you.

WESLEY

And maybe I'll learn a few things about you, too, neighbor.

17

JULIETTE

WESLEY

Heard you needed help picking up something
from the thrift store?

ME

Wow, word really does travel fast in a small
town.

WESLEY

Helps when you have a sister who doesn't stop
talking.

ME

Okay, rude. That's my bestie you're talking
about!

But yeah…I actually could use the help. :)

You don't mind?

WESLEY

Not at all.

ME

Could we go later this week? We can stop by the thrift store in the morning and drop the items off at Lily's after her morning rush?

WESLEY

Sounds good to me.

ME

Always so chatty. :)

WESLEY

Funny.

ME

:)

My fingers tapped the tops of my bare thighs, right under where the skirt of my dress ended, as I sat in Wesley's truck. We were on our way to Lily's after stopping at Golden Finds, the local thrift store. We picked up the loveseat, a side table, and a few other decorations I'd spotted on my last visit. Layla, the owner, had been nice enough to set the items aside for me, making for an easy pick up. I had the decor in a bag at my feet and the two pieces of furniture were in the bed of Wes's truck.

I was incredibly grateful for his help, because I wasn't sure how else I would've gotten the loveseat over, and it was perfect for the café.

Things between Wes and me were better today than our first handful of interactions, but I sensed something was bugging him. He was trying but still keeping his distance. At least today things seemed less tense, but maybe it also helped that we weren't exactly talking. Wes wasn't very chatty, and I tried not to take it too personally. Even when we met with Layla, who Wes knew well, I had done most of the talking. I'd asked how long she'd lived in Golden Falls, how she started thrifting, and when she had opened the store.

I realized Wes was friendly, but he wasn't outgoing. He preferred listening and didn't want to make things about him, which was also how he'd been at the Richards family dinner.

I, on the other hand, didn't do great with silence. I didn't mind it if I was with someone I was comfortable with, and while Wesley didn't make me uncomfortable...I didn't exactly feel at ease around him. I wanted to know *something* about him.

"What're you thinking about?" I blurted.

We were at a stoplight, and he glanced over at me, eyes briefly flicking down to the hem of my dress before meeting my gaze. He rubbed the stubble on his jaw, shaking his head. "Just trying to focus on driving."

He looked so carelessly casual with one hand draped over the steering wheel, the other hanging out the open car window.

"You must be thinking about *something*," I challenged.

He huffed out a laugh. "I mean, one of the things I was thinking about is when I'll be able to get out on the water. Things have been so busy at Lake Ridge that it's been hard to take a day off. Usually, I would've gotten out there a handful of times by now."

"You have a pontoon tied to your dock. Is that what you usually take out?" I thought back to how relaxed and at ease he looked out on the dock.

"Yeah, if there's a group of us going out. If it's just me, I usually take out the jet ski or the kayak. But as long as I'm out on the water one way or another, I'm not picky. Good place to think. Take in the nature." He paused, hesitating. "We usually take the boat out for the Fourth. You should join us."

I raised my brows. At first, I wasn't sure I heard him right, but when he added, "think about it," I realized I hadn't hallucinated. Maybe we could both exist in the same town for the summer.

"I'd love to," I responded quickly, not needing time to think about it. If he was putting in the effort, so would I. Plus a day out on the water sounded nice. "Will you let me know the details? Or should I ask Lily?"

"I'll text you."

"Careful, or we'll be texting regularly," I teased, reaching into my bag to pull out my phone to text Lily that we were getting closer to the café. "And see, you *were* thinking about something."

A low grumble escaped his lips as he hummed. "I was thinking about a couple things." I felt Wesley's eyes on me, but by the time I finished typing out my message and looked over at him, his gaze was back on the road.

"I'm so excited to see it all come together! It's already looking great," Lily said with a bright smile as I approached the counter. The aroma of cinnamon, freshly baked pastries, and rich coffee when you entered Purrfect Blend was welcoming and inviting, like you were getting a warm hug. I immediately eyed the pastries and mentally picked out which ones I'd buy on my way out.

"Me, too. I'm glad I was able to swing by yesterday to take care of the prep ahead of getting the new pieces in today."

"The loveseat is going to look so good in the other room. I'm so glad you were able to get transport all figured out."

I playfully narrowed my eyes at her. "I'm pretty sure you got it all figured out for me. Wes texted me about it. He's out parking the truck."

Her lips pulled into a mischievous smile. "So, you're *texting* my brother now, huh? That's an interesting development. I don't remember giving him your number."

"He had my number already. When he left the flowers on the porch, he'd also left his number, so I texted him as a thank you. And we sort of cleared the air? Or at least decided to start over."

"Wait a second. Back up." Lily raised her hand. "He left you flowers?" Lily's lips parted in disbelief.

"In a flower planter! Not a bouquet or anything," I added quickly. I hadn't thought to mention it to Lily and also assumed she knew when she'd pushed Wes to help me.

"That's...well, that's good." Lily nodded. "I was worried after dinner he'd continue putting his foot in his mouth. And he still might, but at least this means he's come to his senses that he was being a jackass."

I shook my head with a laugh. No arguing with that.

Her face softened slightly. "He didn't know I was renting out the cabin this summer, so he's been a bit on edge since your arrival. It has nothing to do with you. He used to be the one who managed the rental, and a couple summers ago rented it out. I don't really know what happened, but he was different after that."

"What do you—" As if right on cue, the door swung open. And there was Wes standing in the doorway.

18

WESLEY

"Okay if we keep this door propped open while bringing the furniture in?" My eyes darted between my sister and Juliette, who were both staring at me like deer in headlights. I had no clue what they had been talking about, but I clearly interrupted something.

Not getting an immediate response, I reached down for the door stopper on the floor to keep the door propped and returned to my truck.

"A good morning would be nice instead of just barging in!" Lily called after me.

Yeah, it would've, but the only thing consuming my mind right now was the smell of vanilla and daisies. Juliette's perfume was everywhere, including my truck. Between that and the sky-blue dress she was wearing, I had to fight to keep my eyes on the damn road so I wouldn't get us into an accident. Juliette was summer in human form—bright, beautiful, tempting. I didn't know how, but it was easy for her to strike up a conversation with everyone in town.

Fuck.

I was distracted. I couldn't remember the last time I felt the type of rush I did when Juliette texted me. It was…nice.

But we weren't friends, and I was putting my foot down about that. Neighbors, yes. And we could be *friendly*. But not friends.

I wanted to show her I was serious about putting the past behind us and starting fresh, so it was easy to offer to help with the furniture. Plus, it was on my way into town and a way to help out my sister.

Even though I was closer in age with Jade, Lily and I were similar in that we both had an entrepreneurial mindset. But she was a hell of a lot more impressive than me. She was creating something unique on her own, whereas I was building on what our father had done. Both required work, but Lily's dedication and determination were unmatched.

"How can I help?"

I looked over my shoulder to see Juliette. She stepped in front of me, leaning on her toes and peering into the truck bed. What was it about this woman that constantly captivated my attention? Nothing else existed when she was around. I'd never felt this way before.

"I can grab the table first and then we can bring in the loveseat together?" Juliette's words took me out of my thoughts. She turned around, now facing me. She was trapped between me and the back of the truck. Her lips parted ever so slightly as she looked up, her tongue darting along her bottom lip.

Did I have any semblance of an effect on her like she did on me? I doubted it, but I couldn't help to wonder anyway.

"Yeah, sounds good to me." I cleared my throat and stepped to the side. I created some distance between us, but she was still everywhere.

"How do I…" she trailed off, hand tugging on the tailgate's handle.

"Here," I said, stepping closer and setting my hand over hers, "you pull up like this." I guided our hands to release the latch. She watched as the tailgate dropped down smoothly and quickly moved her hand away. She chewed on her bottom lip, distracted.

"What're you thinking about?" I was curious and hadn't had a chance to ask her back in my truck.

"Oh, nothing," she said with a wave of her hand.

I raised my brows, which got a soft laugh out of her.

"I was thinking about how it's nice to be on the same page as you. For once."

"Yeah, it's not too bad."

"You just gotta put up with me for a few months. Summer always flies by, and I'll be back in Chicago soon enough."

I parted my lips to speak but decided against it, not sure how to respond. That's what I wanted, right?

I helped Juliette unhook the cables that were keeping the side table in place. She then got it out of the truck with ease.

"I'll be right back," she called over her shoulder while I started to get the loveseat ready for us to bring in next.

It wasn't that I doubted Juliette—well, maybe I did at first—but she was surprising me.

I expected her to stand back, which would've been fine, but she was ready to help without me even asking. She was putting in the effort, not just with Lily's café, but with getting to know Golden Falls and its residents. I saw it at Hal's and at my parents' house.

I wanted my initial impression of Juliette to be right—that she was here for the summer and would forget about this town as soon as she left. That she'd turn her back on everything from the summer and move on with ease.

I was starting to second-guess my first impression of her.

And that scared the shit out of me.

I pinched the bridge of my nose with a groan as I leaned back in my desk chair. I thought after finishing payroll I'd be able to play a game of pool with Cooper and then head home for the night. But I still had to unbox the new inventory that came in today, and I wanted to check in with Louise to see if she needed anything.

I normally didn't let the various tasks that came with owning a business pile up, but June had been a blur. I loved Lake Ridge, and I wouldn't change this job for the world, but we were growing faster than I could handle, and I needed a couple more people on my team who I could trust.

Luckily, I'd hired two college students who were in town for the summer to help out around the bar, mainly placing my inventory orders, handling deliveries, and freeing up some of my time so I could focus on moving the expansion forward. They wouldn't start until early next month, but it'd be a weight off my shoulders. Eliza was going to be bartending soon, which would be a huge help. Then I'd need to figure out a plan for the fall. One thing at a time.

A knock on the door brought me out of my thoughts.

"Come in," I called out.

"Figured you were still in here," Cooper said as he opened the door, keeping it propped open as he leaned casually against the door frame. "You doing okay?"

I let out a sigh. "Yeah, I'm fine. Another busy day. I'll have some more help soon, which will be huge, especially having Eliza."

"I'm glad it worked out." Cooper nodded. "And are we still on for the Fourth? You bring the beer, and I'll bring food to grill up?"

"Of course, we're still on," I responded with a grin, my mood lightening at the thought of spending a day out on the water with my best friend. It was one of my favorite ways to pass the time, and Cooper and I had taken that boat out countless times during our friendship. "Sounds like a plan. I'll have the cooler and everything, too."

"Is anyone else coming?" Cooper asked, and for a split second, I wondered if he'd already found out Juliette was going to be there, but then he added, "Like is Jade going to be in town?"

My brow furrowed, and I shook my head. "I don't think she has plans to visit any time soon with her work schedule. You should give her a call sometime. You two talked on the phone all the damn time while we were in college."

Cooper's jaw clenched, and his whole body looked tense. He ran his hand along the back of his neck. "Yeah, well, that was then. This is now."

I raised a brow. *Okay, then.* I wasn't sure where that came from, but it was true they spoke way less often these days—if ever. Things seemed fine with them when Jade was in college, but did something happen before she went off to California? I parted my lips to ask, but decided not to pry. If he wanted to talk about it, I was here.

"Anyways, I'm going to head out. Early day tomorrow, and I need my beauty rest," he said, his grin returning, but it didn't quite meet his eyes.

I shook my head with a chuckle. "You and your damn beauty rest," I muttered. "Yeah, rain check on the game of pool, then? I still have some shit to do before wrapping up."

My phone screen lit up with an incoming text.

"Who're you texting? You hate texting," he said, craning his neck to see whose name flashed on the screen.

"No one. I was just—"

In a couple of quick, long strides, Cooper crossed the distance from my door to the desk, swiping the phone before I had a chance to grab it. What were we? Five years old?

"Oh, interesting," he drawled, a smirk on his lips as he passed the phone back to me. "Didn't realize you were a damn liar."

"Whatever." I rolled my eyes.

"So, you and Jules are on texting terms, which is great timing, actually. I wanted to give her the list of trails we'd talked about at dinner. You wouldn't mind giving me her number, would you?"

I sat up straight in my chair, looking between my phone and Cooper. I couldn't tell if he was messing with me or not—or if it even mattered.

"Don't mind at all," I clipped, my cheek twitching as I picked up my phone. Yes, I fucking minded. Juliette was already every-where—I didn't need her texting and falling for Cooper.

"You sure?"

"Yeah, I'm sure. Why do you think I'd care?"

He shrugged, his smirk turning into a full-on grin as he tipped his chin toward my hand. "Maybe because of the death grip you have on your phone."

I swore under my breath as I tapped on Juliette's contact info, seeing the two photos she'd sent moments earlier. One of the café and the other of the cat room with the new furniture and existing furniture rearranged. It looked great. The changes Juli-ette made fit the space and Lily's vision.

I copied her number and pasted it into my texts with Cooper, my thumb hesitating over the send button before tapping it.

Cooper fished his phone out of the back pocket of his jeans, seeing if the text came through. "Thanks, man. Get home at a reasonable hour." He gave me a nod before walking away.

The rest of the night, even as I made the short drive back to my place, the only thing on my mind was if Cooper had texted her and what the fuck they were talking about.

19

JULIETTE

COOPER

Hey, it's Cooper. Hope you're settling in okay. Wanted to do good on my promise of sending you over a few trails. Let me know if you want more info.

ME

Perfect, thank you!!!

COOPER

I'd offer to show you around myself, but the season has been busier than expected. I bet Wes would take you, though.

ME

Hmm you must not make very good bets then.

COOPER

I do alright, actually.

WESLEY

The café looks great. The cats must be happy.

ME

Thanks! And yeah they love the new couch. :)
Working with Lily was great.

WESLEY

You two seemed to hit it off right away.

Everything good at the cabin? Need anything?

ME

I'm all set for now. Thanks for asking!

WESLEY

For the Fourth, feel free to come on by around
noon. We'll get out on the boat, have lunch, and
then spend the rest of the day out on the water.

ME

Sounds perfect! Should I bring anything?

WESLEY

I got it covered.

ME

I really feel like I should bring something.

Oooh I'll bring watermelon! And maybe some
seltzers.

WESLEY

You like not listening to me, huh?

ME

I certainly like it more than listening to you. :)

WESLEY

That checks out.

REALITY WEEKLY

Paradise Love's Tony Pierce claims there's more to the story of
the leaked audio

In an exclusive interview with Reality Weekly, *tech entrepreneur
Tony Pierce claims his words were taken out of context—and suggests
Juliette Campbell knew his intentions.*

The *Paradise Love* saga is far from over, especially if Tony Pierce
has anything to do with it.

Pierce was one half of the fan-favorite couple who went on to
win the hit reality dating show. Pierce seemed to fall for interior
designer Juliette Campbell, and the two quickly stole viewers'
hearts. Until a leaked audio clip revealed Pierce never intended
to continue the relationship with Campbell and went on the
show to boost his company.

Pierce shared his side of what went down in an exclusive interview with *Reality Weekly*.

While Pierce regrets how harshly his words came out, he claims Campbell knew his intentions from the beginning.

"When the cameras weren't rolling and the mics were off, we talked about how the show could help us both," he said. "She knew I was looking to expand my business, and she was looking for next steps for her interior design career."

Pierce said he enjoyed his time on the show and the relationship he'd formed with Campbell. He said his comment about how they'd "never work in the real world" was misunderstood.

"I developed real feelings for her, but I knew things wouldn't work because of our careers and where we lived," Pierce said. "I was trying to spare her feelings in the long run and do us both a favor."

An anonymous source close to the show could neither confirm nor deny if Campbell knew of Pierce's intentions.

"The contestants do have some time off camera without their microphones, so it's hard to say what the two talked about," the source said.

Campbell could not be reached for comment.

Viewers are unsure who to believe.

"We voted for them to win because it looked like they formed a genuine connection. Now we find out they were both in on this plan? Smh," one viewer commented on social media.

Another viewer wrote, "A man trying to blame his actions on a woman. Classic. Nothing he says could make me like him. #TeamJules."

People are clearly invested in how this will all turn out and if Campbell will speak out next. Will she defend herself? Stay silent? Or admit what Pierce said is true?

We'll grab the popcorn.

Follow *Reality Weekly* online and on social media for updates.

20

JULIETTE

ME

> Hi! Thanks again for the invite for today, but I'm not feeling well. I'm going to skip the boat day.

I finished typing out the text to Wesley and hit send. I then typed out a similar message to the group chat I had with Lily and Eliza, wanting to also let them know I wouldn't be able to make it today.

It wasn't a complete lie. Maybe I wasn't sick, but I still wasn't feeling well mentally or emotionally. I'd been looking forward to the Fourth of July plans since Wes invited me, but I didn't know how much fun I'd be. Or how much fun I'd have.

I made the mistake of logging into my Instagram today. Instead of catching up on photos and what people in my life had been up to over the summer, hundreds of notifications and tags directed me to the most recent *Reality Weekly* article. My curiosity got the better of me, and I tapped one of the notifications, which then led me to reading the article. An article all about Tony trying to save face.

I should've stopped reading after the headline, but my eyes remained glued to the screen, preventing me from swiping out of the app.

Once I finished reading, I couldn't stop crying. I didn't care that he wanted to save his image, but why drag me into it? Why lie all about it?

It showed me even more the type of man he was and how I'd put my trust in the wrong person. I was fully aware of that—I didn't need another reminder. Again, I thought back to our time on the show, how the Tony in these articles was nothing like the man I'd gotten to know. It was easy to see his true colors now. How could I have been so gullible?

I thought I had cried all the tears imaginable—tears of hurt, frustration, embarrassment, and anger—after hearing Tony's words.

But nope, there were more. I didn't even know what exactly I was crying over. I didn't want anything to do with Tony, and I didn't want people feeling sorry for me. I was *frustrated* I couldn't escape this.

I'd started to fall under the illusion that *Paradise Love* was behind me, but the article was a giant reminder that people were still talking about what happened. That Tony was still trying to get his fifteen minutes of fame and dragging me into it. Our social media followings skyrocketed while we were on the show, and he wanted to build off the attention. Maybe I should've known this was what I was getting myself into, but I believed this show would be different. I was tired of blaming myself for it and now having Tony blame me for it, too.

I didn't know if I wanted to share my side of what happened. A part of me wanted to say something to clear my name and move on from it all, but another part still hoped this would all blow over. One thing was for sure, I didn't want to go the route of *Reality Weekly* to tell my side of the story. Maybe I'd post something on social media and move on. I didn't want this to be a bigger deal than it already was.

While it hurt in the moment, I was more than glad Tony ended things with me after the show, even if the last thing I wanted now was to find love. This summer was for me to find myself, rediscover my passions, and figure out what I wanted to do next. I wouldn't stop being myself. One day, far in the future, I'd find a man who didn't think of me as a handful, who didn't feel the need to blame me for his issues. Falling in love right now would only be a distraction. I didn't need that.

I was curled up on the couch under a blanket wearing an oversize T-shirt and pair of sweatpants and watching a romantic comedy. I might have been over real love, but I still enjoyed fictional love. Sue me! My hair was in a messy bun, and I could feel how puffy and red my eyes had gotten from crying. I was emotionally exhausted.

The couple in the movie was about to have their first kiss, but a loud knock at the front door had me pausing the movie. I pulled myself off the couch and walked over to the front entry. Confused, I slowly peeked behind the curtain.

Shit. I quickly let the fabric fall back.

What was he doing here?

"Juliette, I know you're in there. I saw you in the window." Wesley wiggled the locked door knob. "Open the door."

Ugh. Did I have to let him in? He had to leave eventually. He couldn't stand out there forever.

"I'm not leaving," he said matter-of-factly, as if he'd read my mind.

A defeated sigh escaped me. I wiped under my eyes and smoothed out my T-shirt before I reached for the door, unlocking it and pulling it open. "Wesley," I greeted.

"Juliette." He peeked past me inside the cabin, tension in his jaw and a crease in his forehead. Hadn't Lily said something about Wes and the cabin?

With him looking inside, I used the moment to take him in. He towered over me and smelled of mint and mahogany. He was wearing a simple navy tee and a pair of black swim trunks, along with his Lake Ridge baseball cap. His facial hair was a little longer than the last time I'd seen him.

My face started to get hot, the flush creeping down to my neck. Maybe I wasn't looking for love, but I could still admire a good-looking man. And Wesley Richards was handsome, rugged, and likely could easily throw me around in the bedroom. Well, not *me*. A woman. He could easily throw whatever woman he wanted around with his strong hands, muscular arms—

Not the point.

"Shouldn't you be out on the water?" I asked. It was nearly noon.

"Lily and Eliza were worried something was wrong." He paused. "And I wanted to make sure you were okay." He tore his gaze away from the living room and looked down at me, his expression softening. "Are you? Okay, that is. You look like you're heating up."

"Oh, um, I'm fine! Totally fine," I assured. I wasn't about to tell him about what happened with the article—or how I was imagining his hands on me. "Anyways, I'm still not feeling well, but thanks for checking on me." I moved to shut the door, but he was faster. His large palm pushed against the door, preventing me from shutting it. He pushed it open enough to step inside.

He took a moment to take in the space. I expected more of a reaction out of him, but his expression was stone. Wesley Richards had an impeccable poker face, and it frustrated me that I couldn't get into his head.

"It looks different in here," he said slowly.

"I'm sorry if I—" I started, not wanting to annoy him with the changes I made.

"I like it. It looks great. Like a fresh start."

I nodded. "That's what I was going for. For me, at least."

He crossed his arms over his chest, eyes focused solely on me. "You just said you were fine, so why aren't you spending the day with us?" As much as I wanted to look away from him, I couldn't. And I especially couldn't when his brown eyes were focused on me. It was the first time I noticed the golden flecks within the dark brown. "Is it because of me? I don't have to be there."

"Wes," I uttered softly. There was something about his words combined with his soft eyes that gutted me. I didn't want him thinking this had to do with him, that I was avoiding him. I knew he wasn't my biggest fan, but we were making it work. We were being neighborly. "No, it's not because of you. I just... I'm not having the best day."

"All the more reason for you not to be alone. C'mon. Being out on the water is one of the best cures for a bad day." Wes took a step toward me, lifting his hand slowly. He hesitated for a split second but ultimately reached forward and tucked a stray strand of dark hair behind my ear, his touch lingering. He ran his thumb along the side of my cheek before pulling away.

The action, and his touch, was so soft, so tender. I stared up at him, speechless, and gave his words some thought. Maybe he was onto something. I'd been looking forward to today since he invited me, plus it was finally my chance to meet Eliza. *This* was the type of distraction that'd be good for me.

"Okay," I agreed slowly. "Let me quickly change into a swimsuit. I have the watermelon and seltzers in the fridge. Could you grab those?"

"I said you didn't have to get anything."

"And I happen to like doing the opposite of what you say."

"Smart ass," he muttered with a chuckle. "So, if I asked you to keep wearing dresses all summer, you'd stop?"

I tossed my head back with a laugh. "Maybe I'd just walk around naked."

That was the first time I'd seen Wesley Richards blush. It was a good look on him.

21

JULIETTE

"You're here!" Lily squealed as soon as Wesley and I came into view walking down the wooden steps. She unlatched the pontoon's side door and stepped onto the dock, quickly closing the distance between us. "Wes said you weren't feeling well. Is everything okay?" Concern marred her face as she set her hands on the sides of my arms.

I nodded. "I'm okay. Just had a rough morning. I'll tell you about it later. Right now, though," I said, looping my arm through hers, "I want to focus on the boat day. I've been looking forward to it all week."

My mind was still distracted by the article, but my mood instantly improved being in Lily's presence. I was so grateful to have her in my life. Regardless of what happened after the summer, I'd definitely return to Golden Falls to visit her.

"I've been so excited, too." Lily led us toward the boat. "And I love your shorts! I need to shop in your closet one of these days."

"Please do! But I can easily say the same about you," I said with a laugh. I hadn't wanted to keep Wesley waiting, so I kept my outfit simple today. I'd thrown on a pair of medium-wash denim shorts that were frayed at the ends and a loose white linen shirt. Underneath, I had a simple red triangle bikini.

Wes walked past us, holding the twelve-pack of seltzers in his hand and the bowl of watermelon under his arm. I'd offered to help, but he insisted on carrying it all. I'd quickly realized how stubborn he was—almost as stubborn as me, honestly— and figured the battle wasn't worth it.

He used his free hand to get the side door open for us.

The chatter of voices became clearer as we stepped onto the boat.

"Cooper, stop moving the cooler around!" A woman, who I assumed was Eliza, swatted Cooper's arm. "I put it in the shade for a reason, and I—Jules, hi!" she exclaimed. The frown she had directed at Cooper immediately turned into a smile when she saw me. "I'm Eliza. It's so nice to finally meet you. I've heard so much about you from Lily!" She took a few steps from the other side of the boat to meet us and pulled me into an embrace. I easily hugged her back, already feeling like I knew her from everything Lily had told me, as well as from the group chat Lily set up for the three of us.

"So nice to meet you, too. I can't believe we're just now meeting!"

"I know," she sighed. "I wish I could've made time sooner, but between the yoga conference and extending my time in Madison, life was more hectic than I'd planned for. But the rest of the summer should be less busy. I'm back to a normal schedule at the studio, so you'll have to come by for a class. My next task will be balancing the studio with bartending at Lake Ridge, but I think it'll be a fun challenge. It'll be great to have some extra cash to really get the studio where I want it."

Eliza grabbed three cold seltzers from the cooler and then gestured for us to sit while Cooper and Wes finished getting the boat ready. Eliza's sleek black hair hit just above her collarbone.

As she reached up to pull it into a short ponytail, I noticed the various small tattoos scattered on her tan arms, fingers, and torso.

Both Eliza and Lily were wearing denim shorts and had their bikinis on already, too.

"I'd love to come by for a yoga class. That sounds perfect. Lily was also saying we should have a girls' night at Lake Ridge before you start." I got comfortable on the boat's cushioned seating that wrapped around both sides. Eliza and I were sitting on one side, and Lily was on the other. In the middle, there was a small table between us that had chips, popcorn, dips, and other snacks ready for us to dig into.

"We need to," Lily agreed. "It's been too long since I've been out dancing, plus we can celebrate your first month in Golden Falls *and* the café refresh being done." Lily turned to Eliza. "It looks so good, Eliza. The changes Jules made work so well for the space, and the cats are happy, which makes me happy."

As I filled Eliza in on the work Lily and I had been doing, the pontoon's engine rumbled to life. I snuck a glance at Wes, who was in the driver's seat slowly backing the boat away from the dock. He eased the throttle forward, the boat gliding further into the lake.

The crisp blue water sparkled and rippled in the sun's golden rays. The wind picked up as the boat went faster, and the fresh breeze felt incredible on a hot day. There were dozens of other boats out on the water already, and I figured the lake would get even busier as the day went on.

It had only been a matter of minutes of us being out on the water, but I already saw Wes relax. His shoulders eased, and what looked like a hint of a smile was gracing his face. I liked seeing him in his element.

"Ladies," Cooper greeted, sitting down next to Lily. He ran a hand through his messy dark-blond hair. "Jules, you look absolutely beautiful, as always."

I turned my attention to him, a laugh escaping me. "Thanks, Cooper," I said at the same time Eliza reached over and threw a piece of popcorn at her brother.

"Stop flirting with our friend," she scolded, before turning to me. "Well, unless you're okay with it. I guess I always forget most women want Cooper flirting with them." Eliza shuddered, immediately taking a sip of alcohol.

"It doesn't make me uncomfortable or anything," I assured. "Besides, Cooper and I are friends, right?" I asked him, and he nodded in agreement.

There was no denying Cooper was a handsome guy. But I found myself comparing him to Wes. His build was similar to Wesley's in that they were both muscular and had that rugged appeal. His hair was lighter than Wesley's, and his face was clean shaven most of the time.

What was it about Wesley that had me feeling more? The guy didn't even want to be friends with me.

"Hell yeah we're friends. Anyone who lets me talk their ear off about the various trails we have around here is immediately a friend. I'm so glad I got the day off today. I can't remember a year when we didn't spend the Fourth out on the water."

"The four of us plus Jade have been doing this ever since we were little." Lily filled me in. "My parents would take us out, we'd grill lunch, hang out on the boat, get a swim in. It was always the perfect day. Then we'd head back to my parents' house and have dinner with Marnie, Cooper and Eliza's grandma. Things have changed a little over the years, but we've tried to keep the tradition going with whoever is in town for the weekend. I'd say this year worked out great, especially with you here, Jules."

I couldn't remember the last time I felt this included. I knew a fair amount of people in my life in Chicago between my coworkers, apartment neighbors, and casual friends, but I didn't have many people I could truly count on, besides my brother. I hadn't gotten any texts asking how I was doing or where I was spending the summer. The people I thought I had in my life in Chicago either didn't notice I was gone or didn't care—neither of which felt good.

And while I'd been excited for today with Eliza, Lily, Cooper, and Wes, I'd also been nervous. These four were close—they'd spent their whole lives together. It was tough sometimes to be the new person trying to catch up with the various years of memories or follow along with stories. Eliza and Lily were best friends, and a part of me wondered if I'd feel out of place hanging out with them.

But it wasn't like that at all. I was welcomed right away. I felt like I could be myself.

As we laughed at another one of Cooper's jokes, I couldn't help but feel like I'd found my people. I wanted to soak up all the time I had with them before summer ended.

My eyes were glued to Wesley as he walked through the shallow lake water with Cooper.

Wes found us a spot near a sandbar to anchor down. Lots of other people had the same idea. While some people stayed on the boat, others were swimming or walking in the water to cool off.

The guys took a break to hop in the water, while Lily, Eliza, and I stayed on the boat. We'd moved over to the shaded seating area and were each a few seltzers in.

Wes was shirtless, the planes of his muscular chest on full display. And I wasn't the only one looking. Every woman out on the water was looking at Wesley Richards, and he didn't even realize it. His back was toned, likely from a combination of working out at the gym and manual labor.

"Jules?"

I heard my name, but it wasn't until Lily reached over and nudged my knee that I turned to her. "Huh?"

"What happened earlier today? I wanted to make sure you were okay." Lily frowned, sympathy in her expression. She had such a big heart, and I loved her for it. She was always looking out for those in her life.

Paradise Love hadn't come up today, apart from when Eliza and I were at the front of the boat and I filled her in on what had happened before summer started.

I didn't mind Lily asking about it now, and I was glad it was just the girls as I talked about it. I was finally making some progress with Wesley, and I didn't think talking about the reality show I was on would help my cause. I wasn't embarrassed about going on the show. It was what happened afterward that made me want to crawl in a hole.

"There was another article." I sighed, bringing my knees up to my chest. "Tony did an interview with *Reality Weekly* saying the audio was taken out of context and that I knew his intentions all along." I rolled my eyes. "He even said he was trying to spare my feelings and do both of us a favor by the way he ended things."

Eliza's jaw dropped. "What an entitled, selfish asshole."

"I'm so sorry you have to go through this, Jules," Lily added. "I'm glad you didn't stay home, though, because now we can keep you company and keep your mind off of it."

"We have your back no matter what," Eliza assured me. "The people in your life who know you know the truth."

"I'm so glad to be spending the day with you both. It's exactly what I needed. Wes said being out on the water would make me feel better, and I guess he was right. I'm honestly still surprised he was the one who invited me and the one who checked on me."

"Eliza and I were getting ready to head over, but he insisted he be the one to stop by the cabin." Lily stood, adjusting her bikini top and slipping out of her shorts.

"Oh, he did?" I asked, trying to keep my voice casual and my expression neutral. In reality, I picked apart every word of that sentence, focusing on how Wes had *insisted*. It would've been easy for him to step back and allow Eliza and Lily to check on me. But he *insisted* on being the one to stop by.

I obviously didn't know what was going through his mind—I rarely did—but I knew Wes did what he wanted to do, when he wanted to do it. The thought of him being worried about me filled my stomach with butterflies.

"Yeah, he was so stubborn and annoying about it. Drives me nuts when he gets that way. It's his way or the highway, so Eliza and I stayed back." Lily rolled her eyes.

Eliza looked at me with a smirk. If she noticed me over-thinking the exchange, she didn't say anything.

"Should we get into the water for a little?" Lily asked.

"Yes, please," Eliza said with a grin, finishing her seltzer. "I need to cool off from this heat, and I think Jules does, too," she teased with a wink.

The water might help with cooling off from the heat, but I didn't think there was a way to calm the brewing curiosity I had for Wes.

22

WESLEY

"What're you thinking about?" Juliette asked, sitting next to me as I drove the boat away from the sandbar. We'd just finished lunch. Cooper used the boat's mini grill to cook up hot dogs and brats, which paired great with the watermelon Juliette brought. Between the food and the drinks, everyone was beat and looked ready for a nap. I thought Juliette had been ready to doze off, too, until she got up.

Asking each other what we were thinking about had become our thing over the last few weeks. I liked having something that was ours. I didn't talk about my thoughts much—it wasn't easy for me—but I enjoyed letting her in. Even if I did have to twist the truth slightly every now and then. Because if I was completely honest, I'd just be telling her that I was thinking about her. Each and every time she asked.

Like right now.

I couldn't tell her what I was actually thinking about. No fucking way.

I couldn't tell her how the image of her in the red bikini was forever engraved in my brain. How I was *still* thinking about her in that yellow bikini from earlier in the summer. Or how the denim shorts she had on hugged her ass like they were made for her. About how fucking hard I'd almost gotten at her comment from earlier—about her walking around naked.

I knew Juliette was a beautiful woman the moment we met—I wasn't fucking blind—but the more time we spent together, the more the attraction grew. The more I couldn't look away. Her long, tan legs. Hips I could easily sink my fingers into. Plump, pink lips that I knew would taste so damn sweet.

We were out on the water—my favorite place besides my house and Lake Ridge—and all I could think about was her. Normally, I was taking in the scenery, the clear water sparkling in the sun, the line of trees in the distance, the clouds in the bright blue sky. But as soon as Juliette stepped onto my boat, none of that mattered. She took all of my attention.

Needing to respond, I settled on, "I'm glad you came out here with us."

A genuine smile bloomed across her full lips. "Me, too."

Her smile was so damn infectious, and I was proud to be on the receiving end of it for once. Earlier today, when I saw her upset and with red-rimmed eyes, it was like I'd been punched in the stomach and got the wind knocked out of me. I had a primal urge to make her feel better, to fix whatever was bothering her.

The way Juliette looked right now—smiling and happy—was exactly how she deserved to always be.

"How about you? What're you thinking about?"

She twisted her lips to the side. "How I forgot to bring sunglasses. I guess it doesn't matter now since we're almost done being out on the water."

I tsked. "Thought you'd have a million pairs of those, city girl." The nickname didn't have the usual bite behind it.

Juliette playfully rolled her eyes. "I have my million pairs in the cabin. I forgot to bring them on the boat."

"Should've said something sooner." Without giving it a

second thought, I swiped the Lake Ridge cap off my head and set it on hers. I reached around to carefully tighten it so it wouldn't fall off with the wind. Satisfied, I leaned back, taking her in. "That should help at least a little bit."

She looked damn good in my hat, and she looked damn good on my boat.

Juliette gingerly reached her fingertips up to touch the fabric, almost as if she didn't believe she was wearing it. "Yeah, this...works. Thanks, Wes." She chewed on her bottom lip as she glanced around, taking in our surroundings as Lily's playlist crooned in the background. "It's truly beautiful out here. I can see why you like spending time out on the water so much."

"I've always felt most like myself when I'm out on the water. Normally, I don't like to be alone with my thoughts. I'm always thinking about *something*, what the bar needs, how to help my parents..." I faltered. "Second-guessing if I'm good enough. If owning the bar is enough. If I'm successful enough. But something about this scenery lets me just...be. Lets me appreciate what I have and really puts it into perspective."

Juliette reached over, setting her soft palm on top of my knuckles. "Of course, you're enough, Wesley."

"You don't have to—"

"Let me finish," she interrupted, giving me a look. "I've seen how people in this town respect you, how they look up to you. I know I haven't been here long, but I noticed that right away. You are more than enough, but you're also more than what you've accomplished. It's so easy to get caught up in it all, in comparing yourself to others and wondering if you're on the right path. I know I've struggled with it, and part of the reason I'm here is to get on the right path. I'm glad you have a place you can go to quiet those concerns, because this town wouldn't be the same without you."

I rubbed my chest, right over where my heart was. *Fuck.* No one had ever said something like that to me, especially after only knowing me for a month. Somehow Juliette knew how to speak to my soul. I didn't deserve it, especially not after how I had treated her when she first got to town.

"I'm glad you found yourself in Golden Falls," I said truthfully. "Hopefully this can be the place for you to figure out what you need. Get you on your right path." I still didn't know exactly what she was running from, and while I didn't have a right to know—we weren't friends—I was more curious than ever.

"I hope so. I really like Golden Falls. I've never felt this way about a place before," she said wistfully, her voice quiet.

"Did that neighbor of yours stop giving you trouble?" The lighthearted teasing in my voice surprised even me.

"Gosh, he really is the worst, isn't he?" She looked back at me, trying to keep a straight face but failing. She burst into laughter.

"Ha, ha. Very funny," I deadpanned.

"Actually, you're not so bad, Wesley. I think this town might be big enough for the both of us. For the summer, of course."

"Yeah, I think it might be."

It didn't take long after that for Juliette to doze off. With everyone napping, I took my time getting us back to the dock. Plus, with Cooper asleep, it meant he couldn't flirt with Juliette. And that was fine with me. I knew he was doing it to get a rise out of me, and he enjoyed every second of it. He'd make Juliette laugh and then goddamn wink at me.

I didn't mind the silence or the quiet, and I also didn't mind being the one driving the boat. I preferred it, even.

I liked being in control of a situation. It was when things were out of my control or when I was caught off guard that my chest tightened.

I thought stopping by the rental would've brought up more emotions, more memories, than it did. Apart from today and when Juliette moved in, I hadn't been by the cabin since Gretchen left.

I'd spent so much time there during Gretchen's stay that I wanted nothing to do with it afterward. I was trying to stop comparing Juliette to Gretchen—it wasn't fair.

But it wasn't lost on me that Gretchen had been in Golden Falls for more than a year on and off and never made an effort to meet my family, to visit Lake Ridge, or to spend time out on the water. She wanted our relationship to be a secret, and that should've been the first red flag. How had I missed all the signs? Looking back, it was easy to point them out.

But the cabin looked like a different place now, no longer marred by Gretchen's stay.

Now, when I looked at the cabin, all I could see was Juliette. I liked the changes she made to the living area to make it more open and vibrant. Just like her.

The more time I spent around Juliette, the more I realized how wrong I had been about her.

There was no escaping the light that radiated off her. No wonder the whole damn town was drawn to her.

She was fucking addicting.

How was I going to break the addiction once she left?

23

JULIETTE

The nap had given me a second wind for the evening.

Once we unpacked the boat, we made ourselves comfortable at Wesley's house, which looked rustic from the exterior but had a modern feel when you stepped inside. I loved the tall windows and open floor plan. He mentioned to me how he made a number of upgrades to the home since moving in and shared how he was most proud of the basement, which included a pool table, dart board, and bar. The decorations were minimal, which I wasn't surprised by, but the home still felt welcoming and lived in.

It was easy to lose track of time. We hung out on his back porch, played yard games, and shared our favorite summer memories from over the years. Most of Lily's favorite memories had to do with pranks she'd played on her older siblings as a kid, including putting Wesley's car keys in Jell-O and filling his pillow case with water balloons.

Once the sun started to set, the group began to disperse. Lily wanted to be back in her apartment to keep her cats company since they were afraid of fireworks. Cooper and Eliza wanted to stop by their grandma's before the day was over.

Which left me and Wes.

He'd surprised me yet again when he asked if I wanted to join him and watch the fireworks from the back porch. I wasn't about to say no. His back porch, and the view he had of the lake, was absolutely stunning and so peaceful. And...maybe I was looking forward to spending more time with him, especially with how nice today had been.

There was some time to kill before the fireworks started, so I stopped back at the cabin to shower and change before meeting Wes back at his house.

I might've also stolen his Lake Ridge cap.

"The sky looks beautiful tonight." I leaned back in the Adirondack chair with a content sigh. Wes was sitting next to me. He was casually slouched back, and I had to keep myself from thinking about what it would be like to run my fingers through his messy, slightly wet hair or over his stubbled jaw. To distract myself, I focused on the thousands of stars sparkling like diamonds against the dark sky. "I've never seen so many stars."

"One of the benefits of living in a small town, city girl." Wesley brought the tumbler of whiskey up to his lips for a sip. I hadn't minded the nickname today. It came out gentler than in the past, no longer sounding like a curse. But it still served as a reminder to both of us that I wasn't sticking around after the summer. "I swear, Golden Falls has the best views."

I brought my knees up to my chest as I shifted in the chair to face him. "So, you've lived in Golden Falls your whole life, then? What was that like?"

"I have, yeah. I spent four years down in Madison for college.

I appreciated the change of scenery, meeting new people and hearing different ideas and experiences. I wouldn't change a thing, but it felt too busy for me, which was part of the reason I moved back. The other part was I knew I wanted to take over Lake Ridge once my dad was ready to sell."

"You met new people and *enjoyed* it?" I asked with mock surprise. "Don't tell the tourists that."

"Smart ass," he muttered, but I caught how the corner of his lip twitched up, fighting a smile. "I complain about the tourists a lot, but Golden Falls wouldn't be able to survive without them. I'm grateful this town can continue to thrive, but I wish the people who visited were more mindful of those of us who lived here year-round. Took better care of the town, didn't litter, were careful out on the lake. That kind of stuff."

"You love this town and want people to respect it. You're not asking for too much."

"And I guess I don't mind meeting new people if I know they're going to be around. I don't trust people easily, and sometimes that can come off in the wrong way." He waited a beat before adding, "I owe you an apology, Juliette. And an explanation."

I finally looked over at him, tilting my head. "What do you mean? About earlier this summer? We put that behind us already."

With the whiskey still in one hand, he tapped his other against his jeans. "I know we did, and I know I left you that note, but I never technically apologized in person, and it's been bugging me. Today made me realize I'm glad you didn't stop trying even when I gave you a hard time. I'm glad you spent the day out on the water with us, with me.

"The cabin had been empty for a while, and I didn't realize Lily was renting it out. That used to be one of my responsibilities before my parents passed it to her. A few years ago, I'd rented the cabin out to a travel photographer for a magazine. Gretchen."

I didn't have a right to be jealous—and I wasn't—but my stomach flipped at Wesley's mention of another woman's name. I didn't like how I wondered if he still had feelings for her.

"She spent time in the area on and off for about a year, taking photos of Golden Falls and the surrounding towns in northern Wisconsin." Wesley let out a deep sigh, and I couldn't tell what came over him. Sadness? Regret?

"I was different back then," he continued. "Less closed off. More open to meeting people. We hit it off immediately, and I don't know if you'd call what we had a relationship, but we had something. She wanted it all to be a secret, though. She told me it was because of her job, which I respected, but then I realized there was more to it.

"She told me she was divorced, but the truth was she was *going through* a divorce. She was technically still married when we were together, and that's why she wanted to keep things a secret. Why she never wanted to meet my family or friends and never wanted to be where people would see us together. She then said her time with me made her realize she wanted to fix her marriage. That she wanted a life in the city with her rich husband over a life here. That I couldn't offer her anything beyond an escape." Wes was looking out at the water but slowly shifted his gaze to me. "When I saw you with your pink suitcase and all those boxes, I assumed you were running from something, too. And I thought I was even more right when I found out you were on a show. I compared you to her without knowing anything about you, and I'm sorry for that, Juliette."

The pieces of our first handful of interactions were clicking into place, and while it wasn't fair, a sense of relief came over me knowing it wasn't anything I did.

"I couldn't figure it out," I said slowly, "why everyone was willing to give me a chance except you."

Wes frowned, his eyes softening. "It had nothing to do with you and everything to do with me. I shouldn't have let my past cloud the future. You're the first person I've told the full story to," he said. "Cooper knows bits and pieces, but I haven't been able to bring myself to explain what happened. Explain that things ended because I wasn't enough for—"

"Because she wasn't the right person for you," I interjected. "You have so much to offer someone, Wes. You just need to find her, and she's going to be a lucky woman." I firmly believed that as I started to see more of the real Wes. "What Gretchen did and how she treated you says so much more about the person she is than the person *you* are."

He let out a huff, shaking his head. "I don't deserve your kindness, Juliette."

"What makes you say that? Of course, you do. You're a good man. Maybe we got off on the wrong foot, but you've made up for it. I appreciate you apologizing again and opening up to me. Things between us are good." But there was one more thing on my mind. I swallowed before asking, "Do you...still have feelings for Gretchen?"

"No, I don't," he responded quickly, without any hesitation. "The way things ended was frustrating, but even then I knew she wasn't the person for me."

I exhaled a breath I didn't realize I had been holding.

"You seem relieved." That half-smile of his was back, and he knocked his knee against mine.

I shook my head with a laugh, appreciating how, even though our conversation was raw and vulnerable, there was an ease to it, too. "Only because I'd hate for you to be hung up on someone who doesn't deserve you."

"And are you? Hung up on someone who doesn't deserve

you?" His hand clenched around the whiskey glass before he set it on the side table, flexing his fingers at his side. I would've given anything in that moment to know what he was thinking. "You were upset earlier today, and no one should be making you feel that way."

I looked into his dark-brown eyes with golden flecks. Eyes that noticed more than I wanted him to. "I also know a thing or two about falling for the wrong person, but no, I'm not hung up on him."

After Wes gave me a piece of himself, I wanted to tell him my truth. Maybe I did come to Golden Falls as a distraction, but it's turned into so much more. "You know that I was on a reality show, right? Do you know anything beyond that or have you read any of the articles?"

"Articles?" He shook his head. "No. I figured if you wanted me to know something, you'd tell me yourself."

That meant more to me than he realized. I went on to tell Wes about why I'd gone on the show, falling for Tony, the breakup, the audio, my vulnerabilities. How Tony said I was a handful. It all felt like a lifetime ago now.

"And then the same tabloid that ran the article with the audio did an interview with Tony, who said I knew about his intentions from the beginning and was using the show to benefit my career, too. He even said he did me a favor by breaking things off."

"Fucking bastard," Wesley muttered. It wasn't the first swear he said as I recounted what happened. "He didn't deserve you. If the guy you're with doesn't worship the ground you walk on, he's not it. Plain and simple." He was clenching his jaw so hard, I thought he was about to crack a molar.

I sighed. "I'm starting to think I trust people *too* easily."

"Not a bad thing, but I can imagine that comes with its own challenges. I like how open you are with the people you meet, but not everyone deserves your light." Goose bumps formed on my skin. The low rumble in his voice both soothed and awakened something in me.

"You don't think it's stupid I went on the show? Thinking that things would turn out well?" I untucked my legs and stood, walking over to the deck railing.

He stood, too, bare feet hitting the wooden deck as he took a few steps to stand next to me. When I didn't look his way, he reached over and took my chin between his thumb and forefinger, tipping it up. He slowly moved his fingers from my chin, cupping my face instead and running his thumb over my cheek. A shiver ran up my spine at the warm contact of his calloused touch.

"You're fearless, Juliette. I can't imagine many other people who would pick up their life and sign up to go on a reality show not knowing the outcome. Or who would pack up their car and drive to a new town. And fully embrace both experiences." His gaze searched my face. "You've brought new life into this town. Golden Falls is better with you in it. And today was one of my favorite days because of you."

"Because of me?" It was unusual how quiet my voice was, but I didn't shy away from it. I wasn't looking for his approval—I knew I didn't need it—but I wondered if he felt the connection building between us. "So, you like me, then?"

"It's impossible to not like you." His thumb moved along my cheek once more before he dropped his hand.

I grinned up at him, trying not to think too much about the loss of contact. "Oh, really? Impossible?" I teased. "Bet you'll be begging to be friends with me now."

And then something truly breathtaking happened.

Wesley's lips widened into a full smile, his eyes crinkling in the corners. What I would've done to capture his smile in a photo. "Sure, baby, I'll beg if you want me to."

I let out an airy laugh, speechless. I was glad it was dark out, because maybe that meant he couldn't see the heat creeping up my cheeks.

He turned to face the railing, and I did the same, looking out at the water. The lake looked different than it did during the day but just as peaceful. I viewed Wesley in a different light now, too. He'd shown me pieces of himself today I hadn't expected, pieces that helped me understand him.

My palms were wrapped around the railing. He inched his hand closer and hooked his pinky around mine, his dark eyes focused ahead.

As the first fireworks lit up the night sky and crackled above us, I couldn't tell if the booming I felt was from the bursts of light or if it was my heart pounding in my chest.

I liked Wesley Richards, and that was a problem.

24

WESLEY

"Earth to Wesley." Eliza waved her hand in front of my face. "Dude, you look exhausted. Did you not get enough sleep or something?"

Or something.

A beautiful brunette with bright-green eyes had been occupying my mind ever since we watched fireworks together a few nights ago. But, truthfully, she'd been in my thoughts long before then.

I sighed, shaking my head. "I'm fine. It's been a long day."

She raised her brows. "It's eleven in the morning. The day just started."

"I got up early today, so it's been a long day for me," I gritted. I ran a hand through my hair, tugging on the strands. "What's with the interrogation?"

"Ah, I see." Eliza nodded with understanding, a sly smile on her face. "You weren't able to get good sleep, so you got up early to start your day."

"Exactly. I—"

"And that's because you haven't been able to stop thinking about Jules."

Louise, who was a few feet away from us, snorted.

I narrowed my eyes at Eliza. "That's not what—" I waved my hand to dismiss whatever she was conjuring up in her mind. "Never mind. Let's get back to onboarding." Eliza was basically a third little sister to me, so it wasn't unusual for her to be giving me a hard time. I just didn't like how she was right.

I had spent too much time these last few days overthinking my evening with Jules and if us opening up to each other changed anything. I saw her differently now. I knew more about her. But she was still only here for the summer, and I didn't want to fall for someone who was only here temporarily. Golden Falls was my home—I had no plans on leaving and no plans on giving up my dreams with Lake Ridge.

But, for the first time in a long time, I wondered what it would be like if things were different. If I initiated texts with Juliette or even stopped by the cabin to see her. If I gave in to that temptation.

I even told her the full story about what happened with Gretchen and my doubts about being enough or how jarring it was that the person I was seeing was lying to me and keeping secrets. The way I was seen as an escape. It wasn't until Juliette came into town that I realized how much my time with Gretchen had impacted me and closed me off from the world.

I didn't want to be like that. I didn't need to be everyone's best friend, but I also didn't want to be the guy who was constantly in a bad mood, constantly doubting people's intentions.

I thought I had been in love with Gretchen, but time made me realize I wasn't. Because you can't be in love with someone you don't know. Love was about seeing and appreciating all sides of a person—even during the tough times—and choosing them first. Every damn time. That wasn't what we had. Not even close.

Gretchen had never been a real part of my life, because she didn't want to be.

It was such a contrast to the way Juliette lived. She was fully embracing Golden Falls and wanted to be a part of it in every way she could, whether that was getting to know the locals, doing her freelance design work, spending time on the boat, or being friends with my sister. She was this town's missing piece.

Which was exactly why I'd been keeping my distance from her this week. I wasn't avoiding her. Seriously, I wasn't. She was likely busy, anyway. Lily said there were a few business owners who wanted to work with Jules, as well as another couple of residents who wanted her help decorating their rental properties.

Yes, I'd gone to my sister to ask for an update on how Juliette was doing. And to see if she'd asked about me. I'd done it discreetly—or so I hoped. Otherwise, Lily wouldn't let me live it down.

I tipped my chin toward the drink station, focusing back on the training Eliza and I had been doing. "If someone ordered a 7 and 7, what would that be?"

Eliza was catching on quickly. It helped she had bartending experience from college. It was a matter of jogging her memory of the drinks our customers ordered, particularly our regulars.

"A 7 and 7 is," Eliza said as she turned around to face the wall of liquor, "Seagram's 7 Crown whiskey and 7Up. With an optional lemon wedge garnish."

"You got it. Any questions come to mind over what we've gone over today?"

Eliza tilted her head to the side as she thought. "If people want to order food, can we do that at the bar, or should we grab a server?"

That was something I'd been thinking through. Lake Ridge had a limited food menu, but I wanted to expand it within the next year. My goal was to turn Lake Ridge into a year-round stop for people. I wanted to serve a limited, creative food menu during the day for people seeking a lunch or dinner spot and transition to smaller bites in the evening and into the night when people came to drink and dance.

Right now, we kept the late-night food menu simple: fries, cheese curds, chips and salsa, and nachos.

"At the bar is fine for now. Make sure to give them a table number, so they can place it wherever they're hanging out if they're not sitting at the bar. During the day, it's not a problem, but things get hectic at night."

Eliza nodded. "I'm excited for the plans you have for this place. You're going to take Lake Ridge to the next level. Already, it's such a draw to get people downtown."

"Thanks. I'm glad to hear you're excited. I hope you know there's no pressure to stay on bartending. There's a spot here for you if you want it, but if you need to step back, let me know. We'll figure something out."

I wanted to create something new and innovative for Golden Falls, taking ideas I'd seen bars and restaurants implement in Madison and other areas of the state. As we expanded the food menu, I also wanted to implement sustainable practices, such as composting and encouraging customers to bring their own to-go containers for leftovers.

I also wanted to lead by example. If other businesses in town took note of Lake Ridge implementing these changes and succeeding, then they'd consider doing the same. Especially if I showed them how simple it was. It was a big dream, but it would be worth it.

Having Eliza's help at the bar, as well as the college students who I hired for the summer, would free up my nights. I knew it would take time to figure this all out, hire the right people long-term, and get the right vendors in place, but the only way forward was to start somewhere. I was excited for the journey, but it definitely added a layer of stress to my already clouded mind.

As long as Juliette was in Golden Falls, I'd be distracted. I just had to get through the summer.

Eliza looked over at me as she was wiping and cleaning her station at the bar. "Your stress is stressing me out. Is he always like this?" She turned to Louise before turning back to me and saying, "Maybe you need to get laid, Wes."

I nearly choked on my own spit. "Jesus, Eliza. I'm not fucking talking about this with you."

She shrugged nonchalantly. "I'm just saying."

"It's a great way to relieve stress," Louise agreed, getting ready to continue Eliza's training by showing her how to stock the bar before each shift.

I groaned. I did not need this. My fuse was short today, and I didn't need any more reminders about how fucking good Juliette Campbell likely looked naked. I had plenty of those thoughts in my mind already.

"I'm going to the back to see what booze I need to order for the week," I grumbled, stalking my way toward the back.

"Jules likes a good Aperol spritz," Eliza called. "Make sure you have the necessary ingredients stocked!"

The first thing I did was add prosecco and Aperol to this week's inventory.

25

JULIETTE

MOM

Thanks for sending the pictures. You look beautiful! Looks like you had a great weekend with your new friends.

DAD

Agreed. Looks like a great time. Glad you are having fun.

MOM

One of your new friends can't stop looking at you in the pictures. He's very handsome!!!

A summer fling might be fun.

ME

Mom, no! No summer fling. He's my neighbor. And Lily's brother.

MOM

Oh, I think he's more than that. Wow, and those muscles. I zoomed in on the second photo. I might need a glass of water to cool off.

ME

Mom!!!

GRANT

I don't think this conversation needs to be in the
family group chat. And if it does, I'd like to be
removed from it.

I PUSHED OPEN THE DOOR TO HAL'S, GETTING USED TO MY ROUTINE
with him. I'd enjoyed getting to know Hal, his history in Golden
Falls, and his everlasting love for his late wife. Before opening
his hardware store, Hal was a general contractor. While he didn't
focus on remodeling projects anymore, he had a lot of knowledge to share. And I sure could use the advice.

"Hey, Hal. I'm here for my weekly visit," I said with a smile as
I entered the store.

"Miss Jules, always a pleasure," he greeted. "What are you
working on now?" He had his notepad and pencil at the ready to
hear about my next project.

When I was working at Luxe Living, a lot of wealthier clients
didn't have a budget they had to work within. I helped with the
vision of the project and getting materials ordered, but my work
ended there. Other members on the team stepped in to work
with contractors, and I moved onto the next client. With my
work here, I was a lot more involved in seeing the process
through, and it required different skills, like repurposing
existing furniture or thrifting. I was making connections with
the various general contractors and businesses in town but was
doing the majority of the work myself. Like for Lily's café. I'd
painted the walls, got the furniture over to her (with Wesley's
help), and arranged everything.

I appreciated the opportunity to be so involved and to use my creativity. The other businesses and rental owners I was starting to work with also had limited budgets, so I knew there would be more of the same—and I couldn't wait. I'd need help, though, especially if I wanted to complete the various projects on time. I was hoping Hal could get me in touch with some of the local painters.

One of the rental property owners who had reached out to me was Louise, who worked for Wesley at Lake Ridge. She owned one of the cabins near where I was staying and wanted to upgrade her rental. She had been struggling to attract business this summer and wanted my opinion on what improvements would make a difference. I was more than excited to work with her, and she already had a few other leads for me.

Eliza and I were also talking about figuring out a plan to modernize her yoga studio.

"I'm working with Louise on her cabin, and I wanted to put some shelves in. I know what I want them to look like...but I have no idea what kind of brackets, screws, or wood stain I need." I gave him a sheepish smile. "Think you can help?"

He grinned, nodding eagerly. "I'd be happy to."

I set my bag on the floor and pulled my laptop out to show Hal my ideas, focusing on the shelves but also showing him my overall vision. With a few small changes, Louise's cabin would feel more modern but still have that rustic feel visitors were looking for. I wanted to open up the living room by moving the storage cabinets to another area of the house and installing shelves instead that would hold local art and other thrifted finds. I also wanted to hire someone to paint the baseboards and change out the light bulbs to a warmer color.

It was easy to get lost in the projects and forget I was only here for the summer. I had an uneasy feeling in the pit of my stomach just thinking about it, so I pushed those thoughts to the very, *very* back of my mind. I focused on Hal instead.

In less than an hour, I had a full shopping list of what I needed for the shelves and instructions from Hal. It shouldn't be too bad—I hoped, at least. Hal seemed to have more confidence in me than I did.

"You'll do great, Miss Jules. I know it. And if you need anything and I'm not available, you can always ask Wes. I'm sure he'd be happy to help."

I raised a brow, unsure if that was a good idea. We were on better terms, sure, but that was part of the problem. Ironic, wasn't it?

At first, I wanted Wes to like me, but now that he seemingly did, I was nervous to be around him. Nervous for the way my body reacted to him. His words from that night were pulled to the front of my mind.

"You've brought new life into this town."

"It's impossible to not like you."

"Sure, baby, I'll beg if you want me to."

Who said that?! Was he just being nice? Was he flirting? Did it even matter? I hadn't seen him since the Fourth, and that was good. Less complicated. I couldn't avoid Wes forever, but I could at least avoid him for now.

"I'll keep that in mind and reach out if I need help," I said to Hal. "I should be okay to start, at least."

"I believe it. Just want you to know you don't have to do it alone."

"Thanks, Hal." I couldn't help the way I got a little choked up. That was the thing with small towns, right? People knew each other's business, but they also were willing to help out. You had people in your corner regardless of where you turned.

"Besides, I saw the way Wesley looked at you," Hal started,

"and word on the street is you two watched the fireworks together. Sounds romantic."

"Hal, how—" I shook my head with a laugh. "How did you hear about that?" That was the other thing with small towns. Word traveled fast. "We're neighbors who got off on the wrong foot and are friendly now. Besides, I'm leaving at the end of the summer, remember?"

Hal hummed, a smile on his face like he didn't believe me. "If that's what you say, Miss Jules."

What did he know that I didn't? And how had Wes been looking at me?

I grabbed my laptop, closing it and sliding it into my bag along with my notes. I gave Hal another smile. "I gotta get going. Eliza, Lily, and I are heading to Lake Ridge tonight. I have a few more things to get done before then, but I'll see you next week?"

Hal nodded, amused. "I'll see you then. You girls have fun. Say hi to Wes for me."

"I likely won't see him tonight, but if I do, I will."

"Okay, ladies, one shot before we leave." Eliza didn't wait for our confirmation before filling three shot glasses with tequila. She had the lime wedges and salt ready, too.

"Tequila?" I scrunched my nose, able to conjure the sharp taste even before taking the shot. It was going to be an interesting Saturday night if we were starting like this.

We had spent the last couple of hours getting ready in the cabin and listening to Shania Twain, Dolly Parton, Rihanna, and other artists.

"Yes! Perfect way to start the night." Lily made her way into the kitchen, her golden curls bouncing behind her. She was wearing a cropped tank with flared jeans that hung loosely on her hips. "How did training and onboarding at Lake Ridge go? You finished your first full week, right?"

Eliza set the tequila bottle down, handing each of us a shot. She had on black shorts paired with a chunky belt and a crochet halter top. "It was good. Honestly, pretty similar to the bartending job I had in college. I'm feeling ready and looking forward to making some extra cash. Everyone is really helpful, especially Louise. She gave me some tips and tricks for making drinks faster and remembering what the regulars order. I will say though"—Eliza had a mischievous smile on her face as she looked over at me—"Wes seemed distracted all week."

"Why are you looking at me?" I squeaked.

"Uh, because it's obvious," Lily said with a laugh. "My brother literally didn't stop staring at you all of Fourth of July, and then the recluse invited you to watch fireworks with him."

"Because we're, well, friendlier these days." Although I hadn't heard much from him this week. Not that I expected to. And not that I wanted to.

Eliza laughed at the same time Lily quickly waved her hand. "Nope didn't need to know that."

"Not like that!" My cheeks flushed.

"Twenty bucks Wesley says something to Cooper about staying away from Jules," Eliza chimed in.

Lily bumped her hip against mine. "We're giving you a hard time. I mean, I still don't want details, but whatever is happening is between you two, as long as it doesn't impact our friendship, I'm happy."

"I appreciate that," I said slowly, "but there's nothing going on." I didn't like how defensive my voice got. I might've developed a *tiny* crush on Wesley, but that wasn't something I needed to share. It wasn't like this would go anywhere. I didn't want complicated, and getting tangled up with Wes would be exactly that.

Lily looked down at her phone as the screen lit up. "Okay, let's take this shot. Wes is going to be here in five."

Of course, Wes was our driver for the night.

"To girls' night!" Eliza said, and we all cheered.

We licked the salt off the back of our hands, knocked our shots back, and quickly chased the burn with the lime wedges.

"That never gets any easier." I shook my head, my face pinched.

"No, it doesn't." Lily coughed. "But we're going to have a blast tonight."

When I looked at the two of them, Lily was struggling while Eliza looked like she was ready for another.

"Couldn't agree more," I said.

I grabbed my purse, slipping my phone and lip gloss inside. I took a final look in the mirror. It'd been a while since I'd gotten fully ready like this. Getting ready on *Paradise Love* with all the other girls was one of the main highlights of being on the show. It was even better to be getting ready with Lily and Eliza.

As I looked at myself in the mirror, I noticed I wasn't carrying tension in my shoulders and my jaw wasn't clenched. Apart from the boat day on the Fourth, I hadn't given much thought to Tony's comments in the *Reality Weekly* article. If that's the way he wanted to go about life, then so be it. I couldn't control it. What I *could* control were my actions, who I surrounded myself with, and what I did next. I was inspired about working with small businesses and felt even more confident I was making the right decision by trying to pursue this as the next step in my career.

I tossed my curled hair over my shoulder and made sure I didn't have any of my lipstick or gloss on my teeth. I was the only one who opted for heels tonight, choosing my favorite pink pair with straps that tied up my calves. My shoes were the same color as my lace corset-style top, and the black leather mini skirt really tied the look together.

We all looked stunning and ready to take on the night. Right on time, too, because there was a knock at the door.

"That's Wes!" Lily called. "Can you tell him I need another couple minutes?"

Well, almost right on time.

"Yeah, no problem," I responded to Lily, crossing the distance to the door and pulling it open.

As I was opening the door, Wes asked, "Let me guess, Lily needs a few more minutes?"

I let out a breathless laugh, opening the door fully. While I expected to see Wes on the other side, I didn't expect to see him casually leaning against the door frame, muscular arms crossed over his broad chest. He was wearing his usual outfit—jeans and a tee—but he made it look so damn good.

As soon as Wes saw me, he adjusted his casual stance, stepping away from the door frame and standing up straight. "Juliette, you look..." he trailed off, shaking his head. His eyes worked their way up my body slowly, his searing gaze burning me everywhere he looked. And I liked the fire. He started with the strappy heels winding up my legs then moved to the pink corset top I was wearing. His eyes lingered at how the top pushed my breasts together before he met my eyes. He swallowed. "You look beautiful, absolutely beautiful," he finished with a rasp.

His jaw was clenched tight, and when I looked down, his hand flexed before he slipped it into his jeans pocket. Almost like he didn't trust himself not to reach out.

"Thanks, Wes." I kept my response simple, because I was positive my brain was going to short-circuit if I tried to string together more words. I'd never had a man look at me the way

Wes did. What could I say to his compliment, apart from that he makes me feel like I'm the most beautiful woman in the world. That when he looks at me it feels like there's no one else around.

A light laugh echoed behind me. "Oh, sure. Nothing at all," Eliza said as she looked between us with a knowing grin.

I expected Lake Ridge to be the type of bar where the soles of my shoes stuck to the floor and the air smelled a little stale. I imagined a small, local bar. None of that was true. Well, maybe my heels stuck a little.

Lake Ridge had something for everyone. Dancing, drinking, hanging out, and bar games. It was easy to see why Wes, everyone in town, and those visiting loved it. The night had just started, and the place was already packed.

"Wow," I hummed, glancing over at Wes, who looked on with a proud smile as we walked in. "I'm excited to finally see it in person. Should've worn my Lake Ridge merch tonight."

Wes raised his brows. "Ah, so that's where my hat went."

"Maybe," I said slowly, turning toward him. "I haven't seen you much this week."

"I didn't think you'd notice."

"I did," I admitted. "I don't know what I was expecting, but I thought I'd at least see you around town."

He nodded. "It's been a busy week. I should've reached out. I... I wanted to... I just..." His words were interrupted when Lily appeared behind me. Wes cleared his throat, not finishing his thought. "Have fun tonight. Here, drinks on me." He fished his credit card from his wallet.

I shook my head. "Oh, you don't—"

Lily reached over and plucked the credit card from Wesley's fingers without a second thought. "Perfect, thank you! I hooked my phone up to the music, too."

Wes grumbled under his breath. Something about going to find Cooper to start their pool game.

Lily hooked her arm with mine, leading me to the bar. "Eliza is ordering us drinks, and then it's off to the dance floor!"

There was a gasp behind us followed by an, "Oh my gosh."

"Hey, Ruby," Lily greeted. "What's up?"

The girl, who looked to be in her early twenties, blinked as she looked between me and Lily. "You're Jules. Or should I call you Juliette, since we haven't really met yet? I loved you on *Paradise Love!*"

"I am." I let out an awkward laugh, and Lily gave my arm a reassuring squeeze. Most people in town didn't pay much attention to how I was on *Paradise Love*. They either knew me as the person staying in the Richards's cabin or as the designer who worked with Lily. "And call me Jules. Ruby, right?"

She must've realized she hadn't introduced herself, because she put a hand on her forehead, looking down with a shake of her head. "I probably came off like a total creep. I'm so sorry about that. Let me try again." She let out a breath. "I'm Ruby. I'm back in Golden Falls for the summer from college and working at Lake Ridge. It's nice to meet you, Jules." Ruby turned toward Lily, greeting her, too.

My shoulders relaxed as I listened to Ruby, a smile easily forming on my face. "It's no problem at all. I'm still getting used to the attention, and it's been nice to get away from it all in Golden Falls. It's nice to meet you, too, Ruby."

"I bet it's been a lot. I love that you were yourself on the show. Funny, wore your heart on your sleeve, not afraid to speak your mind." Ruby's initial excitement was back, her eyes beaming. "I knew from the first episode you were genuine, and I've been excited to meet you. Everyone in town has said such good things about you. I'm so happy you decided to spend the summer in Golden Falls, but I wish you didn't have to go through that to end up here."

"We're really lucky to have her," Lily agreed.

I parted my lips, not sure how to respond. My heart swelled at their words, especially Ruby's. "I, uh, that's so nice of you to say, Ruby. I'm really happy to be spending the summer here, too. And it means a lot to hear about how my personality came through on the show. I haven't seen the episodes. Going through it once feels like enough."

"I don't blame you at all. I actually don't plan on watching future seasons. I doubt it'll do anything—I mean, I'm just one person. Anyways, I'm glad you won. Seeing you on the show... I don't know." Ruby paused, biting down on her bottom lip. "It made me realize I can be unapologetically myself, too. My last ex told me I was *too much*." Ruby rolled her eyes as she used air quotes. "It bothered me at first, but it's his loss. Just like you're a million times better off without Tony."

I didn't realize my appearance on the show could have such an impact on someone. I hadn't even thought of that as a possibility when episodes were airing. "I'm so sorry you had to go through that. Why do men think they can say that to us?"

Ruby shook her head. "Not men—boys," she corrected. "And it's because they don't know how to handle strong women." Ruby crossed her arms over her chest. "Boys are afraid of strong women. Men see the strength in them."

"Rubes, you're way too wise to be in college. Are you sure you're not older?" Lily asked.

"I'm sure." Ruby let out a laugh, a grin on her face. "Anyways, I had to say hi when I saw you, but I gotta go help run some food. The fries here are to die for. You have to try them. We have house made ranch, too!"

"It was great to meet you, Ruby." I liked everyone I'd met so far in Golden Falls, and it was so easy to see myself here. To picture what a life here could be like.

Ruby waved to both of us before floating through the crowd toward the back where I assumed the kitchen was.

"You're winning everyone in town over." Lily smiled as she led me over to the bar, where Eliza and Louise were chatting.

"Long time, no see, Jules," Louise teased. We had recently gotten together for coffee to talk about her rental.

When Eliza started to reach for her purse, Lily waved her hand. "Wes is paying," she informed Eliza before turning to Louise. Lily held out Wes's card. "Could you put our drinks on Wes's tab, please?"

"Oh, of course." Louise took the card with a wink. She set our finished drinks on the bar: a hard seltzer for Lily, tequila soda for Eliza, and an Aperol spritz for me. "Have fun, girls."

It was going to be a fun night, and I wanted to soak up every second of it.

26

WESLEY

I couldn't stop staring at her. No matter how hard I tried to stop, my eyes found her in the crowd. Like there was something pulling me to her.

She was dancing effortlessly, hands above her head, hips swaying side to side, and singing every word. She wasn't wearing a sundress tonight, like she typically did. She'd opted for a short black skirt—one that gradually rose up as she danced, showing even more of her tan thighs.

The pink strappy heels tied around her toned calves were the same color as her top.

There was no missing her. Pretty sure every goddamn man in this bar was looking at her.

Anyone who saw her observed how radiant she was. It was impossible not to. She took attention from the room without even trying. I was damn near speechless when she opened the door and greeted me earlier tonight.

"Got a little drool there, Wes." Cooper tapped the corner of his mouth.

"Oh, fuck off, and take your turn." I tipped my chin toward

the pool table. I ran my hand over my jaw. Had my staring really been *that* obvious?

"It's your turn, actually." His grin widened as he corrected me. "I mean, if you want to give up and hand me the win, you certainly can. I'll win on my next turn, anyway."

With a low growl, I shifted my gaze back to the pool table. We were playing best two out of three, and Cooper had won the first game. I lined up my shot and sunk the first ball into the pocket easily but then missed my second shot.

Cooper only had the eight ball left.

"Eight ball, right corner," he called. The ball sunk into the pocket effortlessly. He leaned the pool cue against the table and crossed his arms over his chest, grinning.

Normally, we were well matched and almost always played a third game to break the tie. That wasn't needed tonight. He'd crushed me during both games.

"Damn it," I groaned, shaking my head. I took a final swig of my beer and set the empty bottle on the ledge along the back wall.

"Funny how on your day off you still end up here. Even funnier you lost these two games so easily. Wouldn't have anything to do with your pretty neighbor, would it?" He nodded over to where Juliette was dancing with Eliza and Lily.

"Lily asked me to drive them over, and I figured I might as well hang out here and kill some time instead of coming back to pick them up. And Louise already gave me crap about being here on my day off."

"Uh huh, whatever you say, man." He finished off his first beer. "I'm gonna go get one more. Did you want another?"

I shook my head. "Nah, I'm good with just one tonight."

As Cooper made his way over to the bar, he stopped by where the girls were. He gave a friendly hug to Lily and Eliza. When he reached Juliette, I swear his hug lingered longer than it should've, his hand resting on the small of her back for a beat. I inhaled through my nose and exhaled slowly.

Cooper was kind, friendly. People in town flocked to him. He easily flirted with the women in Golden Falls and surrounding towns. It never bothered me. If anything, I was surprised he hadn't found someone to settle down with yet, since he certainly had women who were interested.

But seeing him with Juliette, likely flirting with her, too, caused my mind to spiral, a sense of dread falling over me. Was he interested in her? What if she was interested in him?

If Cooper wanted to pursue Juliette, I wouldn't stop him. He was better for her, anyway.

I had no clue what I'd offer a woman like Juliette. She deserved so much more than what this small town and I had to offer.

The two of them even looked like a couple as they walked over to the bar, Juliette trailing behind him.

Fuck it. I was heading over there, too.

As I got closer, her laugh was the first thing I heard.

"You're kidding!" She threw her head back with another laugh, setting her hand on Cooper's arm. I'd never gotten the urge to kill my best friend, but murder didn't sound like a bad idea right now.

"Nope, not kidding at all," Cooper responded.

I hadn't caught what story Cooper had told Juliette, which made me uneasy. I assumed it was likely about something we'd gotten up to, but there were hundreds of those stories.

Louise approached the bar. "These two were always getting up to something." She gestured to me and Cooper.

Juliette grinned at Louise before turning, her hair whipping around and the smell of daisies and vanilla quickly taking over my senses.

"Oh, Wes, hi," she greeted, but her voice sounded different.

Nervous, maybe? Did she not want me interrupting her conversation with Cooper?

"Luckily, Louise keeps us in line," Cooper teased.

Louise rolled her eyes with a smile. "Always a charmer." She set her hands on the bar. "Another Spotted Cow for you, Coop?"

Cooper nodded, looking over at Juliette. "Did you want another drink?"

Juliette bit down on her bottom lip as she thought, and I couldn't tear my eyes away from her. *Again.* "I'm good for right now, but I'll take a soda water and lime."

Louise looked to see if I needed anything, and I shook my head. She placed the beer in front of Cooper and filled a glass with soda water and dropped in a lime wedge before setting it down for Juliette. "Have you two seen what a talented designer this one is and the plans she has for my rental? You got a gift, Jules."

Juliette was working with Louise?

"I'm so glad you're happy with it," Juliette said with a shy smile. I hadn't seen her be bashful often, but it seemed like it happened about her work. "It's been so great working with you and getting to know you. And"—Juliette looked between Louise and Cooper—"I'm going to need more Wes stories, especially ones that prove he wasn't always this grumpy."

I grunted, crossing my arms over my chest. "I'm not grumpy."

"Sure you're not." Juliette drew out the words. I didn't miss the sarcasm in her voice, and I sure as hell didn't miss how her gaze trailed from my arms, up to my chest, jaw, and finally my eyes. Any sense of shyness was long gone. Damn, did I like the feel of her green eyes on me.

Eliza and Lily bounced up next to us. "Jules, we're going to get some fresh air outside. Do you want to come with?" Eliza asked.

"I'm good for right now, but if I change my mind, I'll come find you." Juliette thanked them before the two went off, whispering to each other about god knows what.

"Oh, I love this song!" Juliette's body started swaying, like the pull of the music and the dance floor was too strong and she was already getting lured back.

Cooper gave me a look, but I couldn't figure out what the fuck it meant. I made a face. Did he want to dance with her?

"God, you're an idiot," he muttered, which fortunately Juliette didn't hear. He hit the back of my head when Juliette wasn't looking. "Pull your head out of your ass."

I still had no idea what he was talking about.

Cooper cleared his throat. "Wes is a great dancer," he claimed, causing Juliette to look between us both, blinking her black lashes.

"Oh, well, good for him," she said slowly as she looked between us.

"Yeah, you two should go out there. Go on ahead. I gotta"—Cooper looked around—"help Louise get another keg from the back. Right, Louise? Didn't you need one?" Louise gave him a thumbs-up as he rambled. "So, yeah, you two go ahead."

"Oh, um, you want to?" Juliette tilted her head, her voice softer than usual, unsure. I didn't like dancing. I didn't like attention. But I couldn't say no.

The corner of my mouth tipped up. "Yeah, let's go. One dance."

I'd give anything to replay the way her face lit up.

"Lead the way, then, Wesley."

27

JULIETTE

I HADN'T EXPECTED WES TO SAY YES. IN FACT, I'D MENTALLY prepared myself for him to say no.

Turns out, I should've spent that time preparing to be alone with him. The buzz from my earlier shot with the girls and my Aperol spritz was gone, and the soda water was refreshing with the summer heat. I finished it off and set the glass on the bar.

It was just a dance, and yet somehow, we kept getting pushed together. At least the scowl was finally off his face. Sometimes, I was surprised his face wasn't permanently like that.

But even with his scowl, he was still devastatingly handsome. The more I got to know him, the more good looking he became. Especially now that I knew how kind, protective, and considerate he was. Maybe he still put his foot in his mouth every now and then, but who didn't? What I knew now that I didn't my first day in Golden Falls was that Wesley Richards didn't have bad intentions. He just cared about this town and his family. A lot.

Wes gently, hesitantly, took my hand in his, looking at me almost as if he was asking for permission. I gave his hand a reassuring squeeze in response. I wanted to memorize the way his warm, calloused hand felt on mine. It made me wonder how his touch would feel on other parts of my body. How it'd feel for him to grip my thighs, spread my legs, and—

Oh, god.

No.

This couldn't be happening.

I wasn't thinking about Wesley that way. Nope, not going there.

By the time we squeezed our way through to the dance floor, the song that caught my attention was over but replaced with one equally upbeat. Some people were swaying, others were rocking their bodies side to side. One thing I knew for sure was Wesley and I were not going to look like we were at an awkward middle school dance.

"Are you actually a good dancer, or did Cooper set me up to have you stepping all over my toes? I just painted these, you know." I'd opted for a red polish on my fingers and toes.

He huffed a laugh. "Somewhere in the middle. I'm a decent dancer and won't step on your toes. That I can promise you."

"So, you're decent at it," I said as I set his hand on the curve of my waist, "but you hate it." I held on to his other hand, and it didn't take long for us to fall into rhythm. "Your lip curved at the mention of it and everything. Your scowl turned into *even more* of a scowl."

"It did not," he argued, which caused a laugh to escape me. His grip on my waist tightened in reaction, drawing me closer to his chest. "And one dance won't kill me. It's not that I don't like it. I don't like the attention that comes with it."

"That's fair, but if it makes you feel any better, no one is paying attention to us. Everyone's in their own little world." I had to tip my head back to look up at him. He smelled like a mixture of mint and mahogany—fresh and woodsy. I was glad I hadn't opted for another drink. His cologne was more intoxicating than any alcohol. "I mean, look at us. We're not paying attention to anyone else, right?"

"Right." He hummed in thought while looking down at me, and it took everything I had not to look away. His gaze was too intense, too observant. I wished I could get into his head for a moment to see what he was thinking. I knew he saw me out on the dance floor earlier. Every time I looked over at him, he was already looking at me. It wasn't in a bad way or in a creepy way. Almost like...he couldn't look away. And I couldn't either. We kept finding each other.

But now that we were this close, all I wanted to do was look away. This whole time I'd wanted Wesley to give me a chance, but now I was scared of what would happen if he *did*.

Because the glimpses I'd gotten on the boat and later that night were a version of Wesley I liked. But did he like the version he'd seen of me?

"What're you thinking about?" I asked him.

He let out a deep exhale, finally looking away. Jeez, that sounded heavy. "Is there anything going on between you and Cooper?"

"What?" I swore I heard him wrong.

"Do you have feelings for him?" Wesley questioned. "I'd get it if you want to be dancing with him instead."

I blinked up at him, my mouth open as I shook my head slowly. "Why would you—no, I don't have feelings for Cooper. I'm friendly with him because he's your best friend and one of the handful of people I know here tonight. If I wanted to be dancing with him, I would be. But I'm not, because I want to be dancing with you."

His shoulders visibly relaxed at my words. Interesting.

"Is that—were you jealous?"

The muscle in Wesley's jaw twitched. "No, of course, I wasn't jealous."

"I can't believe you were jealous!"

A low growl left him, and he pulled me closer into his chest, a satisfied smile on my face.

The music quickly picked up.

"You ready?" Wes asked.

I looked up at him, confused. "Ready for—" I started to ask but was cut off when he stepped back. He held on to my hand but dropped the one that had been on my waist.

He spun me around. Once. Twice. Before pulling me into his arms, my back against his chest.

Wesley Richards was full of surprises.

I leaned my head against his chest, tipping it back to sneak a look at him as we swayed. We didn't stay in that position for long —unfortunately—before Wes spun me again, unraveling his hold on me. The whole time, I couldn't stop smiling. My cheeks were even starting to hurt.

We stepped and moved our bodies in a casual rhythm, his shoulders relaxing. Wes was focusing on us—nothing else mattered.

As the song started to wrap up, Wes gave me a final slow spin, pulling me close and firmly placing his hand on my lower back as he dipped me.

I tipped my head back with a laugh, and when I looked back up at him, he was grinning down at me. A full-fledged grin that made him even more devastatingly handsome, if that was even possible. Maybe it was good he didn't smile often. I didn't know if I could take it.

"How did you..." I stammered, unable to find the words.

He pulled me back up. His grin softened, but he was still smiling. "You've kept me on my toes all summer. Thought it was time I repaid the favor."

I gave his chest a gentle push and immediately regretted it.

Because his chest was a wall of solid muscle I wanted to drag my nails down.

"Well, you certainly did. That was...really nice." The song was replaced with a slower one, couples now drawing closer and swaying together. I licked my lips. "We don't—" I started at the same time Wes pulled me closer. His hands found the same position as before—one on my waist and the other holding my hand—but he was more confident this time. His grip even moved down ever so slightly so he was holding on to my hip instead. It was a hot summer night, and yet I craved Wesley's warmth.

"You wanted to dance, so we're dancing."

"You said one dance wouldn't kill you, but what about another?"

"I'll be fine, Juliette."

I rolled my lips, hiding my smile, and nodded. "Okay." I stepped closer to him, tempted to rest the side of my head against his chest as "Love You Anyway" by Luke Combs played through the speakers.

I'd heard this song countless times, but it was the first time I truly listened to the lyrics. About loving someone even if you knew it was going to end in a broken heart. About how it's worth it anyway.

A lump formed in my throat, and tears welled in my eyes. Something about being in Wes's arms in this moment, dancing to this song, and knowing this all had an expiration date caught me off guard. I didn't expect it, just like I didn't expect him.

"What're you thinking about?" He dipped his head closer to me, his forehead nearly resting on mine. His low voice was barely a whisper above the music, but it vibrated through my body and cut through my thoughts.

I let out a shaky exhale, keeping my eyes down. I didn't want him to see me like this. *Oh, nothing. I'm just thinking about how I like you more than I realized and how this is all going to end when summer does. So, even if this did turn into something, it would only be temporary. The very thing you don't want.*

"Oh, uh," I said with an awkward laugh, "just kinda spaced out."

He took a moment to respond, and I didn't like that. It meant he noticed something. "So, you have my hand in a death grip for fun? You're not thinking about murdering me or anything?"

If only. My life would be simpler if that was what I was thinking about.

I looked at our hands and saw what he meant. I loosened my grip immediately. "No, I'm not," I sighed.

He moved his hand from my hip, gently gripping my chin with his thumb and pointer finger. "Juliette," he said softly. "What's going on?"

It was the softness, the tenderness, in his voice that got me. I stepped back from his touch. I didn't hear what Wes said after, because I was quickly weaving my way through the crowd to the back hallway.

The warm buzz from earlier in the night was long gone, but I still needed fresh air. I needed to clear my head. Because the softness in his voice hit deeply. Straight to my heart.

Right now, my heart was telling me I needed Wesley. And that just wasn't going to happen.

28

WESLEY

It didn't take long—maybe five seconds, at most—for me to pick my feet off the ground and follow after her. She only had a slight head start, but she was fast, even in those heels.

"Juliette!" I called out. Luckily, with my height, I was able to see her in the crowd and the direction she was heading—toward the back hallway that led to the bathrooms, my office, and the side exit. With a couple more long strides, I caught up to her, wrapping my hand gently around her wrist to stop her.

"Juliette," I breathed. This woman was going to make me work for it, wasn't she?

She turned, finally, and I expected to see fire in those green eyes. Instead, there was a sadness that gutted me.

"Baby, what's wrong?" The term of endearment effortlessly slipped past my lips. It felt so natural.

She shook her head, still not saying anything. I moved us closer to the wall and used my body to block us from anyone passing by. Luckily, we were past the bathrooms, and people rarely came down this far.

"I don't know what's wrong. That's the thing." She exhaled.

"Well, that's not totally true. I guess what's wrong is that I really liked dancing with you. And I've liked getting along with you."

"And that's a problem?" I could see it bothered her, but I wasn't following.

"Yes!" she exclaimed. The sadness in her eyes instantly turned to frustration. I didn't want her feeling either, and I wasn't sure why I had this pull to make things better. "It was easier to dislike you when I thought you were some grumpy, selfish asshole. But now I know that while you might be grumpy and have your asshole moments—"

"That asshole comment feels unnecessary," I interjected.

"—you're the farthest thing from selfish. You're *selfless*, and you care so much. But, god, Wes," she said with an exasperated sigh. "You have the world's best poker face. I have no idea what you feel toward me, if anything. You said all these things when we were watching fireworks together, but did you mean any of it?"

How could she not realize she consumed my thoughts tonight? That when we danced, I didn't want to let her go. Or how when she tipped her head back during that dip, all I could think about was kissing her perfect neck.

I knew I didn't wear my emotions on my sleeve—I never had —but I didn't realize I was that hard to read. I'd gotten so used to people in my orbit knowing me and being able to read me...and a part of me wanted Juliette to know me well enough to do that.

"Juliette," I said with a chuckle, which made her scowl, "do you really not see it?" I took a step forward, and she took a step back, until her back was against the wall. But she stood tall, arms crossed over her chest, pushing up her breasts. "I don't say shit I don't mean. I meant everything I've said to you."

She raised a brow. "Everything? What about when you said you didn't want to be friends with me?"

"I didn't say that."

"Yes, you did," she argued. "You said—"

"That I didn't think I'd be able to be friends with you. That I couldn't." I paused, watching her face as she remembered our conversation in my parents' kitchen. "Because I didn't think I could be *just* friends with you. I already knew then it'd be tough to keep my distance from you if we got too close."

I let the words sink in, realization slowly flashing across her face.

"Ask me what I'm thinking about," I urged.

She twisted her lips to the side, as if she was considering not asking. But I'm guessing curiosity got the better of her. "What are you thinking about?"

"About things I shouldn't be." I braced my palm on the wall next to her head, caging her in on one side. "Things that mean trouble." I dipped my head down, my forehead resting against hers. We'd been close when we were dancing, but not this close.

This was the closest I'd gotten to Juliette Campbell, and I still wanted more. I was drawn to her like she was the sun—like my life revolved around her—and I didn't care if I got burned.

Her breath hitched as she looked up at me, any sense of sadness gone and replaced with fire. With desire. The air was hot and heavy between us.

"Like what?" she asked breathlessly.

"You." My other hand slowly moved up to cup the side of her neck, my thumb running along her jaw. "I'm always thinking about you. It's impossible to stay away from you, no matter how hard I try."

Her tongue darted out to wet her bottom lip, and she watched the way my eyes flicked down to her mouth. She reached up, her hand resting on my chest and her fingers twitching ever so slightly, like she wanted to wrap them tightly around the fabric of my shirt. "Don't stay away from me, then," she whispered.

I kept my forehead pressed against hers, my lips mere inches away from hers. It would be so *easy* to close the gap. To finally find out what her pretty, sassy mouth tasted like.

I acted before my mind could come up with all the ways our growing connection could go wrong.

"Fuck it," I exhaled and finally gave in to temptation. I gave in to Juliette. I grabbed the back of her neck and pulled her mouth to mine.

Kissing Juliette was utter bliss, and I lived for the soft moans that escaped her. Nothing had ever felt more right. We both surrendered without hesitation.

Sometimes when you kiss someone for the first time, there's some stumbling as you find your stride. There was none of that between us. We moved effortlessly—just like our dancing earlier.

When I slipped my tongue past her lips, Juliette let out another moan, eagerly inviting me into her mouth.

Her nails raked up my arms to my shoulders. Her fingers wrapped around the fabric of my shirt, eagerly pulling me to her until her chest was pressed up against mine. I could feel her pebbled nipples through her top. Which, *fuck*, meant she wasn't wearing a bra.

"Juliette, baby." A low growl formed at the back of my throat. "Should've done this weeks ago."

"Yes, you should've," she mumbled against my lips. "Would've made for a much better welcome."

"Smart ass," I said with a chuckle, pulling away only to kiss along her neck. The same neck that had been driving me wild. She tipped her head back, giving me more access. I wanted to find the spot that would drive her crazy. And I did. Right below her pulse point. I sucked on her skin, eliciting another moan from her. Louder this time. God, she tasted and sounded sweet.

"Oh, Wesley," she moaned.

Nothing would ever sound as good as my name leaving her lips.

I wrapped an arm around her waist, holding her up. I knew this hallway like the back of my hand, so without stopping, I led us to my office while pressing kisses to her soft skin. I twisted the handle and pushed open the door, letting it shut behind us. I reached back and locked it with a click.

My cock pressed against my jeans, and I had never been this fucking hard. All from a kiss—the best fucking kiss of my life.

Juliette's hands were all over my body, and I craved her touch. It didn't take long for my lips to find hers again in a passionate, urgent kiss. I led her farther into my office, my hands tightly gripping her waist.

I stopped once her lower back met the edge of my desk, and without looking, I pushed the stacks of papers off the desk and onto the floor. My hands quickly found her hips, lifting her up onto the desk.

"You're not wearing a bra, but are you wearing panties?" I murmured, my hands trailing down from her hips to her thighs, spreading her legs so I could step between them.

She braced herself with her palms on the desk, leaning back. "Why don't you see for yourself."

29

JULIETTE

Wesley's hands felt even better than I had imagined.

Truthfully, I couldn't think of much that felt better than this. Better than him.

He pushed up my skirt, kneading my ass and revealing the pink thong I had on. I needed his rough touch between my legs, needed to feel him.

He ran his thumb along my hip, tracing the lacy fabric. "Fuck, baby, you're so wet for me already," he growled, his voice deeper than normal. I might've been embarrassed of how wet I was and how easily he was able to tell just by looking, if it wasn't for the look of utter awe on his face. I'd never had a man look at me that way.

"Did you wear these for me?" He kneeled in front of me, hooking both his thumbs into the band of my thong and slowly pulling it down my legs. Once it was off, he tucked the thin fabric into his back pocket.

I rolled my eyes with a smile. "I wore them for myself. Wearing them for you would've implied I knew this was going to happen."

Wes shook his head, his own smile forming. "Always such a

smart ass," he muttered. He rubbed his thumb over my wetness. "And always so damn perfect," he praised while still kneeling.

"Wes," I breathed out, one of my hands running through his hair, fingers wrapping around the strands and giving it a tug. I needed something, anything, from him. Preferably, an orgasm. Or two.

"That mouth of yours always has something sassy to say. What about now?" Wes was able to read me like a book. "Feeling impatient?" He tsked. His rough hands moved down my legs, hooking them over his shoulders and pushing my skirt up even further. "I'm not going to rush this, Juliette. I'm going to take my damn time tasting your pussy. Got it?"

I nodded eagerly.

"I'm going to need you to use your words, baby." His thumb inched closer to my most sensitive spot.

"Y-yes, Wesley," I stammered, legs instinctively opening wider.

"Good girl. Love when you say my name." He ran his thumb along my clit, putting pressure on the bundle of nerves, and my head tipped back immediately, a moan already threatening to escape. "I want you to be as loud as you want to be, baby. No one's going to hear us back here with the music playing."

I bit down on my bottom lip, nodding again. I couldn't get any words out and was afraid if I started moaning, I wouldn't be able to stop. He was barely touching me, and I was already a mess for him.

He hummed, looking up at me with a smirk. "No smart ass comments from that pretty mouth? Who knew all I had to do was touch you like this"—he started to circle his thumb faster against my clit—"to make you speechless."

"I... I want more," I stammered, and his smirk widened.

Not wasting any time, Wes buried his face between my legs. He started with his tongue, tasting and teasing me, while his fingers dug into my thighs to keep them spread. He dragged his tongue through my slit, humming ravenously against my core. My grip on his hair instinctively tightened to hold him in place. I watched as he devoured me, but it still wasn't enough.

I tipped my head back, hips bucking against his tongue. "More," I begged.

Wes moved one of his hands, slowly slipping two fingers inside me.

"O-oh, fuck," I gasped.

His mouth moved to my clit as his fingers worked on me. If his fingers felt this good, I couldn't even imagine how his cock would feel.

When I looked down, Wesley's eyes were already on me. He was watching every way my body reacted, and as soon as our eyes locked, he sucked harder on my clit while methodically pumping his fingers.

"Fuck, Wes!" I cried out, eyes fluttering closed as I chased my orgasm, my hips bucking against his hand. "I'm right there."

"That's my girl. Come for me, baby."

I fell apart within seconds, my back arching and legs trembling. My hips lifted to his mouth, a fire spreading through my whole body in response to the immense pleasure. My cries only got louder.

"Wesley," I breathed, my grip in his hair loosening as I tugged him away, way too sensitive to feel his tongue right now. I struggled to catch my breath—my whole body was on fire.

"So fucking sweet." He stood slowly, like he was in just as much of a daze.

I reached over, hooking my fingers in his belt loops and pulling him to me. He dipped his head, meeting my mouth. I sucked on his bottom lip, tasting myself, which got a groan out of him.

"You're going to be the death of me, woman," he murmured against my mouth.

"You're telling me," I said with a grin. "That was the best orgasm I've ever had." My hands reached for his belt, fumbling to undo it.

I frowned when he set his hands gently over mine. "This was all about you, baby," he said. "Don't think I'm done with you—not even close—but I want you all to myself. I want to fuck that pretty pussy of yours all night. In my bed. You're coming home with me."

I definitely wasn't about to argue with that.

"What are we waiting for, then? Let's go."

30

WESLEY

Leaving Lake Ridge was more of a challenge than I anticipated.

I was getting cock blocked by the Midwest goodbye—when you say you're leaving and then stand there talking for twenty to thirty minutes. Sometimes even longer than that.

Normally, I was pretty swift about getting out of those situations, but with Juliette, it was a little different. Because *everyone* wanted to say goodbye to her. I wish I was exaggerating. First Lily and Eliza, then Cooper, Louise, Ruby...the list went on.

I'd had it at the thirty minute mark—could you blame me? I was about to take the most beautiful woman back to my house. Sorry if I was a little fucking impatient. Since Coop only had one drink—he never did have his second beer since he needed to *help with the keg*—he was going to make sure Lily and Eliza got home safe.

I interlaced our fingers together and pulled Juliette away from her *second* conversation with Ruby.

"We'll talk later, Ruby!" Juliette called over her shoulder, waving. She used that same hand to smack my arm. "Rude!" she said with a laugh.

"You'll be thanking me when I make you come again."

The drive from Lake Ridge to my house wasn't long—about fifteen minutes—but it was long enough for Juliette to fall asleep in my passenger seat. Her gentle breathing and lack of talking were a clear indicator.

I pulled into my gravel driveway and put the truck into park. I looked over at Juliette, taking in her plump, slightly parted lips, peaceful expression, and how the moonlight shone on her face. She was so damn beautiful it was unfair.

I wasn't someone who smiled often, and there I was sitting like an idiot, smiling to myself. I shook my head to snap myself out of it.

Since Juliette was still sleeping, I hopped out of my truck and first unlocked the front door to the house. I then went back, opening the truck's passenger door and unbuckling her. "Hey, baby," I whispered, tucking strands of her hair away from her face and behind her ear. "Let's get you inside."

She let out a soft grumble but leaned toward me and wrapped her arms around my neck. I scooped her up—one hand under her knees and the other under her back. She immediately curled against my chest, her lips finding my neck and pressing a soft kiss there. I was worried the rapid beat of my heart would wake her up.

I wasn't surprised she was exhausted. It'd been a long night for her between the dancing, socializing, and the best orgasm she'd ever had. I wasn't going to forget she'd said that.

I pushed open the front door with the toe of my shoe. Not

wanting to turn the lights on and wake her, I carefully walked to my bedroom, setting Juliette on the bed.

"Wes?" she murmured as I untied the straps of her heels and slipped the shoes off her feet.

"Yeah, baby?"

"Can you get me a shirt to sleep in, please?"

"Yeah, of course." I grabbed a T-shirt from my dresser. I wanted to give her privacy as she changed, so I took the time to grab a couple of pillows and blankets to set up for sleeping on the couch. As tempted as I was to slide in next to her, I didn't want her to be alarmed when she woke up. I'd take the couch tonight.

By the time I got back to check on her, she was tucked under the covers and fast asleep. I smiled again as I left and gently closed the bedroom door behind me.

31

JULIETTE

THE SUN'S BRIGHT, GOLDEN RAYS STREAMED IN THROUGH THE window. I stretched my arms over my head as I slowly opened my eyes, turning onto my side so my back was facing the window. I couldn't help the smile that came across my face, especially when I pulled the comforter up to my chin. It was cozy and smelled like Wes.

I had the best night's sleep in years in Wes's bed. If you'd asked me if I slept on fluffy clouds or Wesley's pillows, I wouldn't know the difference. See, it was possible for men to have their shit together and not just have a mattress slapped in the middle of a room. Green flag.

Not even the fact that I slept in my makeup could ruin the morning, although I was itching to get my mascara off.

I wished I hadn't fallen asleep on the drive over, but between the dancing, conversations, and that mind-blowing orgasm, I had been exhausted. After Wes carried me inside and gave me a shirt to sleep in, I meant to ask him to get in bed with me. But I was out as soon as my head hit the pillows.

Heat flared in my lower belly at the recollection of what happened in Wes's office. How good he was with his mouth and fingers. How hard and fast I had finished. I didn't even finish that hard when I used my vibrator.

Speaking of Wes...

I untangled myself from the sheets, setting my bare feet on the floor and standing.

While Wes's room was comfortable, it didn't have many personal touches, which wasn't surprising. He did have two photos on his dresser, though. The first was him and his father standing outside Lake Ridge and the second was a family photo in his parents' backyard. It looked like the whole group was in the photo: Lily, Jade, Cooper, and Eliza. Hal was in the picture, too.

Slowly, I opened the bedroom door and stepped into the hallway, peeking my head around the corner.

Wes was fast asleep on the living room couch. His hand was behind his head, and the blanket was draped across his lower body, leaving his muscular chest and torso exposed. His usually clenched jaw was relaxed. In fact, his whole body looked relaxed as he took slow breaths. I sat on the edge of the couch, near the middle where his hips were, and gently placed my hand on his arm.

"Hey, Wes. Good morning," I greeted softly. My hand stayed on his arm, but my fingertips itched to trace the sharp, stubbled edge of his jaw.

"Morning, baby." He let out a low groan, his lips quickly pulling into a smile as his eyes stayed closed. "I get to wake up to Juliette Campbell in my house, looking like a dream in my shirt. How does it get better than that?" His voice was low and warm, like a golden summer day.

I bit my bottom lip to hide my smile. "You haven't even opened your eyes yet. What if I look like a mess?"

"Impossible," he said, slowly opening his eyes. His smile widened into a lazy grin that took my breath away. "See, looking like a dream. I knew it." He reached his hand up, cupping my cheek and using his thumb to pull my bottom lip, setting my smile free.

"You didn't have to sleep on the couch."

He shook his head, moving his thumb along my jaw. "You were out the whole drive back and when we got here. I didn't want to wake you or make you uncomfortable in the morning."

"I really appreciate that, thank you."

"No need to thank me, Juliette. It's literally the least I could do."

Maybe that much was true, but I didn't think a lot of men would have taken the steps Wes did to make sure I was safe and cared for. I wanted him to know that. "Doesn't mean I can't thank you."

He seemed so relaxed, so...happy. I hadn't seen this side of him yet, but I liked it. It felt natural. "I didn't take you as a morning person," I added.

"Usually, I'm not, but things are a little different today." He dropped his hand and gave my thigh a gentle squeeze. "Are you hungry for breakfast? I can make us eggs, pancakes, bacon, and hash browns. Coffee, too."

"A whole breakfast feast, huh?" I asked with a grin. "That sounds perfect."

"Okay, that's not coffee anymore." Wes raised his brows as I poured a heaping amount of almond milk into my glass, followed by ice cubes.

"Yeah, you're right. Now it's iced coffee," I replied, which earned me a smirk and shake of his head. "I can make you one, if you want."

"I like mine just how it is." Unsurprisingly, Wesley drank his coffee black.

He was also a wizard in the kitchen. He was nearly done preparing a classic diner breakfast for us in less than fifteen minutes. He moved effortlessly and had a few pans going, timing everything perfectly so it was ready and hot at the same time. I would've burned something by now.

He had pulled on a pair of gray sweatpants and a black tee. I was still in his shirt but had washed my face of last night's makeup. Normally, I liked to shower first thing, but today I was enjoying the lazy morning.

"Breakfast's ready." He pressed a kiss to my hairline, and my legs nearly gave out. He was so surprisingly tender with me, even last night when we were in the hallway. The way he cradled my face and tipped my chin up.

Wes prepared two plates for us and nodded toward the table for us to sit. I followed, and we started our first few bites of breakfast in a comfortable silence.

"When I was talking with Louise last night, she mentioned you had plans to grow Lake Ridge. What're you focusing on?" I asked before taking another bite.

He nodded, grabbing his napkin and wiping his mouth before speaking. "I have my eyes set on expanding the food menu, drawing in customers for both lunch and dinner. I want to bring a chef on board who understands my goals and wants to preserve Lake Ridge's atmosphere but has their own vision of a menu. I'd like to work with local farmers to source ingredients and also minimize food waste as we're doing this. My goal for this summer has been to get staff in place to give myself time to research these ideas and feel comfortable about the hiring process for a chef."

I raised my brows, in awe of his vision and what he wanted for the bar. "Wes, that's amazing. I love the sound of that. It'll make Lake Ridge a year-round, local draw. When do you want to hire someone?"

"The spring, maybe? Having Eliza bartend has been huge, and I hired a few college kids back in town, too, to help me with the administrative tasks. I might need to hire one more full-time person when they go back to college, but the rest of the year is less busy than the summer."

"I'm so excited for you," I said honestly with a smile, trying to ignore the pang in my chest at the thought of not seeing his dreams come to fruition. I'd be long gone in Chicago by then.

We continued talking as we finished breakfast. I told him more about my parents and Grant, my favorite parts about living in the city, and the work I'd been doing in Golden Falls. He shared with me more about the various adventures Cooper and he got up to growing up, what his other sister Jade was like, and how he spent his days when he wasn't working.

"Thank you for breakfast," I said before taking my final bite of pancake. "That was so good." I tipped my head back against the chair with a satisfied smile. "Are you going into Lake Ridge today?" I still wasn't quite sure what his schedule was—he seemed to be at work all the time.

"Thank *you* for having breakfast with me." His gaze met mine. "I am but not until later. Wanted to spend the morning and afternoon with you. Unless you had plans?"

"I'll make time in my busy schedule to spend time with you," I teased. With it being a Sunday morning, I didn't have any meetings or work I had to get done. I'd maybe spend some time looking at inspiration on a couple of projects to get ahead for next week, but that could wait.

I stood from the table and grabbed both our plates and silverware.

"You don't have to do that," Wesley said behind me, and I rolled my eyes.

"Wes, you cooked us a breakfast feast. I think I can rinse some dishes and put them in the dishwasher."

He grumbled something under his breath, and I couldn't help but laugh. While reading him was still a challenge, I was picking up on things here and there. He liked control, he was incredibly stubborn, and he liked to take care of those in his orbit. And I guess that included me now?

Throughout our conversation over breakfast, neither one of us had brought up *that* detail of last night. I wanted to, but I... didn't know how. As comfortable as I was around Wes, I suddenly felt shy. I focused instead on getting the dishes rinsed.

"Hey," he said softly. "Don't hide from me. What're you thinking about?"

I glanced at him over my shoulder. He was leaning against the kitchen counter, eyes studying me. He was too observant for his own good. How was he able to read me so well after only a couple of months?

I focused my gaze back on the dishes. "You. Us. Last night." I sighed. "What it means that I want it all to happen again. Wondering if *you* want it to happen again."

He huffed out a laugh at my last sentence, like it was the most ridiculous thing he'd ever heard. He walked up behind me. Then I felt him. His rough fingers moved my hair to the side. His hot breath against my neck. His hips against me.

"Listen to me, baby," he said against my ear. "Last night was the best night of my life, for so many reasons. But you know what all those reasons have in common? You. I've been thinking about you—dreaming about you—since the moment you stepped into my life." His hands found my hips over the shirt's fabric. His shirt. My legs nearly gave out at the way he dug his fingers in, tightening his hold. "Of course, I want it to happen again, but only if you want it, too."

I gulped then turned, now facing him with my back pressed against the edge of the counter. "I want it, too. I want you, Wesley." His eyes were locked on me, like nothing else in the world mattered. Neither one of us looked away. My chest rose and fell as my breaths sped up, and I raised my brow slightly, challenging him. "And I seem to remember you saying you wanted me all to yourself. Well, are you going to do something about it?"

32

WESLEY

From the moment I met Juliette, I knew she was mouthy and didn't back down.

It was sexy as hell.

I was surprised I hadn't pushed breakfast off the table earlier to take her right then and there. It was a miracle I had lasted this long, especially with her walking around in my shirt, achingly beautiful with long legs on full display. And I knew she wasn't wearing panties since I still had her pair from last night. And no bra, either.

It was my own personal torture—or heaven.

I dipped my head, my forehead against hers and lips inches away as I whispered, "Do you want my tongue, fingers, or cock, sweetheart?"

The whimper that escaped her was music to my ears. She swallowed, rolling her pretty lips before speaking. "Fingers first then cock." Her voice was breathy, heat creeping up her neck to her cheeks.

Fuck. No way in hell was I going to argue with that.

I wrapped my arm around her waist, moving us a step to the side and lifting her up so she was sitting on the counter. I stepped between her legs, both of our breathing speeding up as she wrapped her legs around my hips, bringing me even closer.

"You tell me if you don't like something, alright?"

"I will." She nodded, lifting her lips up to nearly meet mine but holding back, teasing. "But you have to do something first."

A low growl escaped the back of my throat. That damn mouth. I brushed my lips against hers but didn't kiss her yet.

She whimpered, and I could see on her face she was seconds away from begging. I was seconds away from caving.

"Wesley," she moaned, her legs around my hips tightening. "I'm so wet for you."

My patience snapped, and I pressed my mouth hungrily against hers, sucking and nipping at her plump bottom lip. With a hand, I pinned her wrists above her head against the cabinets. The back of my other hand moved slowly along her jaw, down her neck, and over the tops of her breasts. I rubbed her nipple with my thumb, pinching it over the fabric.

"Are you always wet for me?"

She nodded, biting down on her lip.

"You want to come, baby?" I asked.

"Please," she moaned.

"Anything for you."

I let go of her wrists but instructed her to keep her hands up, and she willingly listened. Juliette normally didn't like to do things my way—but when we were intimate, it was another story. I began to peel off her shirt, pulling it over her head and tossing it down on the floor.

I nearly came right then and there. My cock, pressing against my sweatpants, was hard and aching for release. Aching for her.

Juliette Campbell was a fucking knockout. Long legs, curvy hips, full breasts. I shook my head in utter amazement as I took her in. "Oh, baby, I'm going to take my time with you."

She let out a breathy laugh, her smile widening at my words.

With one hand tightly gripping her hip, the other moved between her legs. I dipped my head to where her shoulder met her neck and kissed slowly while rubbing her clit. Juliette arched her back, finally lowering her hands to grip my shoulders. I loved the feeling of her nails digging into my skin and couldn't fucking wait to feel her drag them down my back.

I slipped two fingers inside her, and her head immediately fell back with a moan, eyes fluttering closed.

"Oh, fuck."

My fingers moved in a steady rhythm. I wanted to know what she liked, what she needed. I wanted to, eventually, make her come instantly. I wanted to know her body like the back of my hand.

She tightened around my fingers.

"Are you going to come for me, baby?"

Juliette moved one of her hands to her breast, tugging and toying with her nipple as she whimpered, "So close."

I dipped my head to her other breast, sucking a nipple between my teeth, which got a cry out of her.

"Wes!"

I sucked harder and my fingers moved faster as her body responded to me.

It didn't take her much longer after that to finish, her body rocking against my hand and cries of pleasure leaving her lips as her orgasm racked through her.

I pulled my fingers out, sucking them clean with a groan. *Fucking delicious.* "I could taste you every damn morning and never get tired of it."

Not giving her a chance to calm down from her high, I picked her up, throwing her over my shoulder and giving her ass a firm smack.

"I told you I wanted to fuck that pretty pussy in my bed. And, baby, I'm a man of my word."

33

JULIETTE

WAS THIS REAL LIFE? BECAUSE BEFORE LAST NIGHT, I HAD NO IDEA orgasms like that existed.

I also had no idea Wesley Richards had such a dirty mouth. Pretty sure I could come from his words alone.

He made me feel *so* sexy. Like any woman, I had my insecurities in the bedroom. Was I too loud, too needy, did it take me too long to orgasm?

But I didn't feel the need to pretend with Wes. I felt safe with him. Safe to be myself.

And it helped that he literally couldn't take his eyes off of me. Pretty sure the house could be burning down and he wouldn't notice.

He tossed me with ease onto the bed, and I landed with a grin. I bent my knees and leaned back to watch him.

My core was already aching for him again, and I needed to see him. All of him. I'd gotten a look at his muscular build when we were on the boat. But this was different.

This was for my eyes only.

"You're taking your sweet time, huh?" I asked, raising a brow. The patience of this man was insane.

He only grinned, likely loving the torture he was putting me through.

Wes pushed his sweatpants down his strong, muscular thighs before he did the same with his boxers.

Oh, god.

"Wes—" My jaw dropped. "That's not going to fit." I audibly gulped, and Wes laughed. He *laughed*!

"Oh, baby, it'll fit," he said with another chuckle. "You can take it."

He pulled his shirt off last, revealing his sculpted muscles and a smattering of chest hair. The golden sunlight streaked through the windows, illuminating him.

I needed him, and I needed him now. "I'm on the pill," I said slowly. "And... It's been a while for me, but I got tested after my last partner." My mouth watered as my eyes slowly trailed him. "I... I want to feel you."

"It's been a while for me, too, and I got tested afterward. I haven't been with anyone since." Wes paused. "Are you sure?

"I'm sure. I want you like this." I nodded, spreading my legs for him as another way of confirming. I trusted him and the connection we'd built. I wasn't sure where it would lead—I didn't want to think about that right now—but I knew what I wanted in this moment. I wanted him.

"Fuck," he groaned. "If at any point you change your mind, tell me, okay?"

"Okay."

He hovered over me, teasing my entrance with the tip of his thick cock. He slowly pushed inside me, his forehead pressed against mine.

"You feel like you were made for me." He started to move his hips, slowly at first but then gradually picking up speed once I got used to his size. "Do you feel how perfectly we fit, baby?"

My lower back arched off the bed, pushing my hips into him

as my hands found his back. I dragged my nails down, getting a low groan of "Juliette" from him. His voice sounded desperate, strangled, and that's exactly how his motions felt, too. Like he had to have me.

"How do you like to be fucked, baby?" he murmured against my ear while his hips continued to move steadily, filling me up to a hilt.

"I... I like..." I stammered. How was I supposed to form complete sentences? I felt him smirk. "This feels good, really good, but you can be rougher with me. I also like," I said on a breath, "being on my knees."

He hummed, slowing his hips and leaning back. "You'll tell me if I'm too rough?" His expression was serious. It wasn't lost on me how considerate Wes was, putting me first and making sure everything felt good for me. Letting me know I was the one in control. I hadn't had that experience with a man in the bedroom before, and it made me realize what I'd been missing. And that my standards weren't too high—I just hadn't been picking the right men.

"I'll tell you. I promise."

His jaw clenched, eyes dark with desire as his gaze raked over my body. I could tell he was thinking about all the ways he could have me, because as I looked up at him, that's exactly what I was thinking about, too.

"Well, get on your knees, then."

The loss of his cock when he pulled out was brief, because he quickly flipped me over so I was on my hands and knees, facing the headboard.

He gripped my hips—hard—and pulled me back on his cock. He slipped inside with ease, and the pressure between my legs felt so damn good. His chest was pressed against my back as he fucked me from behind, my pussy aching and clenching around his cock.

I was close already. So close. I just needed—

He reached around, using one hand to stimulate my clit while the other wrapped around my throat, adding the right amount of pressure.

"Wes, I'm so, so close."

"Good, baby. Come for me. Want to feel you come all over my cock."

I chanted his name, the pressure building between my legs and the heat flaring in my lower belly. I closed my eyes, focusing only on Wesley: his cock, his fingers, his hot breath against my neck.

It was enough to send me over the edge. My body trembled as my orgasm took over, cries of pleasure leaving me.

It sent Wes over the edge, too. He let out a low groan, his grip on my throat tightening ever so slightly as he finished inside me. Whatever world we were currently living in was where I wanted to stay.

We both let out a shaky exhale, trying to come back to our senses, to come back to reality. He pressed a kiss to my shoulder before pulling out and lying on the bed with an arm bent under his head.

I followed suit, lying on my side and looking over at him. Neither of us said anything for a moment. We just...existed together. Taking it all in.

Wesley's lips slowly spread into a grin—the same full-fledged grin he had while we were dancing last night. No worries on his face, no crease in his brow, no locked jaw. I liked seeing him so at ease. Because somehow, along the way, that's how he made me feel.

"Don't move," he murmured, sliding out of bed and walking toward the bathroom.

I followed his movements and listened as the cabinet creaked open and water started running. Soon after the water shut off, Wes came back with a washcloth. His dark eyes slowly took in every inch of me, leaving a scorching trail down my body. I hadn't moved—just like he'd requested.

"I like when you listen to me." The corner of Wes's mouth tipped up into a smile.

He slid back in bed, lying on his side facing me and gently nudging me to spread my knees. He slowly wiped the warm cloth between my legs. He was so thoughtful and considerate, taking care of me in such an intimate way no other partner ever had.

A small, content moan escaped me.

"Are you sore?" Wes paused wiping the cloth over my center to look at me, his expression soft.

I nodded. "In a good way." I swallowed. "In a way that...I already want more." I slowly trailed my eyes down his broad chest to where his hips tapered in to form a deep V, not wanting to miss a single detail of his muscular body.

A low rumble formed in his chest from my words. "Well," he rasped roughly, "I want to give you everything you want, sweetheart."

Wes was a man of his word. He took his time with me that morning and gave me exactly what I wanted—both in the shower and in his bed again.

We then got comfortable on the living room couch. I was in another one of Wes's shirts. He told me to pick whatever I wanted to watch, so of course, I picked a romantic comedy.

We were about halfway through the movie. He was sitting on the couch, slouched casually while I lay across with my head in his lap. He was gently stroking my hair—and was more invested in the movie than I expected him to be.

"I want to take you out," he said in a low murmur.

I turned my head so I was looking up at him, a smirk on my lips. "Like kill me? Or on a date?"

Wes barked out a laugh, shaking his head. My whole body vibrated from his booming laugh. I'd heard him laugh before—but not like this. Not this free and uninhibited. I wanted more of these laughs from him, and I wanted to be the one who brought them out.

"On a date, smart ass." His hand moved from my hair to cradle my face. "This Friday work for you?"

"Yeah," I said softly. "That sounds perfect."

"I'll get it all planned. You don't worry about a thing."

I wanted to ask Wes what all this meant, and maybe I should've. But I was scared of the answer. I didn't want to ruin the moment by questioning what this meant for our future. If we had a future.

That was all a later problem. An end of summer problem.

I was leaving, and he was staying. But, for now, we were together.

34

WESLEY

Going into work was the last thing I wanted to do today, especially since it meant I had to leave Juliette. Not only that, but she wouldn't be at my house when I got back tonight.

I had always liked living alone. I liked my space and my privacy. But this was the first time I dreaded coming back to an empty house. I had never felt this way before. Not with Gretchen. Not with anyone.

Until today.

I wanted to finish work, get home, and find her already in my bed. I wanted a repeat of this morning. Again and again.

With how busy yesterday was, I anticipated a slower night tonight. Plus, Sundays were typically slower anyway. It gave me time to help out, if needed, but also get inventory organized for the week ahead.

As challenging as it was, I pushed thoughts of Juliette out of my mind and got to work.

We were getting into a groove at Lake Ridge, and I was proud of my staff for how they were handling the various adjustments and ideas I was throwing their way. Eliza was catching on quickly and was a favorite among both the staff and the customers, both locals and tourists.

It was also nice to keep an eye on her, because I knew Cooper worried about her. As much as he and Eliza bickered, the two of them were close. They had to be after losing their parents so young. Cooper had been fourteen and Eliza had been six when their parents were killed in a car accident during a snowstorm by a distracted driver. Thinking about what happened and how it impacted my best friend gutted me—but it also made me proud of the man he turned into.

I was getting ready to make the drive home, and after hopping in my truck and getting my phone connected to Bluetooth, I tapped Cooper's name in my contacts. Similarly to how I worked, Cooper had irregular hours as a park ranger. Some days were typical nine to five, while others started and ended later.

"Hey, man. What's up?" he answered quickly, but I could tell by his voice he was exhausted.

"Long day?"

"You wouldn't believe it. I had a couple of tougher guided hikes today, but that wasn't even what got me. It was the summer camp kids. They're balls of energy, and I wasn't prepared for it. I think I answered about a million questions today, which is great but exhausting. You remember when we went to those camps?"

I laughed as the memories quickly came back. "I'll never

forget it. We were the ones causing trouble back then and likely giving people headaches."

Cooper laughed in agreement. "Well, you seem to be in a good mood tonight. Wouldn't have anything to do with your pretty neighbor who you conveniently drove home last night?"

I didn't bother to hide my smile since we were talking over the phone. "It might have something to do with her, yeah. She stayed over, and we spent time together before I had to stop by Lake Ridge. She's..." I shook my head. "She's something else. Funny, witty, kind. She's exactly what this town needs."

"Exactly what you need, too?"

"I think she might be."

"Damn." Cooper let out a long sigh. I could tell there was something on his mind. "I knew you had a thing for her—pretty sure the whole town has been trying to set you two up, me included—but I thought it would be something temporary. That you wouldn't go and catch feelings for her."

I didn't want to admit it, but it was true. Juliette and I *were* temporary. She was leaving.

Cooper continued, "Or is it more than a onetime thing? For you *and* for her?"

I didn't even need to think about it. Of course, it was more. But did she see it that way, too?

"I mean, we didn't talk about it. But it didn't feel like *just* a onetime thing." It felt like more, but was I getting ahead of myself? "I'm taking her out on a date later this week, which is partially why I'm calling. I feel so out of practice. I have some ideas where to take her, but nothing feels right."

"I'm happy for you, man, I really am," Cooper said, and I could sense a *but* coming. "But I want you to be careful. You've been down this road once before. I don't want you to put your trust in the wrong person." *Again* was the word Cooper didn't say.

"But this is—"

"Different? Maybe in some ways, yeah. I mean, I hear it in your voice. I saw it on your face when you were dancing with her last night. But the one thing that isn't different is she's leaving. She's not staying in Golden Falls, Wes."

Yes, Juliette *was* leaving. But we still had some time until summer ended. I wasn't naive enough to think I could change her mind—I didn't want to be rejected by someone again, reminded that I wasn't enough—but I also knew that how I felt this morning was something I had never experienced before. There was something pushing me to see what this could be. I was getting pieces of myself back when I was around Juliette. If it didn't turn into anything, then at least I tried.

"You're right. She is leaving, but she's here for another month and a half. I'd rather enjoy this time than stay away from her all summer. Because right now, she *is* here."

"I didn't realize getting you to dance with her would be the turning point," he said with a low chuckle. "Be careful, okay? I remember what happened last time—maybe better than you do. You went dark on us after things with Gretchen ended, and I don't want you to go through that again.

"But," Cooper continued on an exhale, "you've changed for the better this summer. I can't remember the last time you had that much fun at Lake Ridge or on the boat. I imagine that has something to do with Jules. And I like her for you—I really do—I'm hesitant about it because I know how you are when you're passionate about something. Or someone."

Cooper always wanted the best for me, and I knew that. I couldn't fault him for being concerned.

His voice turned more lighthearted. "You better make this the best first date she's ever been on, and with my help, you know it will be. Now, what ideas did you have?"

I rattled on what I had in mind and continued brainstorming with Cooper. I truly wanted to make this the best first date for her. If things went my way, this would be the first of many dates with Juliette.

35

JULIETTE

"So, here's the vision board I put together for the yoga studio," I said to Eliza. I had my laptop set up on the coffee table in front of us as I pulled up the board. We were at Purrfect Blend in the cat room, sitting on the new loveseat I picked out earlier in the summer. Lily said it had been a hit—both among customers and the cats.

Eliza and I had been texting since the Fourth of July about ideas she had for her studio, what she wanted to achieve, and her short-term and long-term priorities for the space. The building her studio was in—the same as Lily's café—was older, so some of the designs and fixtures aged the space. But it helped that the business there before hers had been a dance studio.

Eliza had a lot of inspiration for the space, especially after the yoga conference she went to in June, but was having a hard time visualizing how it would all look together. This was one of my favorite parts. I loved bringing people's vision to life—even before the work started. My favorite interior design rendering software allowed me to digitally recreate whatever space I was working on. I had added in measurements for Eliza's studio and various details about the space, including the lights, where outlets were, the storage area, and more. I created two versions: what the space looked like now and what I was proposing.

"And then here is what it would look like when it's all done." I double-clicked to pull up the rendering of what I had designed, pointing to the various details as I explained them. "I was thinking new floors, new paint color, and decorations as a priority. Down the line, you can upgrade the mirrors and light fixtures. For the decorations, I want to really make the space feel like you. You mentioned you love plants, right? Let's lean into that. Fill the space with various plants, flameless candles, and artwork. Really make it cozy. The candles would be on a timer, so you wouldn't have to turn them on each time. You can program them for when you have classes."

"Oh, Jules." Eliza's whole face lit up, her eyes wide in awe and smile bright. "This is absolutely stunning." She leaned in closer to the laptop. "It's...it's beautiful. It's better than I could have dreamed of. We can really make this happen?"

I nodded. "We sure can. And we can do it on your timeline and budget. The floors will likely take some time to get in, but in the meantime, we can focus on picking the paint color and adding the decor. Does that sound like a good place to start?"

"That sounds absolutely perfect. Since the floors will take a while, can we get those ordered soon? Maybe even take a look today at our options?"

"Definitely," I agreed, pulling up the site so we could browse. "I'm so excited to be working on this with you. I should've asked earlier, but what got you interested in yoga and opening a studio?"

Eliza leaned to grab her coffee, taking a sip before speaking. "Well," she said on a sigh. "I've always found exercise as the best way to take care of my mental health. I'm not sure how much you know, but Cooper and I lost our parents in a car accident.

We were raised by our grandma Marnie, who is the absolute best, but it was tough."

I had heard Marnie mentioned before, but I hadn't realized Eliza and Cooper's parents had passed away. I couldn't imagine how challenging that was for them, and I was appreciative of Eliza opening up to me. I nodded as I listened, wanting to give her the space to continue without interruption.

Eliza wrapped her hands around her mug, looking down. "I don't remember much about my parents—I was six when they died—but I've always loved looking at photos of us as a family and hearing stories from Gram, like how my mom always dreamed of opening a yoga studio. It was going to be her plan after she retired, but..." Eliza's voice broke, tears welling in her eyes. "I started practicing yoga in high school as another form of exercise, and I fell in love. Not only was it an escape and a way to prioritize my mental health, but it was also a way to connect with my mom." She set her mug down, using the back of her hand to wipe under her eyes. "Sorry, I didn't anticipate getting so emotional," she said with a quiet laugh.

"You have nothing to apologize for," I assured her with a gentle smile. "That's beautiful, Eliza. Thank you so much for sharing that with me. Your mom would be so proud of the work you've put in."

"I think so, too. It's been a while since I've shared that story. Most people in town know our history and what happened. My dad was a park ranger, like Cooper, so we're both honoring our parents in what we do but also discovering our own love for it."

"I'm so glad you're trusting me with this project, even more so now that I know how much it means to you."

Eliza turned to me with an abundance of emotion in her eyes. "Me, too. I can't wait to work together to make this a reality." She let out a breath and turned her attention back to the screen. "She would've loved it—I know it." Eliza paused for a moment before turning the conversation back to the project. "For the floors, someone would have to install those, right?"

I nodded. "I'm starting to get to know some of the contractors in the area through Hal. He's been super helpful in making those connections since that is definitely something I wouldn't be able to do on my own."

"Isn't he the best?" Eliza asked with a warm smile. "Did Lily mention he owns this building? He has been such a huge part in both of us being able to move forward with our businesses and making them a reality. I really hope he ends up selling the building to Lily—both so he can get some free time and so she can get that experience."

"If he ends up selling, do you think it'll be soon?"

She twisted her lips to the side. "I *think* so. He's talked about it, a little cryptically at times." She laughed. "I'm sure you've noticed, but he always seems to be one step ahead of everyone. Always knows something. I'm starting to think he might be more in tune with the town gossip than Louise."

"I think you might be right," I said with a laugh right as one of the cats—a brown tabby named Maple—came up to us and rubbed against our legs with a meow. I reached down, letting her sniff my hand before I went to pet her. She immediately started purring from the attention. "Gosh, she's adorable. Every time I'm in here she says hi."

"Isn't she?" Eliza scooted over, patting the space between us for Maple to jump up, which she happily did with a chirp. "Her kittens got adopted quickly at the start of the summer, and now it's just her. I bet she'll find a home soon." With a sly smile Eliza added, "You know, *you* could also take her home with you."

I shook my head. "I wish, but I think I have enough going on right now. I technically still don't have a place to go back to in

Chicago. My brother is helping me solve my whole living situation."

"Another reason you should stay in Golden Falls for longer than the summer."

"If only," I sighed. With Maple lying on Eliza's lap, I grabbed the laptop to look up when floor panels would get here once ordered. "So, it looks like the floors would take some time to get here. Late October or early November." A sudden pit of dread formed in my stomach. I wouldn't be in Golden Falls in the fall —I wouldn't be able to see this project through to the end. Pushing through, I said, "But that would be fine. I can place the order for you, line up the contractor, and you can text me if anything comes up or if you have any questions."

Eliza watched me, and while I thought I was keeping my expression neutral, she reached over to give my forearm a squeeze. "You'll only be a call, text, or FaceTime away. Plus, the drive isn't too bad. You can always come to visit, or Lily and I can make the trip to Chicago. This is just the start of our friendship —it's not going to end when the summer does. You can't get rid of us that easily. We just got you."

I didn't realize, until that moment, how much I needed to hear those words and how much my new friendships meant to me. I had friends in Chicago—but not like this.

It didn't take long for Eliza and me to finalize our next steps for the yoga studio. I placed the order for new floors and had my list of decorations to be on the lookout for, as well as paint shades Eliza was interested in.

Eliza had another hour to kill before her shift at Lake Ridge, so we decided to stay at Purrfect Blend. It was easy to get wrapped up in conversation with her. She was funny, sarcastic, and a great listener. Purrfect Blend was such a cozy place to hang out, and the time flew by. The only thing that changed was Maple moving from Eliza's lap to mine, now curled up with her nose tucked under her paws. There was a constant flow of customers, too, both in the café and in the cat room.

Lily pushed open the door to the cat room, a smile on her face when she saw us. "I thought you two left and I missed it! Gosh, this day has been a blur."

"I honestly don't know where the time went," Eliza agreed. "We were productive for most of our time here, but now we're rotting on the couch. I have to go into Lake Ridge soon for my shift. But, holy shit, Lil, Jules has to show you the design she came up with for the studio. It's absolutely perfect."

"Oh my gosh, yes! I need to see." Lily peeked through the glass pane that separated the two rooms to see if any new customers had walked into the café. "I should have some time to see now." She pulled over a nearby chair and sat down, reaching over to pet Maple. "And actually, I almost forgot to ask—" Lily looked at me with a raised brow. She wasn't angry or upset; she looked amused. "What exactly happened Saturday night when my brother drove you home? And why is he now texting me asking what your favorite pastry from here is?"

"Yeah, what did happen?" Eliza asked with a pleased smile, crossing her arms over her chest. "Because last we heard you were *very* adamant about there being *nothing* going on."

"Oh," I said with an awkward laugh. *That.* It was Wednesday, and I hadn't seen Lily or Eliza since our night at Lake Ridge last Saturday. Our work schedules kept clashing, and I didn't want to tell them what happened with Wes over text. I had planned to tell them both today but was trying to find the right time. No time like the present. "Probably because we're going on a date on Friday?" I offered.

Both Eliza and Lily stared at me with open mouths. And then they started speaking at the same time.

"Oh my god! Tell us everything!"

"A date?!"

"Well, maybe not *everything*," Lily quickly clarified. "There's some details about my brother's love life that I never need to hear. But tell us ninety percent of it. What happened?!"

"But, actually, I knew it," Eliza said. "With the way you two were dancing *and* him taking you home. Sparks were flying. And while I didn't win my bet—because as far as I know he didn't tell Cooper to stay away from you—I was pretty sure at one point he was shooting daggers at Coop with his eyes."

I snorted a laugh. "No way. You're being dramatic."

"I swear!" Eliza raised her hands.

Lily nodded in agreement.

"I mean, maybe. He did ask if I had a thing for Cooper, which seemed so out of left field."

Eliza grinned, nodding as if I had proved her point. "See, exactly. Because Cooper was getting under his skin on purpose. And it worked. But back to this date..."

I filled them both in—leaving various details out for Lily's sake—on what happened at the bar, getting back to Wes's house, and our morning together. And, of course, how he asked me out on a date.

"I have no idea what we'll do, but he said he'll have it all planned," I said with a shrug.

Lily tipped her head back with a groan, playfully complaining, "This would be even cuter if he wasn't my brother. When I told him to be nice to you, I didn't see this coming." She chewed on her bottom lip, something clearly on her mind. "But what does this mean for after the summer? Are you staying?"

After the summer. I was starting to hate those words.

"Um, well, no, I'm not staying. We haven't talked about what it means. I think we're both just focused on the now."

Lily frowned, but I couldn't tell which part of my answer she didn't like. "You've both been through a lot. I don't want either of you to get hurt."

"I know," I said quietly. "Do you think I'm making a mistake getting involved with him? Because I—"

"No, Jules. That's not at all what I'm getting at, and I would never ask you to stop seeing him on my behalf," Lily said firmly. "Will you promise me if things don't work out for whatever reason it won't impact our friendship? That you'll still visit?"

I saw the pleading in Lily's eyes, and I understood her worry. It was all valid, and I appreciated that she was sharing her concerns with me.

"I promise. Of course. I can't imagine my life without you two." I looked at Lily and Eliza, getting emotional thinking about how much they had come to mean to me. Leaving Golden Falls at the end of the summer didn't just mean leaving Wes—it meant leaving Lily, Eliza, Hal...everyone who had come to mean so much to me in a short amount of time.

"Stop it! You two are so mushy! Everything will be fine." Eliza pulled us both into an embrace, playfully rolling her eyes. "Now," she said as we pulled back from the hug, "on a scale of one to ten how good was the sex?"

"Eliza!" Lily exclaimed at the same time I said, "Infinity."

Lily gagged, waving her hand. "Let's talk about the yoga studio or how cute Maple looks sleeping. Literally anything but my brother's sex life."

Eliza and I laughed.

"Okay, fine. Let's fill you in on what we're doing with the studio," I said.

"Thank goodness." Lily breathed a sigh of relief, pulling her chair closer to the table so she could see the laptop.

"I am curious, though, did he—" Eliza started but was cut off when Lily grabbed a pillow from the couch and tossed it at her.

The three of us burst into laughter again.

36

JULIETTE

The next day, Lily and I had plans to get dinner together. It was safe to say we had more catching up to do.

As I closed the front door behind me, I noticed a note taped to the door. I recognized the messy scrawl right away.

> Juliette,
>
> I have everything planned for our date tomorrow night, and I'll pick you up just after eight. In the meantime, get yourself a new dress or outfit for the evening.
>
> I can't wait to see what you pick out— even if it won't stay on for long.
>
> By the end of the night, I want you in nothing but your perfume.
>
> - Wes

Taped to the back of the note was a small envelope and

inside was Wesley's credit card. I shook my head with an amused scoff. Things that only happened in a small town. No where else would you be able to tape a credit card to someone's front door and not risk it getting stolen. I safely tucked the note and credit card into my purse before pulling out my phone.

ME

I got your note. I can't wait for our date. You could've knocked you know! Or texted.

But you really didn't have to leave your card.

Three gray dots immediately appeared.

WES

What's the fun in that? And I'm excited too, baby.

I wanted to. I love seeing you in dresses.

ME

You don't think people will talk if I'm using your credit card to pay?

WES

I don't care if they talk or not. I care about you, and I want you to treat yourself to a new dress and whatever else you want. Stop overthinking it.

ME

What if I happen to be going downtown with Lily and she wants to get something too?

WES

Just use my damn card.

ME

Okay!!! Thanks. :)

WES

See you tomorrow.

I bit down on my bottom lip with a smile as Wes's last text came in. I then went back and tapped my texts with Lily.

ME

Slight change of plans. Want to meet for shopping before dinner?

"Okay, so there *are* some benefits to you dating my brother," Lily teased as we walked through The Main Stitch. It was Lily's favorite clothing store in town and what made it extra satisfying was how the clothes were organized by color.

"I wouldn't say we're *dating*. We're going on a date." I ran my hand along the row of red clothes, the soft fabric brushing my fingers as the metal hangers chimed.

"Oh, please." Lily gave me a look. "Wes doesn't go on dates. And he definitely doesn't get flowers for women, invite them to watch fireworks, and dance with them. He's always too busy working, so the fact that he's asked you out on a date *and* is missing work is big news in Golden Falls. I bet there's going to be rumors that he kidnapped you so you wouldn't leave."

"Lily." I let out a laugh, shaking my head. "Where do you get these ideas from?"

"Small town gossip is both the best and the worst." She grinned. "You hear stories about yourself you never would've expected, but luckily, no one believes them anyway. Gotta stay entertained somehow, especially when things slow down after the summer."

I paused, turning to face her. "You'd tell me if you were mad or upset, right?" Lily hadn't done or said anything to make me think she was upset, but the question nagged at me anyway.

I didn't want her to think I didn't value the friendship we'd built.

Lily tore her attention away from the clothes. Her face always looked kind and gentle, but when she saw my expression, her eyes softened even more. "Of course, I'd tell you. I'm not mad or upset. I promise. I'm just a little anxious about it, is all. You both have big hearts, and I would hate for either of you to get hurt."

"I don't want anyone to get hurt," I said honestly. I had put a lot of work into focusing on myself this summer and on my career. I wanted to keep that momentum.

"I think you two need to talk and figure out what you're both looking for in the time you have left in Golden Falls."

That was a great suggestion, but talking would mean bringing it up. And I didn't feel ready to have that conversation yet.

"Yeah, maybe," I mumbled. "You don't think this is just a summer fling for him, do you?" I thought back to what he told me about his relationship with Gretchen. While I knew deep down this was different, I couldn't help but compare what was happening between us to what Wesley had told me. He had fallen for someone who was passing through once before. The last thing I wanted to do was break his heart and bring up all those emotions.

"I have no idea if it's a summer fling, which is exactly why you need to talk to him." Lily gave me a pointed look.

I guess she was right.

Lily and I continued to make our way through the store, slowly looking over each section and picking out what we wanted to try on. After a marathon of putting on and taking off various outfits, we made our purchases—with Wesley's card.

I settled on a red cotton sundress with thin straps and a gathered bust. The dress flared out at the hips, hitting below the knee. It also had pockets! I couldn't wait to wear it on my date. Lily picked out jeans, two tees, and a pair of sunglasses.

Even with the sun starting to set, the temperature and humidity were still high. Both of us were sweating walking through downtown.

Lily fanned herself with her hand. "So, for dinner tonight, should we order our own entrées or split a bunch of appetizers?"

We looked at each other and at the same time said, "Split a bunch of appetizers."

37

WESLEY

MY CONVERSATION WITH COOPER EARLIER THIS WEEK HELPED EASE some of my nerves, and I was grateful for his help. I was feeling ready for my date tonight.

A foreign excitement coursed through my veins as I drove up the gravel driveway to the cabin. I hadn't put this much thought into a date before, and I'd gotten so used to my routine in Golden Falls. I didn't date much in college or after. College usually consisted of a night out with a girl I never saw again. The last couple of years were more of the same. If Gretchen and I went on a date, it was always out of town and quick. Always a secret, and she was also always on her phone. The more I thought about our time together, the more I realized she was likely always texting her husband, even when we first met.

This date with Juliette would be different from all of that—in the best way. We didn't have to hide, and we could do this all summer if we wanted to. If *she* wanted to because, hell, there wasn't a doubt in my mind that I needed more dates with her. She was incredible and unlike any other woman. I'd never felt this way about someone.

I was constantly thinking about the next time I would get to be in her orbit. She had a pull on me, and I didn't want to fight it anymore.

I pulled up to the cabin in my truck and hopped out, making sure to grab the bouquet of flowers I'd gotten for her. I made my way up the porch steps.

I hoped this would be the best date Juliette had ever been on, but the voice in the back of my mind loved to prey on my insecurities, on what I couldn't give her. On what this town didn't offer that the city did. And not just any city—Chicago. She likely went on a bunch of extravagant dates in the past to shows, restaurants, exclusive events.

I didn't know if I could compete with that. But I would sure as hell try. Sometimes being stubborn paid off.

I knew I could give her a night that showed how much she was coming to mean to me.

With a bouquet of colorful flowers in one hand, I raised my other to knock. I stepped back, letting out a slow exhale.

Within seconds, Juliette pulled open the door, the sweet smell of vanilla and daisies immediately overcoming me. I'd never get tired of that.

"Hey, I'm almost ready!" She waved me in. "Just need to grab my bag and get my shoes on."

"No rush at all," I assured her, my eyes slowly taking her in. "You look absolutely breathtaking." My hand that wasn't holding the flowers flexed, desperately wanting to touch her, to pull her into my arms. Her brown hair was curled, and she was wearing a red sundress that was fitted to her lean frame. The top of the dress was some corset style, pushing up her round breasts, and cinched in at the curve of her waist, flaring out ever so slightly. The bottom of the dress hit below her knee. Her eyeshadow was done, mascara coated her long lashes, and her lips were a glossy pink.

Fuck. This was going to be a long night.

Her face immediately lit up at the compliment, and she twirled. "It's the dress I bought with your card at The Main Stitch with Lily. Thank you for doing that, by the way." She came up to me, reaching up to run her fingers along my stubbled jaw. "You look so very handsome."

"Thank you, sweetheart," I murmured, smiling at her compliment. "And you're welcome for the dress. I like spoiling you."

Her soft touch along my jaw nearly distracted me. All I could think about was pulling her into my arms, kissing her, slowly peeling that dress she looked so good in off her body. I cleared my throat. Patience—we'd get there.

"These are for you." I lifted the bouquet. "I wasn't sure about your favorite color or favorite flowers, but I asked the florist in town to put something together." The bouquet had pink roses and various colorful wildflowers. Pinks, blues, oranges, and yellows. It was lively, bright, and beautiful—just like the woman in front of me. "The flowers reminded me of you."

She looked up at me, a gentle smile on her face. "Wes, that's so sweet. Thank you. I love them." She took the flowers out of my hand and brought them up to her nose. She closed her eyes and inhaled the floral scent. "I love all types of flowers. I don't think I have a favorite. As for my favorite color...pink. I'm a simple girl," she said with a laugh.

Juliette moved to the kitchen, putting the flowers in water. She then sat on the couch to slide on her heels. "What's your favorite color?" she asked.

The corner of my lip tipped up. "I've found myself really liking green this summer."

She nodded with a smile, looking up at me with her bright green eyes, likely not realizing the reason behind my new favorite color.

"And yellow, red, pink."

She tilted her head to the side, looking down at her dress and then playfully narrowing her eyes at me as she stood. Her heels clicked against the wooden floorboards. "Red because of my dress?"

Once she was close enough, I set my hands on her waist, a gasp leaving her as I pulled her closer. "Green because of your eyes. Yellow because of that goddamn bikini you were tanning in. Red because of your dress tonight. Pink because of your lips —and because you love it." I watched the thin column of her throat bob as she swallowed, her lips parting ever so slightly. I loved making her speechless.

"So," she said breathlessly, "is this your favorite dress, then?"

My grip on her waist tightened, the soft fabric bunching underneath my fingers. Her cheeks immediately flushed pink, and I could feel her nipples pebble through the thin fabric, which meant no bra. Again. Was this woman trying to kill me? "It's one of my favorites, yeah."

Juliette leaned forward, pressing her lips softly to my neck, kissing up to my jaw. She smiled against my skin. "One of them? Which one is your favorite, then?"

"The yellow one. With the thin straps that tie into bows."

She paused, pulling away enough to look up at me. Her forehead creased ever so slightly. "I know which one you're talking about but...when did I wear it?"

"Dinner at my parents' house in June."

Recollection dawned on her. "Oh, right! Wait, but that was the start of summer. We weren't—well, you didn't like me back then. You noticed the dress I was wearing?"

"Baby, I noticed everything about you that night—and every night in between. You're impossible to look away from." I reached to tuck a strand of hair behind her ear. "I can't get enough of you."

She looked up at me, and we stayed like that for a moment.

Just looking into each other's eyes like we had all the time in the world.

The corner of my lip tipped up as soon as I noticed her gaze start to shift to my mouth.

She tugged on her bottom lip with her teeth, looking back up at me but this time with hooded eyes. "Maybe we should—"

"Don't you dare finish that sentence," I interrupted with a chuckle. "Because I don't have enough self-control to say no to you, and I'm taking you on this damn date."

"But your note..."

"Patience, sweetheart. We'll get there."

Juliette nodded with a playful sigh, getting out of her daze. She beamed at me, and I knew I would never get tired of the sight. "Let's see what you have planned, then, handsome."

"You're in for a treat, city girl."

I drove Juliette to my favorite spot in Golden Falls, right on the edge of town by the lake. It was a picture-perfect lookout spot that was tucked away from everything and everyone and, in my opinion, had the best view of the sunset. I had initially thought about having a picnic dinner with Juliette by the lake, and we would wrap up by watching the sunset, but Cooper told me there was a rare geomagnetic storm happening tonight—which meant we would possibly see the northern lights. So, instead I picked Juliette up just before sunset, which this time of year was around 8:30 p.m. It would be completely dark by around 10 p.m.

I had blankets and pillows ready in my truck bed for stargazing once the sun set, plus a couple of dips, chips, and a bunch of Juliette's favorite snacks. Lily also made us cookie dough brownies—a recipe she'd been trying out. Juliette always gravitated toward Lily's chocolate treats when she stopped by Purrfect Blend.

"Oh, Wes, this is beautiful," Juliette marveled as she hopped out of my truck.

I backed in when I parked so we could sit in the truck bed and see the water. I grabbed the paper grocery bag, blankets, and pillows from the backseat and rounded the vehicle, opening the tailgate with ease. I had the radio on, too, soft music playing through the windows.

I hopped up in the truck bed and extended my hand to Juliette, helping her up.

"What makes this spot your favorite?" she asked as we got the various snacks, blankets, and pillows set up.

"It's always been a great spot to come to think and unwind. I've never seen anyone else here. Parts of town and the lake can get so busy, so it's nice to know I can come here to get away from it all. This view is why I love Golden Falls so much. The trees, the water, the birds chirping, and various wildlife running around. I don't want this town to lose that, even as more people are coming here."

"It's beautiful. There are so many spots in town that would go perfectly on a postcard, but this is my favorite one so far. Don't worry—I won't share your secret spot with anyone." She looked down at the cheeses, crackers, dips, brownies, and gummy worms I had bought and eyed me skeptically. "Do we have the same taste in snacks or did you buy literally everything I love?"

"A little bit of both...but mostly the second one."

She gave my arm a gentle nudge. "This is supposed to be *our* date. You can't just buy everything I like."

I scoffed. "Says who?"

Juliette laughed, playfully rolling her eyes. "This is already the best first date."

She scooted closer, and I wrapped my arm around her, pulling her into my side and kissing the top of her head.

I could stay like this forever.

38

JULIETTE

Wesley and I could talk for hours now that we were comfortable with each other. He was chatty when he wanted to be! We'd talked about anything and everything over the last couple of hours: favorite music, what we wanted to accomplish in the next five years, what we looked for in a partner, people in our lives who influenced and motivated us. All the while, we made good progress on the snacks.

"What's one place you really want to visit?" I asked.

We were both lying down. I was on my side with my head on his chest and my leg draped over his. He had his arm wrapped around me, his fingertips tracing up and down my skin.

"Alaska," he answered without any hesitation. "Every picture or video I've seen looks absolutely stunning. Plus to be surrounded by mountains and nature like that? It would be perfect. I've yet to see any mountains, so that's at the top of my list."

"Hm..." I looked him up and down. "Yeah, I could see you as a rugged mountain man," I teased.

He shook his head with a laugh. "What about you?"

I thought about it for a moment, about how I'd be ready to travel anywhere if it meant going with him. If it meant continuing *this*.

"I'd love to go to Italy," I finally answered. "The food, the wine, the history. I could easily spend weeks there, but even if I only got a small taste of it, I'd be happy."

"You could probably spend some of the prize money on a trip, huh?" he teased, giving my side a gentle nudge.

"Yeah, probably." I rolled my eyes playfully. "My parents recently bought a house in Florida, so I would like to help them pay that off. Then I want to make sure I have some sort of job. My brother will likely tell me to invest whatever is left, and I'll listen because, annoyingly, he's right. Just don't tell him I said that."

Wes looked down at me thoughtfully. "That's really nice of you to do that for your parents. You should do something for yourself, too. Even if it's not as big as a trip. You deserve it."

I wanted my parents and brother to meet Wes. I wanted these different parts of my life to come together...but would they? I thought back to Lily's words earlier this week about talking to Wesley about our future. Or, I guess, if we even had a future.

I paused, thinking through how to phrase it. None of the versions in my head felt right.

"Wes, what—"

"Baby, look," Wes interrupted as he sat up. "Looks like the sky is showing off for us tonight."

Confused, I sat up. When I looked again, it became clear what had caught his attention. I gasped at the sight.

Lighting up the sky was the most spectacular view I had ever seen. The sky was alive, green and deep purple ribbons dancing across it. The reflection of the northern lights stretched across the still lake, creating a mirrored glow. Time stilled, urging us to soak in every vivid detail together.

"I've never seen something so beautiful," I whispered, taking it in. I knew there were areas in the Midwest, including Wisconsin and Illinois, where you could occasionally see the northern lights if the timing was right, but you had to get far out of the city in order to stand a chance. My hand itched to grab my phone, to capture a photo that I could look back on, but I appreciated the moment. I reached for his hand instead, intertwining our fingers together. "Did you know we would see this tonight?"

"I hoped we would. Cooper mentioned there was a chance, and I figured we might as well try. It paid off."

I nodded in agreement, softly saying, "I'm glad we tried." The double meaning from my words hung in the air. Yes, we still had time, but it was fleeting. Would any amount of time be enough with Wesley? Even if I stayed?

I paused, turning my head and taking in the sight of him under the lights, the way the greens and purples illuminated his sharp jawline, the slope of his nose. But it was the way he was already looking at me, so achingly tender, that had my eyes welling up. I thought back to the Luke Combs song we danced to at Lake Ridge earlier this month. Were we getting into something we knew was about to end in two broken hearts?

"Oh, baby," he murmured without me even having to say anything. "I know."

I bit down on my bottom lip, but it wasn't caught between my teeth for long. Wesley's rough hand cupped the side of my face, and he used his thumb to pull my lip free.

"Did you ever think something could feel this right?" I asked, my voice quiet and hesitant.

Wes used the pad of his thumb to wipe away a stray tear, a soft smile on his face. "No, not before meeting you. Honestly, it still catches me off guard the way I feel about you, how quickly my feelings are growing. But I wouldn't change a thing. I don't regret anything that's happened between us."

"I don't regret anything either. I just... I don't know where this is all going to go." I swallowed the lump in my throat.

"I don't either, and I think that's okay. All I know is..." His large hands found my hips, bunching up the fabric of my dress as he pulled me on top of his lap so I was straddling him. He set his palms on my thighs, fingertips inching underneath the hem of my dress. "You make everything feel easy, Juliette. Everything feels right with you."

My hands found his shoulders, gripping the fabric of his shirt as I leaned in closer. "Yeah, everything feels right with you, too," I whispered.

We knew what was coming, but maybe it was okay to forget about it for a moment. To just be. Together.

I thought about what I wanted out of this summer when I first got to Golden Falls, and part of it was to be more present. To not think so much about what comes next.

And with Wes, all I could do was be in the moment. I couldn't think of a better place to be.

We stared at each other for a beat. Then another. It was silent except for the crickets chirping—and my heart pounding inside my chest. Wesley's hands slowly inched up my thighs until he met my hips. Even on a hot summer night, goose bumps formed on my skin from his touch.

"I want to focus on you tonight, on us," I said. "I want"—I pulled Wes closer by his shirt, my mouth inches away from his —"you."

"I want you, too. So much." A low growl rumbled through Wes's chest. "Do you feel what you do to me, baby?" he asked in a hoarse whisper, rocking my hips over his jeans.

My breath picked up in anticipation. Even though I was wearing panties, the friction against my center felt *too good*. So good that I couldn't take it anymore.

I closed the distance first, my mouth meeting his in a slow but hungry kiss. A moan immediately escaped me from how good his lips felt against mine.

While the kiss started off slow, it didn't stay that way for long. The pace of everything quickened once I parted my lips. Our kiss. My hips. Our hands exploring. The searing kiss was both too much and not nearly enough. More. I needed *more*. I needed everything he would give me.

Wes's hands pulled down the straps of my dress to expose my breasts.

"Fuck," he groaned against my lips. "You're going to be the death of me. Aren't you, sweetheart?"

One of his large hands cupped my breast, toying and tugging my hardened nipple. The pleasure was all consuming, and I rested my forehead against his to catch my breath. "I want you, Wes."

My hands trailed down his chest to his belt, my fingers fumbling to undo it and then his jeans.

He chuckled lowly, his whole chest rumbling. "I'm all yours."

Wes reached underneath the thin fabric of my thong, his rough fingers finding my wet center and rubbing my clit. "Fuck, you're wet and ready for me. Such a good fucking girl."

Within moments, my panties were off and Wes pushed his jeans and briefs down to line up his cock against my aching center as I hovered over him.

"Are you going to ride me, baby?"

I nodded quickly, unable to find the words yet again. I was only focused on how good he would feel between my legs, at the heat pooling low in my belly. With my hands gripping his shoulders, I sank down on his cock, tossing my head back with a moan. "Fuck, Wes," I cried out. I moved my hips slowly at first, adjusting to his size.

With his hands on my hips, he guided me over his cock until I let out another moan. "Just like that, baby. Find what feels good and use my cock." Those were the words I needed to find my confidence, to pick up my movements against his hard length.

"You feel...so good," I moaned.

"You feel like you were made for me," he groaned, pressing hot kisses along the side of my neck, nipping and sucking at the skin, down to my breasts. He moved one hand between us, his thumb finding my clit and adding pressure.

I let out another cry. Steadying myself with one hand, I moved the other to Wes's hair, tugging on the strands. "Wes, you're going to make me come," I breathed.

He grunted against my skin. "That's the goal, baby." He made circles with his thumb, causing my hips to move more erratically. Wes never took his eyes off of me, staring up and looking at me like I was the most breathtaking thing he had ever seen, more mesmerizing than the lights dancing in the sky.

"Oh, fuck!" I gasped, the familiar warmth and pleasure overtaking my body. My breaths were quick and shallow as I chased my orgasm, tightening around his cock with another cry, chanting his name. At the same time, his cock stiffened inside me, his chest rumbling with a groan as his hips moved quickly to push him over the edge.

"Juliette," he groaned, his hold on me tightening as he finished.

We were both panting, a sheen of sweat coating our bodies. I let out a huff of a laugh, and Wes grinned over at me. He gripped the back of my neck, pulling me in for a slow, tender kiss. "I can't get enough of you," he said, pulling away.

"I could say the same about you," I said breathlessly. I

pressed a kiss to the side of his neck, lifting my hips and sitting down next to him. Wes pulled his briefs and jeans back on and buckled his belt. Once he was done, he wasted no time in pulling me into his side, pressing a gentle kiss to the top of my head.

I couldn't think of anything better than being in his arms.

39

JULIETTE

On the drive back after our date, Wes asked me to spend the night with him.

So I did.

There wasn't anything better than waking up next to Wes. Or waking up to Wes wanting to go down on me. I would happily take it all.

We had gotten into a routine as July wrapped up. I found myself in his bed nearly every night. The only times I was at the cabin were when he had late nights at Lake Ridge, which wasn't happening as often.

By the end of July, I had slowly moved *a couple* of things to his house. My toothbrush, favorite snacks, and makeup. And maybe his room looked like a little bit of a disaster with the amount of clothes I brought over.

While Wes claimed he didn't mind the mess I had made (even after he almost twisted his ankle tripping over one of my heels), I was spending the morning cleaning up before starting my work day.

As I checked my calendar on my phone, I saw that meeting with the painter for Eliza's studio was my main task—but that wasn't until later in the afternoon. Earlier in the week, I had gathered decorations and potted plants for Eliza.

Working with Louise was going well, too. I had stained the wooden shelves, and they were nearly ready to hang up. I had a handful of other businesses and people who owned cabins in the area reaching out to learn more about my design skills—likely hearing from around town the work I had been doing with Lily, Louise, and Eliza. As much as I appreciated the business, I didn't feel like I could take on any expansive design projects. Not with the days flying by. I didn't want to be in a position where we were ordering supplies into the fall—when I wouldn't be in Golden Falls.

I was focusing instead on requests where I could move quickly, like update decor and offer them guidance on how to use what they had to change up the space for a timeless feel. I had started to take most of my introductory meetings at Purrfect Blend, so it was a little boost to Lily's business, too.

My plan had always been to be in Golden Falls for the summer and then return to the city. But I'd been starting to wonder what it would mean if I stayed, because with each passing day, I felt an increased sense of dread about leaving this town, leaving Wes. My life here was better than anything I had in the city. People knew me here, I had friends, I had the start of a life with Wes.

I put all my clothes into a laundry basket, carrying it over to the washer to start a load of laundry. Yes, I had brought enough clothes over that I needed to do laundry. But Wes encouraged me to! He frowned any time I mentioned going over to the cabin —I'm not kidding. As much as I liked being around him, he liked being around me.

After starting the laundry, I met Wes in the kitchen. He was dressed in his usual jeans and tee and making a pot of coffee. He looked so very handsome—like always.

"I don't know how you survive with the limited closet space you have." I sighed with a shake of my head. "I would only be able to fit my summer clothes in the space you have."

The corner of his mouth tipped up. "Because I usually wear the same thing, just a different version of it. Helps to keep it simple. Did you want some space in the closet? I'm happy to move my stuff. Hell, if you want the whole closet, you can have it."

I let out a laugh, grabbing two mugs for us. "You definitely don't have to do that. I don't need the space, especially since..." I trailed off, not wanting to finish that sentence. Instead, I switched thoughts. "Especially since I'm doing laundry right now. I'll fold everything and keep it in my suitcase." I cringed. That wasn't much better. Both were reminders of the inevitable.

Wes huffed, taking the mugs from me. He poured a heavy dose of my favorite caramel creamer into my mug and filled the rest with coffee.

"You won't be doing that. Keeping your clothes in your suitcase, I mean. I'll clean out some of the closet for you and a drawer or two. Just until..." Wes paused, before starting to ramble. "Well, if you need more space or less..." He cleared his throat. "What I'm trying to say is we'll figure it out. But I'm going to start by making some extra space for you."

I brought the mug up to my lips to hide my smile. I had never heard Wes ramble before, and it was incredibly endearing. "A drawer or two sounds nice."

"And some of the closet," he reminded me with a grunt.

"Right, of course." I smiled again.

He gestured with his head over to the back deck, and I followed him. We enjoyed drinking our morning coffee out on the back deck—the same spot where we watched the fireworks —when we had some extra time.

We both wanted to focus on the now. Living in the moment

and all that. But had he thought about what it would mean if I stayed? I glanced over at him, watching as he took in the view of the lake. He looked so comfortable here, like he was exactly where he was supposed to be.

For the first time in my life, I felt like I belonged—in Golden Falls and in Wes's life.

But I'd worked so hard this summer to put myself first and figure out what I wanted out of my career, out of life.

Would I be failing if I stayed?

40

JULIETTE

"Hey, Grant, what's up?" I used my shoulder to hold my phone to my ear as I sifted through the hangers in my closet—well, Wesley's closet that had my clothes. He had, of course, made good on his promise, and within a few days, I had way more space than I needed. I let out a frustrated huff when I realized the outfit I wanted for tonight was over at the cabin.

"Jules, did you hear me?"

"Sorry, I got distracted," I admitted, closing the closet door and grabbing my phone with my hand. "What were you saying?" I could practically hear him rolling his eyes on the other end.

"I wanted to check in. Haven't heard from you in a while, and I tried to FaceTime you earlier, but it must've not gone through."

"Oh, weird. Yeah, it must've not gone through."

It did go through. I had declined the FaceTime, because while Grant didn't know exactly what the cabin looked like, he would know I wasn't there. Then he would ask me where I was, and the last thing I wanted to explain was how I had been spending nights over at my neighbor's house. A neighbor who I was quickly falling for.

Grant wasn't overprotective like some brothers were, but I remembered his concern when I told him I was heading to Golden Falls. I knew he wouldn't think getting involved with Wesley was a good idea, and I didn't need that lecture right now.

So, a phone call was safer.

"And if you paid attention to the family group chat, you'd see my updates," I added. "I've been sending photos all summer of what I've been up to and my various projects. Mom and Dad have been loving them."

"You don't even want to see the number of unread texts on my phone. There's no way I saw any of those. If you ever need to get a hold of me, it's best to call."

I rolled my eyes. "Okay, Mr. Ancient. Didn't realize you didn't know how texting worked."

"It's not that I don't know."

"Keep telling yourself that."

"God, you're annoying sometimes."

"You're the one who called me!" I exclaimed.

"Right," he sighed. "So, about your apartment. With all the shit going on with your landlord, I easily got you out of your lease. Everything is still in your storage unit. But I don't know how quickly you'll be able to find a new place. Apartments and condos, especially ones that don't cost an arm and a leg, are renting quickly. I recommend looking now and trying to get that figured out if you're trying to move in early September. I can ask around, too. That's still your plan, right? Or were you leaving at the end of the month?"

As I listened to Grant's words, I tried to focus on the good news. I was out of my lease. Yay! My stuff was still safe in storage. Also, yay!

Then came my mental spiral. As much as I had been trying, I couldn't escape the end of summer and when I was leaving. Silence filled our call as I thought.

"You *are* leaving, right?" Grant asked after a moment.

"Of course, I'm leaving," I defended. "I'm just...trying to figure out my plans. There's still plenty of time left. I'm not in a rush or anything."

"It's August already, Jules."

No it wasn't. It was still—

I pulled my phone away from my ear, putting it on speaker as I pulled up my calendar app. I narrowed in on today's date, and hot tears began to sting my eyes when I realized Grant was right. It was August.

My chest started to feel tight, the walls closing in, my breathing getting more rapid. My mouth felt so dry that I wasn't sure if I'd be able to continue the conversation.

"Right, yeah, I knew that," I lied, swallowing the lump in my throat. "I'll start looking this week. Maybe even tonight. I'll have some time before heading out to dinner." Laura and Mark were having another dinner in their backyard, and Wes and I were going to head over together.

"Let me know if you need any help. I'll see if anyone in the office knows of someone who's renting."

Knowing Grant, he would find someone immediately, and that would make my life easier. So, then why did it feel so wrong?

"That would be great. Thanks, Grant. Let me know if you find anything, and I'll start looking, too. Listen, I gotta run. Talk to you later?"

As I was about to end the call, Grant quickly spoke up. "Wait, Jules, you're having a good summer, right?"

I swallowed the lump in my throat. "The best."

"Good. I'm happy to hear that. You sound different, happier. Whatever is in the air in Golden Falls has been suiting you well. I'm proud of you for getting out there, and I'm excited to see you when you're back. Talk soon."

It was only when the call had ended that it registered how wet my cheeks had gotten, and I realized I was crying.

What was I going to do?

41

WESLEY

I couldn't wrap my head around how it was August already. Apart from summer slipping through my fingers, things were good. Really good.

I loved having Juliette in my house—she was the missing piece in making it feel like home. Everything was brighter with her around.

We had gotten into a routine. We had coffee together in the mornings, and we'd meet up for lunch somewhere downtown. Sometimes she would bring lunch over to Lake Ridge or we would walk around downtown holding hands before heading back home. I normally wasn't big on public displays of affection, but I loved showing the whole town that Juliette was mine. Lily still gave me shit whenever I kissed Juliette at Purrfect Blend, but that was to be expected.

No one in town was surprised to see us acting this way. Either word got around fast, or they saw it coming before either of us did.

I also loved hearing about Juliette's projects and was amazed at both her talent and determination. She had accomplished so much in a couple of months. I loved how much she cared about this town, too. I wasn't the only one getting attached. Even Ruby today asked me if there was a chance Juliette would stick around.

I told her the truth—I didn't know.

While at the start of the summer I was nervous about Juliette being a distraction, I couldn't have been more wrong. She was a motivation. On the nights I knew she was waiting for me, I was more productive because I wanted to get home. Lake Ridge was in a good spot. All summer we had been able to handle the busy season, especially once Eliza started bartending. Things were running smoothly, which made me feel better about hiring a head chef in the coming months. The late night bites, as simple as they were, were already a hit.

When I talked with customers over the last few weeks about the idea of expanding the food menu and being open for lunch and dinner, the excitement was palpable. Lunch and dinner would allow families, as well as couples and groups, to stop by before the atmosphere shifted toward drinks and music. Maybe live music was in our future, too.

I knew hiring a head chef would further put Lake Ridge on the map in the Midwest, especially if we were able to attract candidates who were recognized in the culinary field. It would be a challenge in its own way, because I still wanted Lake Ridge to have a welcoming, casual feel while serving delicious food. But I knew we'd get there.

I had a renewed sense of optimism lately, and something told me it had to do with Juliette.

I got to the cabin later that day to pick Juliette up for dinner at my parents' house. She texted me earlier, saying the outfit she wanted was at the cabin and she decided to get ready there. She let me know she had left the door unlocked.

I knocked on the front door and reached for the door knob, pushing it open. "Hey, sweetheart," I called out.

"Hi! I'm almost ready," she responded from the other room.

"Don't worry about it." I walked over to the couch, sitting down. I thought about the first time I had stepped into this place this summer and all the memories that came with it. Now when I was here, all I could think about was Juliette and the new memories we had made and how she had made the cabin her own.

A weight had been lifted off my chest now that I didn't have to be so guarded all the time. But maybe I'd thought that too soon.

As I reached into my pocket to pull my phone out, Juliette's open laptop caught my eyes. I stared at the bright screen for at least a minute, trying to make sense of it.

It was a list of available apartments. In Chicago.

It felt like a bucket of ice-cold water had been dumped on me. Logically, it made sense. Her time in Golden Falls was wrapping up, and she would need a place in Chicago. But emotionally? I had been holding out hope that she would change her mind. That she'd *stay*.

We had a routine here. We could have a *life* here.

I swallowed the lump in my throat, tilting the laptop away from me and leaning back into the couch. She hadn't even left yet, and it already felt like my heart had been ripped out of my chest.

I didn't blame her if she wanted more, but I thought this could be enough. I thought I could be enough.

Within a few moments, Juliette emerged in the living room,

first looking through her purse and then looking over at me. The smile on her face fell immediately. "What's wrong?" she asked, worried.

I didn't realize my expression had been so easy to read. "I, uh," I stammered, letting out a sigh. "Your laptop was open, and —" I started, and understanding dawned across her features.

She walked over, her heels clicking against the floor, and closed the laptop. She sat next to me on the couch, a heavy exhale leaving her. "Grant called me today. He got me out of my lease, which is good, but that means I need to start looking for a new place. He said apartments have been renting out really quickly and encouraged me to start looking. So..." she trailed off, looking down at her hands. "I did some browsing today before getting ready." I hated how small she sounded, and I didn't like the guilt that was written over her face, either, because she hadn't done anything wrong.

"Hey," I said gently, reaching for her hand. "It's—"

"Don't say 'it's okay,' Wes. I saw the look on your face. This... this hurt you, and I hate that. I'm sorry."

While that was true, I could see it was hurting her, too, and I hated that more.

"It caught me off guard, yeah, but it shouldn't have. We should talk about this and figure out what it all means for us. I don't want you to miss out on a good apartment because we've been avoiding having this conversation."

She nodded slowly. "Us talking about it is long overdue, huh? Can we...not do it tonight, though? I don't want the conversation to be rushed before dinner, and I also want to enjoy this time with your parents."

"Yeah, of course." It made sense, but how long were we going to keep putting it off? We were nearly at the point where we *couldn't* put it off any longer. "Are you still okay to head to dinner tonight? If you don't feel up for it, we don't have to."

"I am." She nodded again, a soft smile crossing her pink lips. "I've been so excited to see your parents again. I wouldn't miss it."

I stared at her for a moment, searching her face. I could see in her eyes there was something she wasn't saying, but I tried to let it go. "You look beautiful, by the way." Her brown hair was curled and pulled back into a ponytail, exposing the slope of her neck. She was wearing a blue and white dress I hadn't seen yet—a slightly longer one that hit below her knees.

"Thanks, handsome." She leaned over, pressing a kiss to my neck, just under my jaw. Her lips lingered, and her grip on my hand tightened. Silence filled the space between us before she said, "Let's get going."

She was leaving at the end of the summer, but even that couldn't stop me.

I was falling in love with Juliette Campbell.

42

JULIETTE

The drive to Laura and Mark's was quiet. It wasn't an uncomfortable silence, but I could tell Wes had a lot on his mind. And I did, too.

With one hand draped over the steering wheel, his other hand was holding mine. As I looked out the side window, I thought back to my first dinner at Laura and Mark's at the start of the summer and how much had changed since then. If you told me that Wes and I would be arriving at a future dinner together, hand in hand, I would've thought I was being pranked.

But...that's exactly what was happening.

Everyone in town knew about Wes and me, and I liked that we didn't have to hide anything. I loved how affectionate he was with me, whether we were at home or out in town. But this was the first time I was seeing his parents since we started to spend time together.

Things were a little bit tense between us, and I hated it. I had totally forgotten about my laptop, and I hadn't wanted him to find out that way. The look on his face pained me, even thinking about it now. I knew we decided to pause the conversation for the sake of tonight's dinner, which had been my idea, but there was so much I wanted to say to him.

I didn't want it to seem like I was running away from Golden Falls, or from him. I didn't want to break his trust and make a haste decision. I didn't want to be like his ex. I wanted to stay—I just didn't know if that was the right decision. The one thing holding me back was my career and ensuring that I had my own life here and wasn't clinging onto Wes's life.

"I'm sorry again." I looked over at him with a frown. "For earlier."

Wes stopped at the red light and looked over at me, and I didn't deserve the gentleness in his eyes. Shouldn't he be frustrated with me? Angry? "I know you are, Juliette. You apologized already, and you didn't do anything wrong, okay?" He gave my hand a squeeze, but there was hesitation in his eyes.

"Tell me what you're thinking?" I asked.

He looked forward, continuing the drive to dinner. We were less than ten minutes away.

"I'm thinking," he started slowly, "that we've both been avoiding this conversation, and we're getting to the point where we can't put it off any longer. You need to figure out your plans and I...need to figure out what comes next." While I knew Wes cared about me, I also knew his life would continue after I left. Eventually, he'd find someone to settle down with. My heart ached at the thought. "But I also don't want that hanging over us tonight. I love that you've been excited for dinner. So have I. It'll be almost all of my favorite people in one spot. How can I not look forward to that?" he asked with a small smile. "What do you say we try to enjoy tonight? The rest will be waiting for us."

I slowly inhaled through my nose and exhaled, nodding. I looked down at my hand in his, setting my other hand on top and running my fingertips over his knuckles. "I say that sounds like a great plan."

We were the last ones of the group to get to Laura and Mark's. Similar to the first dinner, Mark was finishing up dinner on the grill with Cooper's help, and Laura was talking with Lily and Eliza.

I tightened my grip on Wes's hand. As excited as I was for tonight, I was also anxious. What if Laura and Mark didn't want me to be with their son because I was going to break his heart? What if they didn't understand what was going on between us, especially with summer wrapping up?

I knew our relationship was between us...but I also knew how important family was to Wes.

"Look who finally decided to show up!" Lily exclaimed as Wes and I walked through the yard to where everyone was gathered. Lily's eyes fell to our clasped hands, and she let out a squeal. "Okay, yeah, this is adorable!"

Laura got up from her seat, a smile on her face. "I'm so happy you two were able to make it." She didn't seem fazed at all by Lily's comments, which led me to believe she had found out one way or another that I was spending time with her son. "You look beautiful, Jules," she said, pulling me in for a hug.

"It's so good to see you again. Thanks so much for having me," I responded before pulling back. A part of my worries evaporated with Laura's words and her embrace.

She then went on to hug Wes. I tried not to listen, but I could hear Laura whisper to him, "I love seeing you so happy."

Laura then looked at us both, motioning for us to join her at the outdoor table. "Come on and get comfortable. Dinner's almost ready, and it's a beautiful evening. I'm glad we were able to get everyone together, especially since temperatures are supposed to increase later this week into next. Make sure you two are getting enough water and taking breaks inside if you need them."

There was an August heatwave expected to roll through the Midwest.

Wes let out a small huff, a smile on his face as he rolled his eyes. "Mom, thank you, but we don't need the reminder."

She gave him a look. "I'm your mother, Wesley Richards. Of course, I'm going to give you the reminder."

"I appreciate the reminder," I piped in. It was true, but I mostly wanted to tease Wes.

Laura turned to me, hooking her arm with mine. "And that's exactly why you're my favorite tonight."

I looked at Wes over my shoulder and laughed when he shook his head. He had a smile on his face, and that's all that mattered.

One of my favorite aspects of having dinner with the Richards family was the constant conversation. There was never a dull moment as we sat around the table, from Lily and me sharing how Eliza kicked our butts during yoga to Cooper talking about all the ways a six-year-old put him in his place during recent programming he helped run for the summer camp kids.

And, of course, I had to share the story about how I had accidentally scared Wes a couple days ago when he got home from work.

"I don't think he's ever yelled so loudly," I said in between laughs, while everyone else was cracking up, too.

"I had no idea you were over!" Wes defended, the corner of his mouth twitching. I could see how badly he wanted to smile. "And then you pop out of nowhere without making a sound. That's not natural."

"Only thing that would've made it better was getting it on video." I reached over for a napkin, blotting the tears from laughter from under my eyes. "Maybe next time."

"Oh, I'd pay good money for that." Cooper rubbed his hands conspiratorially.

"I'll see what I can make happen," I said with a grin, to which Wes wrapped an arm around my chair, pulling me closer only to tickle my side. If I thought I was laughing before, it was nothing compared to this. "Wes!" I said in between laughs, swatting his hand away.

He stopped after a few moments, leaning over. "Better watch it, city girl," he murmured against my ear, pressing a kiss to my temple.

I blushed, but luckily the table's attention had already moved on to the next conversation.

I took a moment to soak it all. How comfortable I felt around everyone. How they had welcomed me in. I hadn't been part of a bigger dinner like this since my parents moved to Florida, so it was nice to get that this summer.

"I'm so glad we made it tonight," I whispered to Wes.

He looked down at me, a smile on his face. "Me, too. And I'm sure there's still more antics to come," Wes said as Eliza was pushing Cooper's phone away.

"Jeez, Cooper! Warn us next time—"

"Oh my god," he said, annoyed. "I literally did, Eliza." Cooper let out an exasperated sigh. "I said, 'Look at this snake I saw while out in the parks today,' but you weren't listening—"

"I also didn't hear you say anything," Lily interrupted, siding with Eliza.

"Of course, you didn't, because you were talking to her!" Cooper hung his head and looked over to Wes for help.

"I heard him loud and clear," Wes chimed in.

With Laura and Mark not getting involved, the group looked in my direction.

My eyes widened. "I don't want to get involved in this!"

"Jules is automatically on our side. That's just how it works!" Eliza said to him with a sarcastic smile.

Cooper rolled his eyes, running a hand through his dirty blond hair. "I need another beer."

Wes reached over to the cooler, pulling out two bottles. "One step ahead of you."

Once dinner wrapped up, Laura and I teamed up in the kitchen to get the various plates and silverware into the dishwasher. Cooper and Wes were starting a bonfire while Mark cleaned the grill. Eliza and Lily had called Jade for a few minutes to catch up.

"I appreciate the help, Jules, but I really want you to know that I'm fine in here," she assured me for the fifth time.

I let out a gentle laugh. "I'm happy to help. Really. It'll go faster with the two of us, and then you'll be able to see the revamp we did to Eliza's studio." Eliza promised to show Laura the photos once we got settled around the fire.

"I'm so excited to see. I remember all the ideas Harper, Eliza and Cooper's mom, had for her own studio, and I love that Eliza is making it her own. She reminds me so much of her." Laura had a wistful smile on her face.

"You two were close, I take it?"

"Very much so. Harper was my best friend, and we talked about how it would be a dream come true if our kids were best friends, too. And it happened. Maybe Harper and Rob aren't here to see it themselves, but I see them every day in Cooper and Eliza. I love those kids like they're my own, and that'll never change. That's the nice thing about family. It isn't defined by blood." Laura looked over at me. "And it's easy to bring someone new to the mix at any time."

"Oh, um, I appreciate that—"

"I might've overstepped, and I apologize for that, but I want you to know you always have a place here. Regardless of your plans after the summer. You're always welcome—please don't forget that."

"That means..." I paused, clearing my throat. "That means the world to me. Thank you, Laura." I set the final couple of plates into the dishwasher as I gathered my thoughts. "I'm not sure what my plans after the summer are. I like it here, a lot, but I never planned to stay." I hadn't said any of this out loud, but talking to Laura was natural, especially after her kind words.

"Well, Jules, that's the thing. Plans change, and that's okay. The only constant thing in life is change. Doesn't mean it isn't scary—because it is—but it's also beautiful. Because it means even if things aren't going your way one moment, they might the next." Laura turned the water off, drying her hands with a towel. "You're going to figure out the right thing for you. I know it," she assured me, giving my hand a squeeze.

Laura's words were exactly what I needed to hear, but it didn't mean things were any easier. I thought back to the start of summer—about how much I needed change. How I found that change in Golden Falls. That was a perfect example of things not going my way, but now I was here, and it felt like everything was right. Except I was never meant to stay.

So, what happened next?

43

JULIETTE

Laura's words played on repeat in my mind over the next couple of days. Wes and I were going to have our conversation the next day, but he got called into work with how busy it was. Between our schedules, we kept missing each other and hadn't had a chance to talk about what was next for us.

It did allow me extra time to think, though, and I felt ready to tell Wes what I wanted. I wanted to stay. I wanted to have a life with him in Golden Falls.

And then my former boss called. Or, I guess, she was kind of still my boss? While I had taken a step away from Luxe Living, I never *technically* quit. I was on a temporary leave.

I was at Lily's apartment, which was a couple floors above Purrfect Blend, and we were waiting for Eliza, who lived in the apartment across the hall from Lily's, to show up.

As Lily was finding us a movie to stream, I leaned back against the couch. My relaxation was short-lived. My eyes widened in disbelief when Cheryl's name flashed across my phone screen.

"Oh my god," I breathed out, picking up the phone and showing Lily.

She let out a gasp. "Wait, why's Cheryl calling you?"

I shrugged. When the phone let out another ring, I tossed it in Lily's direction like it had burned me. Lily caught it and tossed it right back.

"I'm not going to answer it!" she squeaked. "You answer it. Before it goes to voicemail."

"Fine," I said with a defeated sigh, knowing I only had a few seconds to pick up. I cleared my throat, trying to sound like I hadn't been freaking out. "Hey, Cheryl. How are you?"

"Jules," she responded. "It's so nice to hear your voice. It's been quiet in the office this summer without you. I wanted to check in on how things are going. Have you been doing okay?"

Put the call on speaker, Lily mouthed.

I pulled the phone away from my ear and tapped the speaker button before answering Cheryl. "I've been doing a lot better. Thanks so much for asking. The summer has been what I needed, both personally and professionally."

"I'm really happy to hear that. You have a gift, Juliette." She paused. "Does that mean you're not coming back to Chicago?"

I looked between the phone and Lily. "I'm...considering staying."

Lily clamped her hand over her mouth, her bright-blue eyes sparkling with excitement. I hadn't said those words out loud to anyone.

"Listen, you know that I support you doing what's best for you. But before you fully make up your mind, I'd like to run an idea by you. I was thinking about our last conversation before you left for the summer, and I might just have a project that would interest you. Could you come into the office so we can discuss it in person? I'd reimburse you for gas and other expenses, of course."

I stammered, unsure how to respond. Cheryl's words hung in the air, a silence filling the room. I hadn't expected that.

I muted the call for a moment, looking over at Lily.

"You should at least see what she has to say," she whispered with a sad smile. "You'll regret it if you don't."

I knew Lily was right. If I was going to make my decision, I needed to know all my options.

I unmuted the call. "I would love to hear you out, Cheryl." I paused. "Let me know when would work, and I can plan on driving down for a couple of days. I don't want to commit to anything beyond that."

I heard Cheryl clap her hands together. "Wonderful! And I understand. I'll email you the details, and I'll see you soon. I'm excited to see you, Jules. I have a feeling you'll like this new direction."

That's exactly what I was afraid of. I had a feeling in the pit of my stomach that Cheryl was going to make me an offer I couldn't refuse.

"I'll see you soon, Cheryl," I said, wrapping up the call. I stared at the phone, a shaky sigh escaping me. "What if this changes everything?" I asked Lily.

"It might," she said with her own sigh, scooting closer to me on the couch. "But I would hate for you to make your decision without hearing your boss out. I mean, it has to be big if she wants you to come down in person, right? And you've put so much into your career this summer."

"I guess so. She's always preferred face-to-face conversations over talking on the phone, so I'm not surprised. But, yeah, I guess with her covering my travel expenses down there, there must be something she can't show over Zoom."

Both Lily and I groaned, leaning back against the couch, as the door opened.

Eliza pushed the door open, a box of pizza under her arm. She looked at me first and then at Lily. "What happened to you two?" she asked, confused, sliding off her sandals and making herself at home. She set the box of pizza on the coffee table in front of us, and Lily immediately opened it and grabbed a slice.

"We need the comfort food," Lily said before taking a bite.

Meanwhile, I filled Eliza in on what happened over the last half an hour.

"Well, that's the last time I'll be late." Eliza raised her arms and let her hands fall against her thighs. "But, seriously... that's..." She shook her head.

"Mhm," I hummed as I took another bite of pizza. "Horrible timing?"

"Or..." Eliza tilted her head to the side as she thought. "It could be an opportunity for you to really think about what you want—and how you can get both. If that's what you want."

I thought about her words. Could I really have both? Because how was I supposed to pick between my heart and my career? And why was it so challenging as a woman to have both?

I nodded slowly. I thought about the start of the summer, how when I first started working with Lily I had the idea of pitching to Cheryl how we could work with small businesses. "I think it starts with me going to Chicago for a couple of days."

44

WESLEY

I RUBBED MY EYES AS THE SUN PEEKED THROUGH THE CURTAINS IN my bedroom. With a groan, I rolled over to the other side of the bed, feeling for Juliette's body. Instead, I was met with cold sheets. I hadn't even felt her get out of bed this morning.

The last few nights had been long at Lake Ridge, including last night. While I had hoped to see Juliette, I had to keep pushing back the time I could leave, ultimately texting her to go to sleep and not wait up. When I got home, I only had enough energy for a quick shower before I passed out in bed. I slept like a fucking rock. It wasn't lost on me that I had been getting good sleep recently, and I knew exactly why. I slept significantly better with Juliette in my bed.

I reached over to grab my phone, seeing it was just after seven. I didn't have to be at Lake Ridge until this afternoon, but I hoped today I would at least be able to get home at a decent time. I wasn't sure what Juliette's plans were, but I wanted to either take her out on another date or cook us dinner at home. Whichever she preferred.

I got out of bed and pulled on a pair of gray sweatpants, making my way out to the kitchen. I desperately needed coffee.

As I poured myself a cup, I spotted Juliette out on the back deck, a phone pressed against her ear as she paced back and forth. She worried her bottom lip between her teeth, her free hand coming up to rub her forehead.

After she finished her call, I heard her heavy exhale even before she pulled open the sliding glass door.

"Everything okay?" I asked.

Lost in her own thoughts, it took Juliette a moment to register I was in the kitchen. "Oh, hey, handsome. Good morning." She crossed the distance between us, leaning up to press a soft kiss to my jaw.

My hands instinctively found her hips, my grip tightening ever so slightly. "Good morning," I said slowly, drawing out the words as I watched her continue to chew on her bottom lip. "Juliette, hey, what's going on?"

She swallowed, looking up at me hesitantly. An uneasiness came over my body, and I froze. She didn't have to say the words—they were written all over her face.

"You're leaving?" I asked her in disbelief, letting go of her hips and creating space between us.

"Kind of." Her face paled, and she quickly shook her head. "Only for a couple of days."

It felt like my heart was being ripped out of my chest. "You're going back to Chicago?"

"My boss, Cheryl, called last night when I was at Lily's. She has something to tell me but wanted to do it in person. It sounds like a job offer of some sort. I... I don't know if I want it, but I would like to at least hear her out. There's also an idea I had that I wanted to talk with her about. I've been feeling stuck in my career, and part of why I came to Golden Falls was to find my place again. If I don't go and talk with her, I'll always wonder."

I ran my hand over my face. Fuck, I wasn't ready for this. You'd think I would be—considering we had all summer to prepare. "And if it's your dream job? What then? Are you going to move back to the city?" I couldn't stop the questions from firing off. It was hard enough to wrap my head around Juliette leaving for a couple of days. But Juliette leaving forever? I knew that was a possibility, but... I had also let myself hope that she'd stay here.

While we hadn't had the chance to talk since dinner at my parents' house, I had done a lot of thinking. I wanted Juliette to stay, and I wanted to ask if she'd consider moving to Golden Falls.

But I couldn't do that now.

I couldn't hold Juliette back. I'd seen firsthand how talented she was. How she took someone's vision and ideas and turned them into reality. Lily's face brightened any time someone complimented the café, and she wasted no time telling them it was Juliette who did the work. Louise bragged about her renovated cabin to anyone who stepped foot in Lake Ridge. Eliza loved how the yoga studio brought an increased connection to her parents, especially her mom.

I would never ask Juliette to give up an opportunity that could accelerate her career. Her talent was bigger than Golden Falls. The last thing I wanted was for her to live a life of regret if she stayed. She had to go take this meeting. She had to make this decision.

"I don't know any of that yet." Juliette turned, pacing up and down the kitchen. "I'd like to at least talk about it with you once I know more. I've been looking for motivation in my career, and this could be it. Would things still work between us if I lived in Chicago?" Juliette's voice was quiet. "Would you consider moving to the city?"

"I don't know, Juliette," I answered honestly. I couldn't see long distance working with our schedules, and I also couldn't see myself leaving. My life was here...but I also knew her life and career were in the city. I didn't discredit that at all—I simply had no fucking clue how this could work. "You can have your career here, in Golden Falls. Things have been going so well over the summer—"

"They have been, but that was never part of the plan, Wes. It's worked for the summer, but how sustainable would that be? Ultimately I'd run out of clients, right? I don't know if I can pick up, move, and start over—"

"You wouldn't be starting over," I said, exasperated. "You've lived here for the past three months. You're part of this town." How did she not see that?

"I just... I don't know what to do."

"Then let's figure this out together."

"I want to. I do. It's just—" She sighed, looking up at me. "I need to go to Chicago first. And then I'll come back, and we'll figure it out, okay?"

I didn't like that she had to leave. I hated the uncertainty. We'd been living in this limbo state all summer, but now the days were running out.

"When are you leaving?" I asked.

"It's all coming together quickly. I'll leave tomorrow morning and be gone for two days, maybe three. If I'm down there I want to see my brother, too," she said with a small smile.

We had today together. Would it be our last day before everything changed? How the fuck were we supposed to pretend like everything was *normal*.

"What're you thinking?" I could see the emotion in her eyes, the pleading.

That I love you. That I'm terrified to lose you. "This is a lot, Juliette. That's what I'm thinking. I don't even know where to start. I get why you're meeting with her—I do, and I will always support you—but doesn't mean it doesn't scare the shit out of me. I don't know what this means for us. If there's even an us after the summer."

"I know." She closed her eyes. "I don't know what it means, either, but I need to do this, for me, for my career. And then when I get back we'll talk about what it means for us." She let out a breath, opening her green eyes to look up at me. Green eyes that were usually so bright and filled with life, now dulled by sadness. "Trust me?"

Juliette was asking a lot of me, especially after what happened with Gretchen. I'd trusted the wrong woman before and gotten burned. But Juliette wasn't my ex. She hadn't given me reasons not to trust her.

I nodded slowly. "I trust you."

I believed she'd come back. I just didn't know how long she'd stay once she returned.

45

WESLEY

"Hey, Hal," I called as I pushed open the door to the hardware store with my shoulder. "Wanted to check on you with the heat. I brought you some water and an iced coffee from Lily's." I lifted up the water jug in my right hand and the iced drink in my left.

The heatwave my mom had warned us about spiked today—just as the air conditioning at Lake Ridge was acting up, making it hotter than normal in the bar. I decided to close the bar until things cooled off and I was able to get a repair guy in. I assured my staff that even though the bar was closed, they would still get paid for their usual shifts—I didn't want my decision to close to impact them.

No one argued with me, likely because they sensed how irritable I'd been since Juliette left this morning. You would have thought by how much I missed Juliette that she'd been gone for days. Nope. It'd only been five hours. Maybe six.

While my staff usually gave me a hard time, everyone was walking on eggshells around me, and I hated that. I didn't want to be that type of boss.

I just had to get through today, tomorrow, and the day after. Three days. I could do that.

Hal, who was sitting by the front counter, looked up from today's copy of the newspaper. He read the *Golden Falls Gazette* every day.

"Wesley," he greeted, sitting up. "I didn't expect to see you today, son." He folded the newspaper and took off his glasses, setting both on the counter in front of him. "Well, don't just stand there. At this rate, the iced coffee will be hot." Hal waved me over.

I let out a chuckle, shaking my head. I set the water and iced coffee on the counter, my eyes focused down, then began tapping my fingers steadily. I could feel Hal watching me carefully, which didn't help the tension in my shoulders.

Out of corner of my eye, Hal reached for the iced coffee, the plastic creaking as he swirled the straw around. He hummed as he took a sip. "This is great. Did Lily put all her fancy syrups in there?"

I swallowed and finally tore my gaze from the counter to look at Hal. "She did, yeah. Said it's supposed to taste like a s'more."

Hal took another sip. "You know what? That's exactly what it tastes like."

Silence filled the space between us again, and while Hal had started our conversation entertaining small talk, I knew it wouldn't last long.

"You're stalling. You'd do the same thing when you were a kid." I heard the smile in Hal's voice before I saw it. "There's something on your mind, Wes. Spit it out."

I ran my hand over my beard, silently cursing the hot stinging behind my eyes. I wasn't someone who got emotional easily. Not that I had anything against it—it just wasn't me.

But the thought of losing Juliette was unbearable. Like the

walls were closing in on me, like my chest was too tight, like my heart was going to come out my throat. But my heart wasn't in Golden Falls anymore. A five-foot-four brunette took it with her when she went to Chicago.

I cleared my throat. "Juliette is in Chicago for a few days, meeting with her boss about a potential job opportunity. She'll be back soon, but..." I trailed off, hoping Hal would get the idea and cut me some slack. I thought wrong.

"But what?" he asked, nodding for me to keep going.

"She's only been gone for six hours, and I'm sick to my stomach," I blurted. I took a breath and continued, "I'm happy for her, and I think it's good she's hearing her boss out, but the thought of her leaving Golden Falls? I can't... I can't even begin to think about it. I just got her. I can't lose her."

I could handle three days without Juliette if it meant I would get forever with her. It was the other outcome that had my mind spiraling. I had spent all of yesterday and this morning replaying our conversation—or, more so, the things I didn't say. Telling Juliette I loved her was on the tip of my tongue, but I couldn't get myself to say it. Not because I didn't want to. But because I didn't want to hold her back.

I saw how she'd been struggling, and I knew that would carry into today. I wanted her to have a clear head going into her meeting with Cheryl, because at the end of the day, I wanted what was best for Juliette.

Hal hummed. He gestured for me to pull up one of the nearby chairs. I listened, rolling it over and sitting. I leaned forward, elbows resting on my knees.

"Is the issue her leaving Golden Falls or leaving you?"

"Well, leaving me." I paused. "But... I live here. I've grown up here. Lake Ridge..." I trailed off, shaking my head. It didn't feel right saying *my whole life was here*. Because that wasn't true. If Juliette wasn't here, none of that mattered.

Hal watched me come to the realization. "Parts of your life are here, Wes," he said with a nod. "They always will be. And when you get to be my age, you might think about the bar, and the town you grew up in from time to time, but the one thing that will constantly be on your mind?" With a fond smile, Hal looked over at a photo he had hanging up of Vera, his late wife. "There's not a day that goes by that I don't think about her. About our time together. About her smile, her laugh. And while I miss her immensely, I have decades of memories with her to look back on. I will always wish we had more time together, but I know, deep in my heart, that we made the most of every moment together."

"Damn it, Hal," I said with a chuckle, getting choked up over how fondly Hal spoke about Vera. Vera was loved around Golden Falls. It rocked everyone when she passed away, but especially Hal. They were together for decades.

"I've seen the way you look at her, Wes. From the very first moment I saw you two together, I knew she was exactly what you needed. That's exactly how it was when I saw my Vera. I was lucky that she'd moved to Golden Falls, but we had our own challenges over the years and both made our sacrifices. But we always put each other first, because we knew what we had was once in a lifetime."

"I think that's what we could have. I'm in love with her, Hal, and I didn't get the chance to tell her."

"Well," Hal said slowly, eyes twinkling. "You'll get a chance to tell her when she's back. You haven't lost her, Wes. Don't give up so easily."

I was about to respond when my phone vibrated in my jean pocket. It was a text from Juliette.

JULIETTE

Hey! I made it to Chicago. I'm getting ready for my meeting. I thought I'd see my brother tonight, but he has to work late, so I'm going to see him tomorrow. Then make the drive back the next morning.

I miss you.

I quickly typed back a reply.

ME

I miss you, too. Good luck today. You're going to kick ass.

She immediately sent back three heart emojis.

I stared at the screen, particularly the contact photo I had added for Juliette. It was a photo of her from the Fourth of July in my Lake Ridge cap, her green eyes sparkling and her smile bright. I remembered taking the photo. She was reaching for my phone, laughing how she didn't want me taking a picture because she *didn't look good*. Yeah, right. She always looked stunning.

My eyes lingered on the Lake Ridge cap. Apart from my family, the bar was one of the main reasons keeping me in Golden Falls. I loved this place—I had big dreams for it—but plans changed. As my mom often reminded us: *The only constant thing in life is change.*

I tapped my fingers against my jeans, slipping my phone back into my pocket. Hal was right—as always. I couldn't give up. I had to go big.

"I'm not giving up, Hal," I assured him. "I have an idea, and I think this just might work."

The next day, I'd gotten updates here and there from Juliette, but I was itching to talk with her in person once she was back. I was spending the day at Cooper's house. He lived on the outskirts of town, making for an easier commute to the surrounding state parks. He suggested we play a game of pool, and I appreciated having something to do with my hands and mind. I was feeling better than I had yesterday. Because now I had a plan. After wrapping up my conversation with Hal, I'd spent the rest of the day looking through paperwork and figuring out the best way to put my plan into motion.

"I'd like to sell the bar." I watched as Cooper missed his shot by a mile, likely caught off guard by my words.

His jaw dropped. "W-what?" he asked. "I think I fucking misheard you. You want to *sell the bar*? Get to talking, Wes, because I'm not following."

I focused on lining up my shot. "Juliette gets back from Chicago tomorrow. If the way she feels about me is the same as I feel about her, I want to make this relationship work, but I don't want her to feel pressure to move here if she doesn't want to. She has worked so damn hard on building her design portfolio and has talked with such excitement about her career. I know for a fact she has big dreams, and I can't stand in the way of that." I made my first shot then moved to line up my second. "Yes, my family is here, but it's really Lake Ridge that's tying me down. I can open a bar anywhere, but there's only one Juliette Campbell." I set my pool cue down when I missed my third shot.

Cooper shook his head slowly, and I saw something pass over his expression. Something nostalgic.

"I'll support you no matter what, man." He lifted his head to look at me. "If this is what feels right... I wouldn't want you to live with the type of regret that comes with not following her. I wouldn't wish that upon anyone."

Cooper sounded like he was speaking from experience, but I couldn't remember him being in a relationship with someone who would leave that kind of impact. I remember him being out of it when Jade left after her college graduation, but...no—there was no way. Shaking the thoughts out of my mind, I said, "A woman like that is one in a million. I'm not missing my chance."

He crossed his arms over his chest, a grin quickly appearing on his face, removing any semblance of the emotion from earlier. "Well, I'll be damned. My best friend's in love. Well," he sighed, "let's get this plan in motion. Who better to help than the guy who helped plan that awesome date, huh?"

I shook my head at my best friend—at my brother, really—and couldn't help the grin that crossed my face. "Let's get this plan in motion," I repeated.

46

JULIETTE

"I'm so proud of you, Juliette," my mom said over the car's Bluetooth speakers. I was driving back to Golden Falls and called her from the car about an hour ago. We had a lot to catch up on—a whole summer's worth of updates.

"Thanks, Mom. That means so much to me." I couldn't help the smile that came across my face at her words. I just finished telling her about my trip to Chicago and what I was going to do.

"I hear the happiness in your voice. It's been a while since you've been this excited about your career, and I love how confident you are in your decision."

"I know this is the right thing for me and for my career. I...I really hope it goes well."

"Oh, honey, I bet it will," my mom assured. "And I wanted to say...I called it from the beginning!"

I rolled my eyes with a laugh. "You sure did, Mom."

"Have a safe rest of your drive, Jules. Let us know how everything goes."

"I will. Love you. Say hi to Dad for me."

"Love you more. Talk to you soon."

I hung up the call and lightly tapped my fingers against the steering wheel. I still had two hours left in the drive until I was back in Golden Falls. Ever since I left a few days ago, I had been counting the hours until I'd be back. Until I could see Wes.

I was in love with him. It was that simple.

I reached over for my bag of sour gummy worms, grabbing a piece of candy and taking a bite. I couldn't believe how different this drive was compared to the start of the summer. And also how similar it was.

Like at the start of the summer, it was time for a new adventure. I told Wes before leaving that I wanted to make this decision together. But I knew what I wanted.

I hoped it was what he wanted, too.

One bag of gummy worms, a Diet Coke, and an order of medium fries later, I pulled into the gravel driveway leading to Wes's house. When I texted him before starting the drive, he replied that he would be waiting for me at home. *Home.* I liked the sound of that.

Yesterday, the group text between me, Lily, and Eliza was blowing up. According to Eliza, Wes "had the biggest stick up his ass known to mankind" that first day I was gone. She sent another message with a bunch of upside down smiling face emojis begging for me to come back.

I had no clue what was going on. Wes hadn't mentioned anything out of the ordinary, but I would find out soon enough.

After parking the car and cutting the engine, I moved quickly toward the front door. My suitcase could wait.

I was about to push open the door, but he beat me to it,

opening it with a breathtaking smile. "You're back," he sighed with relief.

Relief coursed through my body, through my bones. I felt it as soon as I got into Golden Falls, but I especially felt it now standing in front of him.

I nodded, unable to keep the smile off my face. "I'm back."

Not wasting any time, Wes took a single step forward, closing the distance between us and wrapping his arms around me.

I flung my arms around him in return, burying my face in his neck and inhaling his cologne as he lifted me off the ground. God, he smelled good. He smelled like *home*.

"Wes, I missed you," I whispered, my eyes starting to water, "so much."

My heart was pounding, and I wondered if he could feel it as he held me. There was so much I wanted to tell him, and this conversation was long overdue. But my chest wasn't closing in and panic wasn't setting in like it did earlier this summer. I felt butterflies. I was right where I belonged.

Wes stepped back into the house then kicked the door closed and set me down.

"Baby, not nearly as much as I missed you." Wes felt deeply, but he didn't always show it. Seeing his eyes start to water too was nearly my undoing. "If that's what three days without you does to me, I don't want any time apart. Hear that?"

"I don't want any time apart from you, either," I croaked. I parted my lips, about to speak, but Wes beat me to it.

"I know we agreed to figure it out together once you got back, and I don't know what your decision is...but I can't go another minute—*another second*—without telling you how I feel. How much you mean to me. How I would do anything for you," Wes rasped, his voice low and raw.

"I love you, Juliette." He cradled my face in his large hands, using his thumb to swipe away my stray tears. "You've brought light into my life. Now that I know what it's like to have you, I don't want to live any other way. I want to wake up next to you every morning. I want to slow dance with you. I want to cook you breakfast. I want to build you your dream closet. I want to buy you all the goddamn dresses in the world. I don't want you to change anything. You're not too much—and I hate that anyone made you feel that way. You're fucking perfect."

"Wes," I said softly, my voice cracking. Those tears that had been threatening to make an appearance finally broke through. "That's what I was going to say. To you." I shook my head with a laugh. Stubborn man couldn't even let me be the first one to confess my love.

In the span of a few months, Wes managed to understand me better than anyone. He knew my insecurities, my vulnerabilities, what made me happy, what I wanted out of life. I'd spent the last few days thinking about how I couldn't live life without him. Now I finally got to tell him.

"As soon as I left, I wanted to turn right back around," I admitted. I rested my hands on his chest, my fingers wrapping around the soft fabric of his shirt. His heart was beating as quickly as mine. "Wes, this summer is the happiest I've ever been, and that's because of you. I got pieces of myself back—my creativity, my passion, my drive—and I also fell in love with a man who values all those things about me, who truly sees me and wants what's best for me."

I paused to take in this moment, to take in Wes. I wanted to see his face when I told him. "I love you, Wesley Richards. I am so in love with you. I never want you to think that you're not enough—because you're everything. You're kind, thoughtful, protective. I love your sense of humor. I love that you brought me all the flowers in the rainbow because you didn't know my favorite color. I love how calm and patient you are. I love how much you care about those in your life. I love—"

Wes's lips spread into a smile, and he interrupted me with a kiss, his mouth hot against mine as he backed me up against the door. My hands moved to his arms, then his shoulders, and then tangled in his hair as my lips moved against his.

"I wasn't done." I smiled against his mouth while also making no attempt to stop the kiss. If anything, I pulled Wes even closer.

He chuckled against my lips. "I couldn't wait any longer to kiss you, show you how much I missed you." Wes moved his lips from mine, pressing hot, slow kisses along my jaw to my neck.

"Wes," I breathed out. My fingers wrapped around the fabric of his shirt, itching to pull it over his head. I nearly started to rid him of his shirt when he spoke up again.

"I know that this doesn't fix everything," Wes mumbled against my skin. "I don't want you giving up your dreams, your career, for me. I'd never ask you to do that."

My brows furrowed, and I looked at Wes as he pulled back. "What are you saying?"

"I have one more thing, sweetheart." Wes took my hand into his, leading me toward the kitchen. Various papers and documents were messily scattered on the table.

"I don't care where we settle down, as long as I'm with you. I want to be by your side as you take the world by storm. I've spent the last couple of days figuring out the logistics of selling Lake Ridge. I figured it would be easier to move to Chicago this way."

I was at a loss for words. Lake Ridge meant the world to Wes, and he had so many plans for his business. He hadn't even asked me to move here. The gesture overwhelmed me in the best way. He was willing to do anything for us.

I quickly shook my head. "Wes, you can't do that."

"I can try to open another bar or start another business anywhere. There's only one you."

I let out a breath that sounded like a half sob, half laugh. One that, from the look of Wes's face, was not the reaction he was expecting. I turned toward the table, scouring the pages before facing him again. "Please tell me you haven't signed these papers yet. You can't move to Chicago."

He shifted from one foot to the other, running his fingers through his hair and tugging on the strands. "W-what are you saying?" he stammered.

"Moving to Chicago might not be the best idea," I said slowly, "because I'm moving to Golden Falls. I even brought more of my stuff up." I nodded in the direction of the driveway where my car was parked. "So, if you want to be with me, I think we should stay right here. This is where we should start our life together and build upon both of our careers. I want to see everything you have planned for Lake Ridge and support you as much as I know you'll support me."

I wasn't sure if he had heard me at first, because he just stared at me, but when it clicked, Wes's booming laugh filled the room. God, he was so handsome when he smiled. He wasted no time in pushing the papers off to the side and lifting me onto the table. He pressed his lips against mine in another kiss.

"God, you drive me crazy, woman," he said with a grin against my lips. "Why didn't you say that when you got in?! You're moving here? Really? What happened?" he asked, and with each question I got a kiss, one to my lips, a few on my neck.

I let out a laugh, tipping my head back. "Because as soon as I got in, you were going off on your romantic love confession!" I grinned up at him, my fingers wrapping around his shirt and pulling him even closer to me. I didn't want any space between us.

He paused, breaking the kiss. "What about your job? What did your boss pitch to you?"

"Funny enough, she pitched to me what I wanted to talk to

her about. What I've been doing in Golden Falls—working with local businesses and offering interior design services at an affordable rate, making it more accessible. She wants to open an interior design firm affiliated with Luxe Living that's dedicated to that. When I told her about my work over the summer, she was even more convinced that I was the right person to lead the team. I told her I would love to work with her only if I could live in and work from Golden Falls. And she loved the idea."

"Juliette, that's amazing. You're going to have a team and everything?"

I nodded eagerly. "It'll be a remote team. We're going to be able to work with clients over video chat, but I also want to hire people who are passionate about the towns they live in and their local businesses. I'm going to be able to work with Golden Falls businesses, as well as the surrounding towns. I might do some occasional travel, like to Madison or Milwaukee, but Cheryl and I will hire someone based near Chicago as one of the first members, so I don't have to make that drive as often."

Wes stared at me with awe in his eyes. It only made me feel even better about how this was all turning out. "I knew you were amazing, but damn, baby. I'm so proud of you. I can't wait to see the life we build here. Together."

"Together," I repeated, loving the sound of that. "It's going to be perfect." I saw it coming together so clearly—us living together, going on more dates, traveling, getting married, starting a family. This was only the beginning.

I went on *Paradise Love* because I wanted to fall in love with someone who would be by my side during the highs and lows of life. Someone who loved me no matter what. Turns out, I should've packed my bags and come up to Golden Falls. Luckily, it all worked out the way it was supposed to.

This summer helped me find a renewed sense of passion for

my career, life, and love. I couldn't wait to see what Wes and I would accomplish together.

We stared at each other for a moment, and when my eyes flicked to his lips, his gaze hardened. His hands found my hips. His grip tightened, fingers digging in possessively.

"I love you, Juliette Campbell," he murmured. His whole chest vibrated from his words. His calloused hands slipped underneath my tank top, fingertips brushing softly over my skin.

"I love you more, Wesley Richards," I responded, a mischievous smile crossing my lips. "And I want to show you how much."

47

WESLEY

Juliette was a woman of many surprises, and I'd learned to go with the flow. So, when she pressed her hands against my chest and guided me to sit...I fucking sat. Fire and desire sparkled in her green eyes.

Juliette made me want to be the best version of myself in every way. I was insecure at the start of the summer that I wouldn't be enough—that Juliette was too good for someone like me. Well, I was going to be the man she deserved each and every single day.

She was mine, and she *loved me*.

I still couldn't fucking believe it.

We had our whole lives ahead of us. I was going to propose to this woman—no doubt about it. I even had an idea of how I was going to ask her, but I was trying not to get ahead of myself. That time would come. For now, I was reveling in the fact that she loved me. That she was moving here. That were together. That we both chose *us*.

My eyes were locked on Juliette as she dropped to her knees in front of me. Her hands moved over my jeans up my thighs to my belt, her fingers moving swiftly to undo it.

"I also want you to show me how much you love me," Juliette said, a confidence in her tone that I was forever obsessed with. "I want you to kiss me." She undid my belt, pulling it through the loops and dropping it to the ground. "Take me." The hiss of my zipper cut through her words. "And show me who I belong to."

God, this woman.

"But first," she continued, pulling down my jeans and boxer briefs, "I want to taste you."

I started to reach for her, but she leaned away.

"No touching...yet," Juliette tutted. She had a sly smile that made my cock even harder. I was so gone for this woman, and I wouldn't have it any other way.

I let out a reluctant grunt as I listened and moved my hands away from her.

Juliette ran her tongue slowly along my cock before guiding it into her mouth. She bobbed her head slowly at first, humming against my length, before picking up her pace. One of her hands wrapped around the base while the other was resting on my thigh, nails digging into my skin.

Maybe I couldn't touch her, but I still knew what she liked to hear. "You're taking my cock so well, sweetheart. Just like that."

Juliette moaned against my cock, the vibrations sending a shiver up my spine. My hands flexed at my sides, itching to touch her and wrap around her wavy brunette locks.

"Fuck," I hissed. "You drive me crazy, baby." I reached for the back of her neck, fingers tangling in her brown waves to pull her head back. "I think I went enough time without touching you, don't you think?"

Juliette moved her mouth from my cock, looking up at me with bright green eyes. "I guess so," she teased, drawing out the words. With her hands on my thighs, she pushed up, now standing between my legs with her arms draped loosely over my shoulders. "Where are you going to touch me first?" she asked, running her tongue along her bottom lip. My eyes followed the motion. "Are you going to feel how wet I am for you?" Juliette dipped her head and lowered her voice to whisper. "You're all I've been thinking about."

She was all I'd been thinking about, too. My hands found her hips first. I was going to take my time with every inch of her body. I slipped my fingers underneath her tank top, slowly, teasingly inching up her back.

"You tasted power, and suddenly you're asking all the questions," I teased lowly. Truthfully, Juliette had all the power over me. She always did, and she always would. "You told me what you wanted—for me to kiss you, take you, and show you who you belong to—and that's exactly what I'm planning to do, baby."

I stood, carefully stepping out of my jeans, and picked up Juliette. I easily tossed her over my shoulder and gave her ass a playful smack over her denim shorts before heading to the bedroom.

48

JULIETTE

I let out a squeal as Wes tossed me onto his bed. He was on top of me within seconds, his kiss hot and urgent but also slow and careful, like we had all the time in the world. Because now we did.

I moaned against his mouth, my hands slowly moving down his broad chest to the hem of his shirt. I wanted to feel every inch of him. "Need you," I panted as I pulled the shirt over his head. The palms of my hands met the planes of his muscular chest, my nails digging into his shoulders as my touch moved higher.

Wes moved his lips from mine, dragging his nose against the side of my neck with a growl. "I'm all yours, Juliette," he said lowly. He left a scorching kiss to the spot I couldn't resist just underneath my ear. "And you're *mine*."

Wes leaned back to slowly peel off my clothes, admiring my body as each piece of fabric came off. Once my shorts were off, he lifted my leg, kissing up my calf, inner thigh, all the way to my center.

He hooked his hand underneath the side of my panties and

gave a sharp tug, my eyes widening. My panties were nothing more than a scrap of fabric in Wes's large hand.

"Wes! You're either stealing my underwear or ripping it!" I scolded him with a laugh, to which he grinned.

"You told me to show you how much I missed you. That's exactly what I'm doing."

He hooked his hands underneath my thighs, pulling me closer and dipping his head between my legs. He ran his tongue along my slit, humming eagerly. "I've been starving for you, sweetheart." His thumb circled my clit while his tongue tasted and teased my entrance.

Wes pulled away after a moment, slipping two of his fingers inside me. He pumped them rhythmically and rapidly.

"Wes!" I gasped with pleasure, my back arching off the bed and my fingers wrapping around the sheets. I wasted no time in pulling him toward me, kissing and sucking on his bottom lip. Tasting myself on him.

"I can't wait to feel you," he groaned.

"What are you waiting for then? I'm ready for you."

"Fuck, baby. You want my cock that badly?"

"Yes," I breathed, spreading my legs for him. "I want you. I *need* you. Please," I begged.

His hand wrapped around his cock, and he slowly pushed inside of me. The pressure between my legs caused my head to fall back and a moan to fall from my lips.

"Baby, you feel like heaven. You're my goddamn angel," Wesley groaned. He started moving his hips slowly, letting me adjust to his size before he increased his speed.

I reached for his shoulders, pulling him closer to me so I could get my lips on his neck, his jaw, all the way to his mouth. I kissed him slowly—a sharp contrast to how quickly our hips were moving.

My legs wrapped around his waist tighter, and I moved my

hips in unison with his. My moans filled the room, and I didn't hold back on letting him know how good he was making me feel, how much I needed this. How much I needed him. Forever.

"I-I'm close, Wes. So close."

"Come for me, sweetheart," he urged. "I'm right there with you." He moved his hand between us, adding pressure to my clit while he continued to move his hips. Wes reached up to grip the headboard with one hand, his muscles flexing. "I. Love. You." He punctuated each word with a thrust.

It was what I needed to be sent over the edge. My vision blurred, filling with stars as the pressure built, built, and built. I let out a cry of pleasure as my orgasm exploded, my back arching off the bed, closer to Wes. Wes continued to move his hips, a groan escaping him as he finished, too.

He collapsed on the bed next to me with a content sigh, immediately wrapping an arm around me and pulling me into his side. We were twisted up in the bedsheets, and something told me we wouldn't be leaving this bed any time soon.

I curled up next to him, pressing a gentle kiss to his neck before resting my head on his chest. "I don't think I'll ever get tired of hearing you say you love me," I murmured.

Wesley pressed a kiss to the top of my head. "Good, baby, because I plan to show you and tell you each and every day how much I love you."

I tipped my head back to look up at him, taking in the man I was deeply in love with. I wondered what our life would be like five, ten, fifteen, years from now. But I didn't want to get ahead of myself. I wanted to focus on today—the day we chose each other.

Wes tenderly gripped my chin with his thumb and forefinger, tipping my head back to meet his gaze. "I love you so much," he whispered.

The way Wesley looked at me when he told me he loved me
was the same way he had been looking at me all summer.

REALITY WEEKLY

Paradise Love's Tony Pierce files for bankruptcy after losing multi-million dollar deal
Tech entrepreneur Tony Pierce was on the verge of closing a life-changing multi-million dollar deal—until investors learned about his behavior after winning the hit reality dating show. Now, he's facing bankruptcy.

Tony Pierce, who was one half of the winning couple on the latest season of the reality dating show _Paradise Love_, has been soaking up his newfound fame over the summer. Photos of him in his luxury sports cars, at fancy restaurants, and partying at exclusive events are all over his social media.

But there's one thing that's notably absent. News of his recently failed business venture and pending bankruptcy. Karma sure has a way of catching up, doesn't it?

Sources confirmed Pierce was days away from securing a lucrative tech deal, which he intended to use to support his new lavish lifestyle. The deal fell through when the leaked audio clip resurfaced and investors found out how Pierce treated his co-star Juliette Campbell. In the clip, Pierce called Campbell a "handful" and said he went on the show to boost his company.

"They didn't want to be associated with someone who publicly deceived his partner and those around him," an insider source with knowledge of the deal said. "The way he used Juliette and the way he spoke about her came back to bite him. No one wanted to invest in someone who lacked integrity and treated others this way."

Court filings obtained by *Reality Weekly* show Pierce is now filing for bankruptcy after burning through his *Paradise Love* winnings and losing out on the multi-million dollar deal. He's trying to secure a spot on another reality dating show, but no one wants to cast him, according to a source close to Pierce.

Pierce could not be reached for comment.

Pierce's co-star, on the other hand, appears to be thriving. Campbell, who also couldn't be reached for comment, recently posted a series of photos on social media. The caption started out with "Found my paradise," followed by a couple of paragraphs of Campbell sharing with her followers how she found genuine friendships and love this past summer. Her caption also cleared up that she was not aware of Pierce's intentions, something he claimed earlier.

The photos show Campbell smiling with her friends, spending time out on the water, and a few selfies. But fans were buzzing over one photo in particular—a mirror selfie with a mystery man who had his hands on Campbell's hips while pressing a kiss to her temple.

Swoon.

We weren't able to identify the mystery man or find him online, but maybe that's a good thing. We do have a question though: Where can we find a man like that?

Follow *Reality Weekly* online and on social media for updates.

49

JULIETTE

ME

It's official! I'm moving to Golden Falls.

MOM

Oh, honey! That's wonderful. We are so excited for you!!! I can't wait to hear more.

DAD

We'll have to plan a trip to visit you soon. I'm sure your brother can help you with the move if you need it.

GRANT

Sure, it's not like I'm swamped at work or anything.

But, seriously, I'm really happy for you, Jules. You deserve it.

ME

I love you guys. So much. I can't wait for you to meet Wes.

MOM

We love you, too, and can't wait to meet him. From what you've told us, he sounds wonderful.

Grant, what is going on at work? Make sure you're getting enough sleep.

GRANT

I'm fine, Mom. Things have just been busy.

MOM

I'll give you a call later this week. Surely you can make some time for your mother.

WHEN I GOT TO GOLDEN FALLS A FEW MONTHS AGO, ONE OF MY hopes was that things couldn't get worse. Never in my wildest dreams did I think everything would get *this* much better.

It had only been a week since I got back from Chicago. A week since Wesley told me he loved me. A week of getting into my new routine.

Within a few days of me being back—and once Wes and I finally left his bed—we decided it made sense for me to move in with him over trying to find an apartment. After all, we had basically been living together all of August.

The reaction from those closest to us was better than we could have anticipated. I didn't expect any negative reactions, but I wondered if they'd think we were rushing into it. No one did. If anything, everyone was relieved we made this decision and they didn't have to intervene.

When I told Eliza and Lily that not only was I staying but I was moving in with Wesley, Lily wouldn't stop smiling. Eliza pulled me into a tight hug and said, "We wouldn't have let you leave anyway." It sounded ominous, but I swear she meant it in a loving way.

My parents were more than eager to meet Wesley, especially

after getting the chance to talk with him over the phone and video chat. They had plans to come up to visit us, and Wes said they had to come next summer so he could take them out on his boat. Wes was already in the family group chat. I was hoping Grant could make a trip up here soon, although he seemed to have his plate full between work and whatever was happening with Scarlett, his ex-wife who was apparently still his wife.

My mom claimed she called my relationship with Wes from the beginning, but I didn't think anyone saw it coming better than Hal. When I told him I was sticking around, he wasn't surprised. Like, at all. He simply said, "Well, of course, you are," and went back to reading his newspaper.

The attention from *Paradise Love* resurfaced with the most recent article, but it quickly faded. For me, at least. I didn't think Tony could say the same.

Truthfully, I hadn't expected Tony's actions to catch up with him. Men weren't held to the same standards as women, whether that was on reality TV or in the real world. I thought a different show would want him to increase their ratings, which would likely lead him to breaking another woman's heart. So, it was good to see there were consequences. Hopefully, he learned from them. And if he didn't? Well, the devil worked hard, but karma worked harder.

I initially hadn't planned to post photos on social media from my summer, but I thought about my conversation with Ruby at Lake Ridge. About how watching me on the show made her realize she could be unapologetically herself and how one of her exes called her "too much."

I thought about what my brother said at the very start of the summer. How people didn't pity me but instead related to what I went through.

That's who I posted those photos and the caption for. I wanted to show them I found a group of friends and an incredible man who didn't think I was a "handful." Someone who loved things about me others, including myself, had been critical of. I wanted it to be a reminder not to settle and not to chase a person who didn't deserve your light.

Selfishly, I also wanted to clear up Tony's accusations about how I knew his intentions to fully close that chapter of my life. I didn't have regrets about going on the show, because it led me to Golden Falls—to Wes—but I was ready to fully move on.

I didn't plan on posting on my personal social media often, because my focus shifted to the new account I had created—Campbell Creations. Cheryl had allowed me to name the new design firm I was leading.

With my arms crossed over my chest, I stared up at Wesley's house—our house, now—knowing without a shadow of a doubt this was exactly where I needed to be. I looked around, admiring how beautiful Lake Golden looked in the sun and the stunning view I would get to appreciate every day from here on out. I'd get to see Golden Falls when the leaves started to change color in the fall, when the snow fell in the winter, and every season after.

I walked closer to the steps, raising my brow. "What do you think you're doing? This is private property."

Wes turned around with an amused grin, waiting to roll his eyes until he was facing me. He had two moving boxes stacked in his arms. "Very funny," he deadpanned. "How long have you been waiting to use that one?"

"Oh, I don't know, a few months, maybe? I was playing the long game," I mused.

He let out an amused huff.

"If you're lucky, I'll let you stay with me." I walked past him to pull the door open for him.

Wes followed me inside, setting down the boxes and immediately wrapping an arm around my waist, pulling me into his arms. "I'm the luckiest man in the world with you by my side, city girl." He tipped my chin up with his thumb and forefinger. "This is only the beginning. I have big plans for us. Just you wait."

"I'm more than happy to wait. Forever, remember?"

"Forever," he murmured, pressing a kiss to my mouth.

I melted into his arms, wanting to remember this moment. The start of our life together.

When I got to Golden Falls, I thought this summer was for me. Turns out, it was the summer for us.

EPILOGUE
WESLEY

THREE MONTHS LATER

November

I didn't think I would ever get used to waking up next to Juliette in my bed, her leg draped over mine and her hand resting on my chest. Well, *our* bed, now, in *our* home.

I was one lucky bastard.

It was a no-brainer having Juliette move in once she decided to move to Golden Falls permanently, even when she brought *all* of her belongings from Chicago. That woman had a lot of clothes. The closet was solely hers at this point, but I didn't mind at all.

I didn't need much to be happy. In fact, I only needed one thing.

Juliette.

I wanted to eventually pick out a home together—whether that was buying or building—but starting right here was perfect. Anywhere with Juliette was perfect.

This was the same house my parents started their lives together, and now it was our turn.

With my arm wrapped around her waist, I pulled Juliette closer, my lips meeting the smooth skin of her neck.

"Wesley," she breathed, tilting her head to give me more space.

I moved my mouth, pressing slow, hot kisses along her soft skin to wake her up. "Good morning, sweetheart," I murmured.

Her eyes slowly fluttered open, and a lazy smile came across her face. "Good morning, baby."

With my lips continuing to move along her neck, my hand snaked between her legs, pushing aside her sleep shorts and feeling between her legs. "Wet already? Naughty girl. What were you dreaming about?"

"You," she breathed with a moan, back arching and legs spreading wider for my touch. "Always you."

"Good. Because I woke up fucking starved."

She moaned in response.

I pushed the covers down, settling between Juliette's legs and pulling off her pajama shorts. Her pretty pink pussy was glistening and on full display for me. I dipped my head, pressing soft, slow kisses to her inner thighs. Her hands found my hair, threading through the strands and tugging roughly. I knew exactly what she wanted, but I was going to take my time getting there.

"Patience, baby," I murmured.

My mouth moved from her inner thighs to her center, getting a taste. *Fucking delicious.*

I groaned against her, my fingers digging into her thighs to keep her legs nice and spread for me.

"Feels so...good," Juliette cried, starting to buck her hips against my mouth as my tongue picked up speed. As soon as I slipped two fingers inside of her and moved my mouth to her clit, I knew she was close.

Within moments, she reached her peak, breathless moans

escaping her. She took a moment to catch her breath, her cheeks flushed and hair messy. Juliette leaned up on her elbows and looked down at me.

I couldn't hold back my grin at the sight of her gorgeous smile. I brought my fingers up to my lips, sucking them clean with a groan.

"Delicious," I hummed.

Her hands found my shoulders, and she tugged me up so I was hovering over her, my forehead pressed against hers. She traced her fingers over my jaw, a tender moment between us before her eyes flicked down to my mouth and she captured my lips in a heated kiss.

I'd never get tired of starting my days with Juliette like this. Kissing her, tasting her, hearing her soft moans.

She was everything I had ever wanted, and I was going to show her over and over how much she meant to me.

The *only* reason we got out of bed was because my family was coming over for dinner. And I'd never been more pissed at myself for inviting them over.

But now that I was out of bed and dressed, I knew it would be a nice night. We were having my parents over, as well as Lily, Eliza, Cooper, and Hal. Marnie, Eliza and Cooper's grandma, was also joining. Like everyone in Golden Falls, Marnie had already become fast friends with Juliette. We were also going to FaceTime Juliette's parents, who I talked to pretty regularly once Juliette introduced us virtually. They were planning to visit soon.

Tonight's dinner was a delayed moving-in celebration for

Juliette. The last few months got away from us—between her getting settled, getting Campbell Creations up and running, and everyone getting into a new routine now that summer was over. But better late than never to get everyone over to see how we'd made this house our own.

I enjoyed summer in Golden Falls, because it meant being out on the water, but my favorite time of the year was fall. Nothing beat the view of seeing red, orange, and yellow leaves on the horizon, the vibrant colors mirrored on the surface of the lake.

I grabbed my car keys, getting ready to head downtown to pick up our catering order of Italian food for dinner. Staying in bed all day also meant we didn't have enough time to cook said dinner...but it'd be fine. I knew my family, and they would be more than happy to have a good, warm meal picked up from Pasta Fresca.

As I was about to leave, Lily's car pulled up the driveway. I did a double take at the time, wondering if I was behind, but nope—she was hours early.

"Are you expecting Lily?" I asked Juliette, who was sitting on the couch. She shook her head and closed her laptop.

Confused, I unlocked the door, and within moments, Lily came barreling inside. She didn't look upset, but she was frantic. She quickly started talking and waving her arms around.

"Hal wants to sell the building! Which is great. It's what I wanted! It's what we've been talking about. How he wants to take a step back, and how I'm ready to buy the building from him and take on that additional responsibility. So then why in the world is *Gabriel Nelson* included on the email of Hal expressing how he's interested in selling the building. Gabriel Nelson!" Lily shrieked. She let out a frustrated exhale.

"Gabriel Nelson, as in Hal's grandson?" Juliette asked slowly, looking between Lily and me.

I parted my lips to respond, but Lily spoke first. "Yes, my new enemy!"

I had never seen Lily like this. Her cheeks were red, her blonde hair was a freaking mess, and her hands were balled into fists at her sides. It was honestly terrifying, and Juliette likely had the same thought as her eyes widened at Lily's outburst.

"Yeah, that's him. He's, I don't know, probably twenty-eight at this point? He's younger than me—I know that." I stretched my hand out to Lily, gesturing for her phone. "Show me the email."

Lily let out a breath, handing me her phone with the email on the screen. Juliette stood and came to my side to look at the email, too.

"Hal was telling me about Gabe this summer when I'd stop by the hardware store," Juliette said. "Gabe's really smart and business savvy, apparently, but Hal is worried he's losing touch with what's important. I asked Hal what he meant by that, but he totally pretended like he didn't hear me."

"Gabe? No," Lily scoffed. "We are not on a nickname basis with him. Nelson Group is successful, but they're ruthless. They're focused on luxury apartments and commercial space. They would rather see a big coffee shop chain in the building than my café."

Juliette and I both scanned the email, and I quickly saw that Lily was right—Hal was offering to sell the building but said he wasn't sure what that would look like yet. He wanted to talk to Lily and Gabriel in person, meaning Gabriel needed to come to Golden Falls.

"There's no way Gabriel is going to show up here," I said with a scoff, shaking my head.

"What's Hal planning with this?" Juliette asked, looking between Lily and me. I had been thinking the same thing. Hal was always steps ahead—what were we missing? "Hal loves Golden Falls. He wouldn't be so careless with the building just to see it turned into something that hurts the businesses and people in town."

"Maybe he doesn't think I can handle the responsibility?" Lily offered, her shoulders slumping. This news devastated her—she'd been saving for months for this day, rarely taking any days off and pouring nearly all of her profits back into the café.

"I don't think it's that, Lily," I assured her. I knew how much Hal cared about my family, especially Lily. He'd always had a soft spot for her. "Maybe we're worrying for nothing—"

Juliette gasped.

"What?" Lily asked with wide eyes.

"Gabriel responded." Juliette held the phone up so we could both see the most recent email. "He said he'll be in Golden Falls next month."

THE END

BONUS EPILOGUE
FIVE YEARS LATER

The Golden Falls Gazette

Interior designer finds a home in Golden Falls
Juliette Campbell is celebrating five years of Campbell Creations and looks ahead at what's next.

When Juliette "Jules" Campbell, 32, arrived in Golden Falls five years ago, the last thing she expected was to stay longer than a few months—and she certainly never expected to call this small town home.

Campbell said her summer in Golden Falls came at the perfect time. The interior designer from Chicago was feeling uninspired in her career and personal life.

"Since choosing to make Golden Falls my home, all I've had is inspiration," Campbell said. "It's so special to live in a town where people are invested in your success and are cheering you on."

Campbell is celebrating five years of her interior design firm Campbell Creations, which she started soon after moving to Golden Falls permanently. She has worked with small businesses and residents across Wisconsin and the Midwest, providing her design expertise at an affordable and accessible rate.

Her favorite part is meeting new people and seeing what projects they bring her.

"There is nothing better than bringing someone's vision to life," she added.

Campbell co-owns Lake Ridge, a bar and restaurant that has garnered both local and national attention, with her husband Wesley Richards. Lake Ridge has been lauded for its innovative head chef, comfortable atmosphere, live music, and partnership with local nonprofits. Travel magazines have called Lake Ridge a "must stop" for anyone traveling through northern Wisconsin.

"Lake Ridge wouldn't be what it is today without Juliette's creativity and vision," Richards said. "I can't think of a better partner—both in life and in business—than my wife. The sky is the limit for her."

It's been a busy five years for the couple, and Campbell said they don't plan on slowing down any time soon.

Continue reading on page 5A

Juliette

When the bedroom creaked door open, I sat up in bed, folding the newspaper and placing it on my nightstand. I'd finish reading the article later today. Right now, my full attention was on my daughter, who was crawling toward me, and my husband, who was slowly walking behind her.

Rosalie let out a happy squeal as she reached the bed, babbling "mama." Wes scooped her up in his arms and lifted her onto our fluffy white covers. Rosie let out another squeal, grinning wide and showing off the two bottom teeth that were poking through.

"Why hi there, little lady," I cooed, bringing her to my chest and pressing a kiss to the top of her head. "Have you been helping your dad with breakfast this morning?"

As happy as Rosie was to see me, she was immediately distracted by Maple, our brown tabby cat, who was lying on the bed next to me. The same Maple from Purrfect Blend during my first summer in Golden Falls. We adopted her a few months after I moved here permanently. I had infinite photos on my phone of our cat and Rosie cuddling together, and I didn't know of a sweeter sight.

"She sure was," Wes said with a chuckle, standing at the side of the bed and looking down at us. "Her helping me means she's staying out of trouble. I'd say this morning was a success." Wes let out a content sigh. "Good morning, sweetheart."

"Hi, handsome." I looked up at him with a smile, still unable to believe how lucky I was that this was my life. I couldn't imagine a world without my husband and daughter—luckily, I didn't have to.

He leaned down, tipping my chin up and pressing a tender kiss to my lips. "Breakfast is ready," he murmured against my mouth.

I inhaled the delicious smell of pancakes, eggs, and bacon, and my stomach immediately rumbled. Sundays were one of my favorite days. Not only did Wes cook breakfast, he also loved spending the mornings with Rosie, which meant I got extra time in bed *alone*. Time for myself was even more precious now that I was a mom, and I was so grateful that Wes and I had such a strong partnership. Being new parents came with its challenges, but it was so rewarding. Seeing Wes become a father—and melt at the sight of our daughter—was something I'd never get tired of.

I couldn't believe five years had already flown by.

Campbell Creations was doing better than I could have imagined, and so was Lake Ridge. I was incredibly proud of Wes and the work he put into his business—well, our business now. Wes brought me on as co-owner about a year after I officially moved to Golden Falls. He proposed not too long after that.

We were a team in every sense of the word. I was so grateful to have a husband who supported my dreams, but I was especially grateful to have a husband who recognized how much I supported him, too. A husband who put me first, who would do anything to support me, and who showed me how much he loved me each and every day.

For the first two years of our relationship, we lived in Wesley's house—the one next door to the cabin. When we began to think about starting a family, we knew we'd need more space, so we decided to move forward with designing and building a home that was uniquely us. We now lived on the edge of town in an area that was more private but still close to our friends, family, and downtown.

Our home had a beautiful view of Lake Golden, and just like that summer, we spent mornings drinking coffee on the back porch. We'd made so many memories over the last five years, and I couldn't wait to see what the next five brought.

"I think it's time for breakfast, huh?" I asked Rosie, just as Maple got up, arching her back and stretching.

"Here, I'll trade you," Wes said with a wink, grabbing Rosie from my arms and handing me a folded up note he pulled out of his back pocket. By now, I knew exactly what the notes were for. Pretty sure I had hundreds at this point. I unfolded the paper and read the messy scrawl, unable to help my smile.

> Juliette,
> I'd like to take my beautiful wife out on a date. Tonight at seven.
> Yours,
> Wes

Wes didn't really ask me out on a date in his various notes—more like told. But it wasn't like I was going to say no. I married the guy!

"Your parents are in for the weekend and are going to watch Rosie tonight to give us some time alone," Wes said with a smirk on his lips.

As much as my parents loved living in Florida, they were *much* more excited to be grandparents. They moved to Green Bay a year ago, which allowed them to be a two hour drive away from Golden Falls. It was also easy for them to visit Grant and his family.

"I have plans for you," Wes murmured, a devilish smirk on his lips before he turned around.

I licked my lips, watching as he walked out of the bedroom, admiring how perfectly his jeans hung on his hips. I swung my legs out of bed, sliding on my slippers and following Wes out of the bedroom and into the kitchen.

I couldn't wait for his plans. I couldn't wait for any of it.

But I would gladly take my time getting to all of it.

After all, we didn't only have the summer anymore. We had forever.

THANK YOU FOR READING!

If you enjoyed *The Summer for Us*, please consider leaving a review on Amazon, Goodreads, or social media! Reader reviews are so important to indie authors, and it would mean the world to me if you left an honest review.

Let's connect!
Sign up for my newsletter
Social media: @authorizabelakamila
Visit my website: www.authorizabelakamila.com

ACKNOWLEDGMENTS

In the summer of 2024, I set out to write a romance book. I didn't know if it would be any good or if it would see the light of day, but I wanted to try. Plus, I had more time and energy in the evenings after switching careers.

While I've always considered myself a writer, for a long time, I didn't think I was creative enough to write fiction. I wanted to prove myself wrong.

And I did, because you just finished reading my debut and met characters that have lived in my head for months. It feels so special to share this world with you.

So many people made this dream of publishing a book possible. Words can't express how grateful I am for their support, although I'll try to do it anyway.

To Michael: Each and every day, you make me feel supported, loved, and like I can do anything. Even when I was unsure of myself and this story, you encouraged me to keep going. My best days are because of you and the way you make me smile, laugh, and feel like everything's going to be okay, even when it's scary. I couldn't have done this without you and am so lucky to have you by my side. I love you so very much.

To my parents: You have always supported my love for reading and writing—from growing up to now—and that's the reason I was able to write this book. You've always believed in me and have been my biggest supporters, regardless of what I'm doing. I'm forever grateful for that, and I love you both.

To Alison: I'm so incredibly grateful for your friendship, and I can't thank you enough for creating the book cover of my dreams. Not only that, but the art of Wes and Jules watching fireworks?! And the café! You brought this story to life, and I'm so glad we were able to do this together.

To my in-laws, friends, and family: Thank you for your encouragement, support, and excitement about my book! I've loved talking about this journey with you, and I can't wait for you to read. Depending on who you are, there might be certain sections you'll want to skip...

To my editors Nicole and Andrea: You two are the literal best, and I had the best time working with you. I can't thank you enough for helping me turn this story into what it is today. Between your helpful feedback, kind words, and answering my questions, you made this process feel less lonely and intimidating.

To my wonderful beta readers Annika, Danie, Katie, Liz, Michaela, Rachel, Rose, Sydney, Vanesa, and Wren: Thank you for helping me make it the best it could be. Having you along for the journey made this process feel real, and I loved your excitement for this book. Your comments, reactions, and feedback gave me life!

To Destiny: Thank you so much for formatting my book and answering any and all questions as I've started this author journey! It's been so amazing having you in my corner.

To my ARC readers: Thank you for signing up to read early and taking a chance on my story. I know the TBR is endless, so the fact that you took time out of your day to read my book makes me so happy.

To you, the reader: I can't thank you enough for picking up my debut. I hope Wes and Jules's story made you smile, laugh, and reminded you that you are wonderful just the way you are. You don't have to change for anyone.

And lastly, to me: You did it! I'm so proud of you for trying something new and putting yourself out there. Now, stop crying over these acknowledgments, and go back to writing your next book.

ABOUT THE AUTHOR

Izabela writes contemporary romance that will have you kicking your feet one moment and blushing the next. Expect swoony heroes, sassy heroines, delicious tension, and witty banter.

She lives in the Midwest with her husband and two cuddly cats. When she's not writing, she's reading romance on her Kindle, watching a romantic comedy or reality TV, enjoying the outdoors, or spending time with her friends and family.

To stay up to date on Izabela's upcoming projects, connect with her on social media @authorizabelakamila or visit her website www.authorizabelakamila.com.